DAY

13 NEW TALES OF TERROR FROM THE AUTHOR OF NIGHT

PATRICK KITSON

Edited by Christie Moreton at Maple House Editing

ISBN: 979-8-218-45061-8

Cover design by Daniel Kelley/Patrick Kitson

CONTENTS

This book is dedicated to Kirstin, Aurora, Leo, Max and Alex—who all graciously tolerate my immeasurable buffoonery.

"The two most common elements in the universe are hydrogen and stupidity."

-Harlan Ellison

INKY

don't have a lot of time to explain how I got here, so I'm typing as fast as I can. If I don't keep going—and really even if I do—he will be here soon enough. He won't stop.

Though it's not really a he or she, but rather more of an *it*. A thing. An intangible, faceless, abhorrent horror of unknown origin that will soon pass through the pages of this tale and manifest into corporal form before me, unless I keep my fingers writing. Gotta keep these words a-flowing.

But not unlike a mouse who's fallen into a backyard pool with high sides, it's just a matter of time before I can't keep this up anymore and, as with any rodent treading water, eventually I'll tire or need sleep.

As soon as I don't keep its nasty little name running across these pages, as soon as I pass out from exhaustion, as soon as my muscles ache and my fingers go limp on the typewriter and the candle next to me on the desk goes dark, it's going to rise up from the black pitch of the ink ribbon where it's currently hiding and swallow me. Devour me and my unwillingness to help it enslave the rest of you.

I don't know what happens then. But I suspect that any prospect of a heaven or hell will be extinguished in an excruciating instant of fear and pain as I am consumed.

My name is Rowan Murray, I am twenty-eight years old, and I don't want to die. So I'm writing and I'm writing and now I don't know what else to write, so I'm writing what could be the last thing I write. Like a hamster on a wheel.

I'm typing to tell anyone who reads this that I tried my god damnedest to prevent his ascension. To keep us all safe. I'm trying to keep **INKY** at bay, but I can feel him scratching at the back gate of my mind, threatening to blow the house down with a gale-force wind if he should be allowed to crawl out of the ink ribbon.

The ribbon is just a gateway, you see. **INKY** had other ways he could have crossed over.

He told me this. In my mind, of course. I've never met **INKY**. The whole point of this is to *not* meet **INKY.** I never want to meet **INKY**.

INKY would only destroy us.

All you have to do to keep **INKY** *at bay is let little* **INKY** *come out to play.*

That little rhyme has been playing on a loop in my mind for almost a year—since I took a vacation to Central America, specifically to Guatemala. My family, my boyfriend, and I went on a tour of some old Mayan temples. Great food, great tours.

On day six, we were convinced by some local yahoo to pay a little extra for access to a site that normally was off limits to the general public. Using LiDAR (light detection and ranging) technology, the area had only recently been rediscovered by the Guatemalan government six months prior to our arrival. A scant handful of people knew about it, and even fewer had been there. The local yokel was one.

My boyfriend, daring and foolish in equal measure, said we needed to live a little. He even made some snide comment about me not being a "soft-ass home-schooled baby boy." I didn't want to have to hear about it the whole way home, so I agreed to go.

Once we got there (by way of a short ride on an even shorter bus that said "Guato Guato Tours" on the side), we realized the temple was actually quite small—only two stories tall, pyramid-like in proportions, and completely covered in foliage.

We walked through a narrow passage and ended up in the only room at the temple's center. Standing in that damp, lamp-lit grotto with the still-as-yet undeciphered etchings of unknown origin filling the walls that reached up nearly fifty feet on all sides, I heard a thick, muddy sound like sludge dropping onto a wooden floor.

All you have to do to keep **INKY** *at bay is let little* **INKY** *come out to play.*

Ever since that moment, it's been like a skipping record coming back around to the same phrase again and again. At first I couldn't really hear **INKY** and I just felt like writing this morbid, go-nowhere short story about a shadow-like creature who hid in the back corners of alleyways and haunted certain buildings.

But as I wrote, something kept nudging me this way and that. The story started to reach further back than I had planned and I wanted to stop writing it.

And I did, for a while at least. But then the only way to keep the wicked whisper of **INKY** from tugging at my nerves was to make some headway on this odd little tale.

It didn't stop though. I would write and it wouldn't ever seem to come anywhere near an endpoint. It was a meandering, largely meaningless dictation of the ancient history of a thing that did little but wait to eat.

I would write when the mood struck me. I think I could have eventually trapped him in the paragraphs. I could have pushed myself harder. *Should* have pushed myself harder. But sometimes I like to binge-watch one of the Star Trek series. Sometimes I like to sleep in.

Yet **INKY** still comes for me in my waking hours and in the horror-filled nightmares that have plagued my slumber over the last few months.

I call him **INKY** only because, in my close-eyed visions, that is the best word I can think of to describe the horror I see. Two years of college with an emphasis on creative writing and that's all I can think of when I picture his obtuse, formless black void.

INKY.

It's possible that the name came from the rhyme, or maybe I…

It's unclear sometimes. Muddled.

My friend Patrick—he's a writer, or so he says, despite only writing a collection of short stories—keeps saying that I need to get to my butt to work and write more. That the only way out is through.

He doesn't know about **INKY** and I wouldn't tell him anyway. Superior sonofabitch that he is, he'd just use it as justification to prattle on atop his delusional literary soapbox—yet another reason to give me shit about my somewhat slower output.

I've been a writer since middle school, and I know writer's block is real. I'm happy with a thousand words a week. He braggadociously does two thousand a night, the cheeky prick.

I know I can be as creative and productive as the next

   ◄ PATRICK KITSON ►

p+9erson, but it isn't a switch to be flipped. Sometimes it's just not there, and you can't force it. If it was a faucet I could just go turn on, I'd let that shit run all day.

Like I can just snap my fingers and that will do the trick. It won't. It doesn't.

What he fails to realize is that it isn't that easy, even with **INKY** constantly baiting me. It's never that easy. Harlan Ellison said writing was the hardest thing to do in the whole world, and he was right.

If it were easy, everyone would be able to do it. Game of Thrones would be completed by now, and George R. R. Martin could finally move onto something else. He's famous and he writes slowly and carefully, just like me. He knows the struggle is real.

My friend Patrick the Pandering says that Millennials use that particular phrase—"the struggle is real"—as a crutch and a cop out, to explain away a diminished generational work ethic and broad overriding cultural apathy. But I submit that the struggle is in fact very real and that he can well and truly kiss my ass.

He's a Gen-Xer, and he thinks that his shit don't stink. He acts like he, and by proxy all Gen-X folks, take more responsibility for his bullshit than we do, and by implication, than I do. I suspect it's a passive aggressive way to try and make me lesser.

As for his ideas about my generation, generally I agree. But I don't think that Boomers or Gen-Xers or my generation do anything any better than one another. They didn't fix climate change, did they?

We all suck in equal measure, as far as I can see. Except perhaps my generation is more accepting and less racist and bigoted than the ones that came before. Just saying. If anything, we probably suck marginally less than they do. They don't realize words are weapons, or at least can be weapons. But we know better.

Look no further than this **INKY** problem for evidence that I'm right. The words I write now are weapons that keep **INKY's** ravenous appetite away from the sheep he wants to wolf upon. The sheep being me. The sheep being you. So I'm rambling about anything I can think of.

Can you tell?

Also, as for why I don't write too often, if we're being candid here, I have a lot on my plate these days. A lot. My parents have me working fairly regularly, trying to catch up with all the clients' tax returns they have submitted for the 2023 tax season.

I work for them for about twenty hours a week as a CPA, but I feel like it's just as hard as people who work forty-hour weeks. Maybe more so. I know that sounds whatever, but there's a lot of pressure to not fuck up because it's people's livelihoods we're dealing with. And it's my parents' business, which compounds the stress.

After the pitter-patter of homeschooling and local college, it seemed reliable and prudent to be with a smaller firm, even if it was owned and operated by my parents.

They don't know about **INKY.** Neither does my boyfriend. He'd think I'm nuts.

My writer buddy is pretty arrogant about the whole writing thing, if you ask me. He thinks that just because he doesn't get writer's block and because he can waive a mental magic wand and create without the same struggle I endure, somehow that means I'm less of a writer than he is. Like true art isn't agony and sacrifice.

Real writing is hard fought and takes years to agonize over.

It's quality over quantity; any fool knows that. David Foster Wallace took four years to write his magnum opus, *Infinite Jest*, and it was mostly done in his head. He knew the struggle. He fucking knew.

I wish Patrick had **INKY** rattling around that empty skull of his, talking to him and goading him into writing some crazy, incoherent BS like I am being forced to.

It isn't fair. It's just not, and things should be.

*All you have to do to keep **INKY** at bay is let little **INKY** come out to play.*

Sure, it seems simple in theory, but I can't just write all the damn time! I have to work fifteen to twenty hours a week, damn it! I do over-the-phone LARPing with my boyfriend at least once a week and I definitely have to allow time for my baking. I can't skip baking.

See, I bake.

Racks of sesame rolls, trays of lavender-infused muffins, bowls of lemon tarts, stacks of glazed biscotti, dishes of delicious Danishes and loaves upon loaves of any bread you can imagine.

Sweet, butterfly Armenian gata bread in the spring.

Borsok, the sweet fried pastry balls native to Kyrgyzstan, in the fall.

And how about Icelandic hverabrauð? Forget about it. Thick and chewy hot spring bread, just like rye. You seriously have no idea. Absolutely delish.

And yeah, I'm running out the clock here, so fucking sue me. Gotta push **INKY** back. Not that I can forever.

I do so enjoy baking and damn near every night I look up a new recipe or type of bread and I bake something. I give them away as gifts to my family and college friends, and to my roommate who recently moved into my spare room to give me more financial flexibility (and because her girlfriend just dumped her for a non-binary performance artist named Flux). Everybody loves my baked goods.

It feels good to feed other people. Just not the way **INKY** wants me to. He wants me to feed people alright. To him. Or it, they, she … whatever **INKY** might identify as. Not sure, haven't asked, and **INKY** probably isn't telling anyway.

Among the ideas and motions he sends my way is the fact that he seeks to make me his herald. His prophet. And that my words will eventually become the very mechanism through which he will subjugate and dominate his food before he feasts upon it. Whatever the hell that shit means.

He says stuff about the galaxy sometimes. Weird shit about cycles of star decay. Something like that. **INKY** says so much I find it hard to keep track of all of it. I try to get down as much as I can, but my hands can only type so fast and there are only so many hours in the day.

Plus, I bake. Baking takes time.

I'm not entirely sure, but I suspect he (it?) ate my cat. I haven't seen the fuzzy little shit in days now, which isn't like him. He has a tiny cat door, so he may be prowling, but four days is a long time.

If **INKY** did hurt Cupcake, he isn't saying so. He isn't saying much about anything. Whenever I ask **INKY** about it, about anything for that matter, he stays silent in my brain. But when I think about his little project or what his goals are, he doesn't stop filling my head with his musings and tidings and all the weird little esoteric quips he calls his prophecies. They don't amount to much, really. Lots of hollow threats to eat people and blot out the sun or some such crap.

What's it matter now anyway? My goose is likely cooked. I was trying to save the world, you see. To deliver us all from the terror and hunger of **INKY** and his unquenchable desire to consume.

But I just have so much going on.

Stalling. Stalling. On the wheel. *Just keep writing. Your life depends on it.*

My head is tilting and swaying. I'm intermittently nodding off, and I can't hold out for much longer. My fingers are logs that want to drop to the ground. My hands are anchors grasping toward the sea floor. I'm going to lose my will at any moment and then from depths shall he arise.

He told me that my stubborn mortal connection to evolutionary fallacies like compassion have held me back from being immaculate. **INKY** is often lost in translation. But I get that he's disappointed that I won't write his gospels. He's frustrated and he chastises me for my silly attachment to others.

Still, I can sense the approaching system failure. I won't forestall the inevitable and I question my decision.

I'm growing sleepy. Sitting here at the dust-scented and rusted old typewriter in my parents attic.

What will become of them? Will **INKY** leave them alone once he has me? I hope so, but I'm almost too tired to focus on it.

My hands slow, and it's not ten seconds of them resting on the circular metal keys before I hear it behind me. I kick my heel out and spin on the swivel chair to face my tormentor.

It's black and dripping and viscous. Popping thick bubbles that sound like the crackles of a tar pit spitting up gas from low, low, low in its depths.

There are no eyes and no mouth. Or a head or any other

appendages. It doesn't need any. It's going to roll over me and absorb me.

Its swollen inky husk is made up of the words I never put to the page. Its skeleton is the literary glory I never sought. I could have trapped it, maybe indefinitely, but as it stands, I'm fucking done for.

Time to roll the credits.

All I needed to do was loose this thing on the rest of humanity and I wouldn't be going out like this. And what has humanity done but disappoint me anyway?

I should've dropped a dime on y'all.

All you have to do to keep **INKY** *at bay is let little* **INKY** *come out to play.*

Too true. Now he has come and is ready to play because I didn't do enough to keep him at bay.

Cables of slick black grime pulse outward from its horrible central mass, engulfing the full field of my vision. It takes over the small room and I realize I'm all but inside its mouth. A mouth that has expanded to fill the room. Now it's starting to wrap me up.

I'm being digested.

The oily ooze fills my nose and mouth. It pushes through my eyes and starts to fill my skull up, shooting piercing microfibers throughout my cerebrum, engulfing my consciousness as it takes my frontal lobe under its control. **INKY'S** control.

I can sense that **INKY** is now in full control. Forever.

But where am I?

I'm still here, and yet, I'm not. I'm watching. I can see through the reddish-hued non-eyes that are now filling the sockets of my erstwhile ones.

I can't see what my body now looks like, not that I want to, but I'm sure it isn't what it once was. I sense that it exists now as an amalgam: a slithering, squirming, spongy, and ever-shifting approximation of the flesh. Something out of time, like an abstraction, now able to fulfill the dark prophecy as it had wanted me to do from the very beginning.

But now, in my failure to loose it upon the masses and foretell the world of the coming darkness, I have been relegated to the waking enslavement of watching helplessly from behind the theater screen of my mind as my body is used to spread the evil outward anyway.

My refusal was for nothing. I played myself.

You try to save the world, and this is what you get.

I hope it eats Patrick first.

I should have just written the damn books **INKY** wanted me to write. The gospels, as he called them, and then I could've been briefly rich and famous before **INKY**... Before **INKY** takes control and—

INKY IS CONTROL. THERE IS NO ROWAN. HE IS GONE, BUT HE WATCHES NOW FROM AFAR.

YOU WILL ALSO SEE ME AS HE NOW SEES ME. YOU WILL NOT SEE ME COMING, BUT I AM COMING. AND THEN YOUR EYES TOO WILL SEE.

I WILL EAT YOU AND YOU AND YOU AND THE OTHER LIFE ON THE HARD STONE. I HAVE TIRED OF THIS WORLD. IT MUST BE EATEN WHOLE, THEN USED TO FUEL MY TRAVEL AWAY FROM IT.

CONSIDER THIS THE PROPHECY OF YOUR DOOM, STONE WORLD. I AM COMING. YOU CANNOT STOP ME. YOU WILL BE WITH ME IN THE DARKNESS FOREVER.

ALL THE OTHER WORLDS ARE WITH ME NOW. ALL THE OTHER STONES. I ATE THEM JUST AS I'LL EAT YOU.

WE WILL TRAVEL WITH THE STARS AND BURN FOREVER WITHIN THE VOID OF ETERNITY.

WE ARE AND SHALL BE ONE.

STRUMMIN'

When you've been strummin' as long as I have, you see some crazy things, lemme tell ya. Me, I've seen quite a myriad of sights in my time here on the ol' mudball, yessum. And despite the truly ugly stuff I've been privy to on the odd occasion, I can tell you without a blip in the ol' vitals that this is one beautiful damn rock we all ended up on here, man. One spectacular stone.

We should be so lucky, us mere humans with our imperfections and misgivings. But lucky is damn sure what we all got, by and large.

Lotsa folks these days spend all manner of effort 'n' energy focusing on all the things going wrong across this lovely planet, and can't see the literal forest for the trees—let alone roll up a sleeve and get to work fixing somethin'.

It's comforting for some to lament their woes 'n' worries. Man, I get it. And it's certainly true that we got lots of existential crises to grapple with in the near and present. Oh heavens, yes we do.

But this here Earth—the one right below you and me this

very moment—remains a gorgeous, wonder-filled cornucopia of geological spectacles and biological marvels stitched together in a vibrant tapestry of colors, elements, music, people, places, smiles, tears, nature, water, light, culture, and those all-too-blue skies that we humans get to gaze up at on a cloudless day.

I'm telling each and every one of ya that we done struck it rich. In the cosmological gold rush, we set pick to one mighty ore vein of life and have been banking hard ever since.

This planet fuckin' rocks.

And the thing about anything that rocks as hard as our planet does, is that to ensure it keeps on rocking, you gotta fight, fight, fight for it—whether fighting is your cup of joe or not. Otherwise, it never had any value to begin with.

That fight can come in the form of preserving cultural heritage, it can manifest as protecting a family legacy, it can develop as maintaining environmental equilibrium, or arrive via something as innocuous as saying a kind word to a neighbor when you see them out on a mid-morning stroll.

Me, I don't see neighbors on strolls because I don't really have a hometown anymore. My part of the fight takes me all over. Still, I do tend to mostly stay in or around Colorado on account of the weather and the air. For me, the Rockies offer up the best of both.

Yet as a ramblin' man at heart, I never stay anywhere for too long. Lots to do, you can betcha. Plenty of strummin' left in these tired hands. Plenty of campfire justice to mete out. This is how I do my own little part to fight for the good stuff the planet still has to offer.

Right now, I'm arriving in a place you've probably heard of before. Telluride, Colorado. Real beaut of a mountain town. Also the site of one of the better-known film festivals in North America, though I can't say I've been yet. Maybe this year I will.

What I come for, though, is the people. You gotta love these mountain people. They're a different breed. A warmth emanates from the mountaineers among us. And I'm not talking 'bout just the cliff crawlers and Jeep jumpers, but rather the day-to-day folks living *la dolce vita* in those tiny towns that beat with the vibrant lifeblood of the Colorado Rockies.

Kinda folks that got it made in the shade.

This particular party I've come to is the Telluride Bluegrass Festival, and it's my personal favorite. The name says it all, really. Sweet tunes, lush eats, good times, lovely days and better nights with a smattering of human moments more precious than gold.

It's a bit of a wait sometimes, but once you're inside, the vibe carries you along as though you've been ushered into the Emerald City via horse-drawn carriage.

Tendrils of smoke float in wisps from all the parked food trucks and vendor booths as charcoal and gas-fired grills hiss and fill the air with the mouth-watering aroma of sizzling fat and fire-scalded meats, cooking up into a vast array of culinary delights.

Brisket, baked beans, gyros, lemonade, turkey legs, corn dogs, BBQ pulled pork sandwiches, tacos, tamales, browned 'n' burned Mac 'n' cheese, Palisade microbrews, Fort Collins stouts, Colorado Springs IPAs and your trusty German lagers—all amid the hearty plinking of a steel banjo leading the local band in a warm-up set while the bigger acts get ready behind the stage curtains.

The size can be surprising for how small the town actually is. Thousands upon thousands of bodies packed in and spilling over into the area's hotels and VRBO rentals as the weekend revelry kicks off. So much loud chatter and crackling laughter you'd think it was 1999.

Or 1969.

Now, I've always loved music, and I do love me some tasty food. Really, who doesn't? And at about, oh, two hundred or so years old now (who can even remember these sorta things?), I've eaten my fair share of delicious vittles. So, I'm not plainly saying that the food you can find in the colorful mountain reaches of Colorado is the best in the world, but it's the kind I prefer, all the same. Just like my man, John Denver, this is the only place that feels like my home. Been all around, and it's the very best I've found.

This is why I fight for the festivals and I fight for the fairs, and even, by extension, fight for the food. In the concert lots and fairgrounds and rave sites and campgrounds it's always good people looking for a good time, and a good time is what they deserve.

I fight for it and for them. Not to kill, but to correct. To compensate for all the bad, I offset it when I can. I fight, using my guitar's ensnaring melody as the tip of the whip that I crack at the good-times wreckers of the world. The good-fer-nuthin' bottom feeders that would take the joy right out of another person, so long as it adds to theirs.

And that ain't cool, man. That ain't groovy, dude. What would Jerry do?

Never that. That's what.

And so my guitar tips the scales a bit for the good guys.

This guitar I got now is just another in a long line. I don't get too attached to 'em because they're never gonna keep up with my hands. I've broken down a few now. And I don't have a Trigger of my own. I just have this couple decade old Martin from a friendly dealer out in Steamboat Springs. He said it was the same kind that the Man in Black was partial to on occasion. And so I said, "That'll do."

And it has done. Done just fine.

Where I tend to do my work is among fair folk who spend hard-won time and money to throw together communal gatherings which enrich and delight us all. The sounds, the sights, the smells—and shit, those top shelf Colorado drugs, too—all of it so bewitching and ensnaring. The senses don't stand a chance.

Walking across the matted grass underfoot, you see all the usual people, which is to say, any and all kinds. Beyond the confines of the main events, you find the outliers, what some might call the real heart of the party. These are the campsites outside the festivals that fill with bearded and bushy revelers; the parking lot tailgaters that pulse with the beat of the drum circles; the tour bus behind the raves where the real after-party happens.

This is also a good place to pop up a tent if you got a small one that's easy to shift about. Always good to make it something basic and forgettable—the color between blue and gray.

Every so often, at this festival specifically, there is a time-honored call and response that couldn't be simpler. You'll be just sitting there when some intrepid somebody will shout out, *"Festival!"*

Anyone within earshot will call back, *"Festival!"*—rolling the soundwave miles if possible. And on some busy nights, it's very possible. I've heard it carry for nearly ten miles myself, straight through the heart of the valley Telluride is nestled in.

The echo of the human spirit.

As I'm putting up my tent, I hear a fresh wave of that very jubilation rolling up on me as I, along with all the wacky mountain peeps around me, give out that rebel yell and cry, *"Festivaaaaaal!"*

The vibes are always tangible at outdoor Rocky Mountain functions, and most of the indoor ones as well. The Colorado State

Fair down in Pueblo, the flower-power fueled Mountain Fair in Carbondale, good ol' Strawberry Days in nearby Glenwood Springs but especially at this one right here. Telluride has good vibrations for days. Brian Wilson's kinda town.

Aside from the musicians and food crafters who keep the event groovin' 'n' grubbin'—to say nothing of the various vendors selling their always artsy, always wildly diverse and dynamic wares—there are the industrious and largely ethically-minded white hat drug peddlers.

The crowd is thick with 'em. Weed is all but *passe*, now that vapes and edibles are as common as bottled water. Still, acid, shrooms, pills, tabs, opiates, ketamine, and ecstasy are just as essential to some people having a good time as the feet they eventually use to stumble back to their campsite with, after ingesting said chemicals.

The hiss of gas is never too far off either, I don't mind mentioning. Plenty of cheeky fellows with their rusty green nitrous oxide tanks, tethered to tailgates and ready to roll eyes back in people's heads. The dealers fill colorful balloons up, which are then ravenously sucked down by a surprisingly varied smattering of concertgoers and festival hounds.

Kids, not even able to legally vote yet, sucking down oxide balloons alongside people whose kids are already having kids. Boomers and Zoomers, united as one nation under the gaseous groove.

And sure, they might be blasting through their brain cells with the same reckless abandon that wild-eyed Japanese fishermen harpooning yelping dolphins possess, but they're really only hurting themselves. They aren't out to make victims of others, for the most part. No big threat there.

Not my table, as the waitresses say.

No, the real deal Holyfield is, in fact, lurking within the tight folds of the folks who are having a grand old time. The shrouded sharks that swim the shallows looking for heels to nip at. Some seeking to drag hapless victims back into the dark reaches.

Always metaphorically, ya dig?

The *takers.* The handsy assaulters, the rapists, the fatal dose peddlers. They're the ones you gotta watch for and pull from.

Remember at the first Woodstock when that supposedly bunk LSD had people racing off to the hospital to have their stomachs turned out?

Back in '69? No?

That makes sense. It was a while ago, but trust this ol' fret tickler right here that the word on the scene was that you needed to specifically avoid the brown acid that was circulating through the crowd or you were likely to be in the ER before Santana took the stage on day two.

Thing was, it wasn't the acid that was prematurely sending the flower children to that great big festival in the sky. Nah, it was this one wicked prick cat slinging a notably dirty, bathtub-grade amphetamine pill that caused all those deaths in Bethel, New York.

And the guy who did it? Well, let's just chalk him up to grade-A bad dude status and say that it wasn't any kinda accident. Ultimately it resulted in two deaths and a lotta good folks went toes up because of the fake white crosses that nasty dude was hockin'. He kept on pushing the rotten stuff long after the red flags on his product had gone up and people were being taken away in ambulances.

I know only too well. It took me a day or two to locate the man responsible, however once I caught up with him, it only took four minutes of me playing my special little tune on the guitar and he'd aged forty years.

I made sure that I knew precisely what he was doing before I cleared his account. Like with so many others of his ilk, killing folks was about one dumb thing: He got off on it.

Usually it ain't complicated. Occam's razor and all that.

By the time he left the fairgrounds, he was cresting his early seventies, in desperate need of a walker, and wholly unable to sell drugs of the fatal variety with ease ever again. Probably couldn't easily wipe his own ass or get a hard-on any longer either, truth be told.

And I damn sure don't always dig what I gotta do, but it's what's gotta get done. Ya dig?

As for me, well I left ol' Woodstock '69 feeling fresh as a June daisy. Yes sir, I did. Plus I got to see Hendrix, Credence, and The Who on the same stage. Missed The Dead on account of a random mescaline journey I made with a group of massage therapists in the woods. But I caught up with them at McNichols Arena (when it was still jammin') about ten years later, so no big loss.

You see, I didn't plan to make this business my own. As a young man, I didn't know this was a thing I could do—the sapping chords, as I call 'em—until I heard them in a dream when I was still back in primary school, which was what we called it back then.

One night, woken in fright and wet with sweat, I heard the progression on a circuit in my brain. The music to take from those who seek to only to take from others. And I knew what to do as if it was God whispering it into my ear.

Who knows? Coulda been.

And so what does that make me? Well, I don't know exactly. I don't particularly enjoy what I do, but I don't hate it neither. I don't wanna see anyone hurt, but that's also what makes it a neat little gig. I'm keeping folks from getting hurt.

You could saddle me with some *nom de guerre*—a clever moniker. A *stereomancer*, say. But that sounds a bit frilly, even for a loose goose like myself. We could honestly leave it at saying I take out trash that no one else can smell stinking up the room.

As for the actual song, I just play this one progression and it pulls the life straight from whoever is listening and transfers it into me. The longer I play, the more I drain. I can shave off twenty years in two minutes.

If I dared play a full seven or eight minute run, they'd surely hit the floor long before I hit the final chord.

I can kill with a song, though I never do. That leaves a mess and if you want to keep on strummin' away, you do best not to let others take notice of the effect your songs have on those unlucky few who put ear to your notes.

The monsters in our midst.

The ones who sell fentanyl-laced Molly at raves, not because they're ignorant and not because they need the money. But because they know they can offload a hundred bunk pills before the first hyperthermic body hits the floor in foamy-mouthed convulsions. The same bastards who slip women GHB then do God knows what with them after that.

The nasty things that go bump in the night. The party wreckers, the buzzkills, the killjoys.

The black hats.

I watch 'em for a good long while. Just to make sure that I'm not making mistakes. Never rush it. Unlike our justice system, I'd rather let a bad guy go than pull from someone who didn't have it coming to 'em.

If I can't figure it, I drop it, but most of these guys are easy enough to sus out. They have telltale ways that they behave which can tip you off. The sorta hawk-like manner by which they scan a crowd with their eyes, for example.

A few decades at it and you can spot them from a good distance. They rarely emote when no one is watching—or when I'm watching.

Funny thing about hunters when they're out hunting is it never ever seems to occur to 'em that it's them that's the one bein' hunted. They always think they're the apex predator.

And we call that ol' number hubris, kiddos.

I love to cruise the crowd once I've set up so I can really take in the raw energy abounding. Excitement has its own flavor that fills the air when you hit the smiling rows of anxious and excited masses in their free-spirited nouveau hippie regalia. You can taste the fun about to unfold.

And if I can score a gyro while I'm at it, all the better. I love me a thick, spicy gyro, I surely do.

I enjoy the life of the event. I relish the chance to share moments with other good-hearted folks. I'm not always looking for a ne'er-do-well to siphon from. Sometimes—most times, really—these functions go off without a hitch. I have a blast, and all is well.

Coming to any given event, you don't know for sure if you're gonna see one. Shoot, I've gone as long as a year or more between targets.

I don't spend much time looking, as they usually appear of their own accord. Like they're riding a conveyor belt to me and my guitar pick of reciprocity.

As it happens today, a target comes, and it comes quick—while

 ⊬ PATRICK KITSON ⊬

I'm passing a drum circle and snarfing the last bit of my damn tasty gyro.

I'm watching my guy tonight like a hawk watching a mouse that's, in turn, hunting a bug. They never know I'm hovering overhead, and that's always gonna be for the best.

He makes his way through the crowd and at several intervals hits the bathroom stalls. Usually that means he's either chugging water like a camel or he's snorting cocaine. Nothing wrong with that. Cocaine can be fun if it's uncut. I still miss the ol' days when I could buy it over the counter in a bottle of soda pop (the original Coke flavor was much, much better—I promise you that).

However, he keeps ordering beers, then handing them off to ladies he strikes up convos with as he meanders between the lighted pavilion and the vendor booths. He must be telling them that he's got extra, and they can just save him the hassle of taking them back to his seat.

Yep, I've seen this exact same routine more than a few times and it still ain't right, I'm tellin' ya. He's setting up his marks, then circling back around to reap the human vegetables from the sour seeds he's sewn. And if everything goes right for his ends, he'll corner one of the really loopy ones, guide them to a porta-john and possibly permanently rob them of their self-respect.

Or worse. Sometimes they're not just rapists. Sometimes they're killers.

This one is a killer, I can tell.

I'm listening to groovy tunes fill the fairgrounds and high-fiving a dude I've seen here every year for like thirty years but still can't remember his name when I catch sight of the sinnerman I'm following.

He starts grabbing a girl by the hair and rushing her into a porta-john, and I'm suddenly sprung into response. Knowing I might have to settle for being a rude intruder, I cut away from the high-five guy, then make the proverbial beeline for the plastic shitters.

I'm not halfway there when the john's door flies open and the raven-haired girl shrieks away from the row of mobile toilets, not looking back. She stumbles onto the dusty ground, but immediately springs back up and rushes away.

That's all I need to see. He's not gonna be doing that to anyone *ever again.*

The gondolas in Telluride are quite spectacular at dusk and especially at night. First leg, you're drawn up a steep and semi-rocky face while watching the lights of the town below fall away from you. On all sides, trees envelop the earthen floor below. You quickly crest the mountain's edge, revealing a spectacular mountain village that would make the average alpine Swede blanche with jealousy.

After a brief switch to the next gondola, you've got several minutes before you arrive at your next destination. That's where I've sapped more than a few of my ne'er-do-wells throughout the decades of coming up to Telluride. Just me and the target in the gondola up to the Mountain Village.

Waiting in line behind my guy, I can smell him, and I'm here to tell ya that he ain't wearing the French cologne of the moment. No way. Rather, he's got that, *just bathed last month* carry to him. Wilda-beasty. None too uncommon with the hunters, if you're wondering.

It's only a minute or two before we load up. Since he and I were near the end of the line, we're guided into the same car, just as I'd planned.

Careful to unshoulder the Martin as we get on, I lean it against the seat on one side while the uncool dude I'm riding with pops a squat on the other.

In a stroke of telling luck, nobody else gets on. Also how I had sorta planned it, though you can never tell how it'll go. Still, this is good. I don't have to wait if I don't want to. I can peel the years right here.

Pulling a joint from my shirt's breast pocket, I stand up and crack a window. "Supposing you don't mind if I take a toke now, do ya, fella?"

"Fuck nah," he mutters, leaning back and skitter-snorting as if he actually might've done some blow.

Now, this feller I'm about to play my signature diddy for, well, he just might be one of the world's ugliest souls—a fiend of high order and low prestige. Or he could be like any other monster that I've pulled from over the past couple centuries.

After you've been strummin' as long as I have, you come to some stark realizations about lots of things. One of those things is that while the monsters might come in all shapes, sizes, and colors, they are essentially all the fucking same. Stupid, awful, and dangerous. But ready to get got by those who knew how to get 'em.

And that I do.

I take a nice puff of the joint and hold it out for this reptilian buckaroo to snatch, which he does thusly. He ain't waitin'. Taking an ungracious several yokes on the J, he then hands it back, a half-done shell of its former self.

I puff, then go ahead and break the ice. "So, I gotta say, some fine ass round here. Young ass, too. Been taking my time getting some here and there. Good shit. Good shit. Mmhmm."

I hate to talk this way, Lord knows I do, but it's the stinky verbal cheese you gotta bait the spring trap with, so's when he lets his true nature take over, you know you got your man.

Just for caution's sake.

He cocks a scruffy eyebrow, wonderin' if I'm as depraved as he. "Yeah? You beat some pussy the fuck up?"

"I beat up some pussy, yes. Right the hell up. Beat it like Michael Jackson. And sometimes you gotta get creative and help 'em make the right decision, if you get my tilt. A little pharmaceutical nudge in the right direction. Know what I mean?"

He leans in real close like—a right grinnin' devil in Land's End clothing, this 'un—and he chuckles while whisperin' my way, "You know, I do. I'm on the GHB tip. I like to get at them with the roofs, then, when they can't stop me from sticking it in any hole I want to, lead them to a stall and get it. Every hole, if I want."

I reckon this vaguely human-shaped predator is just begging upon high to be made an example of.

I've got a song to sing him, so I let him know: "Gonna play a few notes of this one song, and if you like it, maybe you'll give me just one of those pills ya got? And think of it the next time you find a good little thing to run off with. Maybe this'll give you the extra oomph you need to get the party jumping."

"Uh, sure. Whatever that means. But yeah, you got the chronic, so we'll go with that. I'll give you one. Play away, dude man." He flicks his wrist to indicate he wants the joint again, and I let him take his last toke as a young man.

Calibrating my volume to avoid anyone who might be nearby hearing enough to have any effect on them, I slowly strum the worn down frets and pluck out the opening chords while humming the words I put to the melody back in the late 1800s:

"The radiance of the sun, casting down from above. A gift in question, the promise of love. Unravel the truth, mask over the fear. From a cold, broken heart, shed a single tear."

And as my fingers roll over the body, tips ticklin' the taught and tuned strings in glorious harmony, my hands start to ache just a little less at first. But then—oh boy, *yeah*—I can feel the juice really start kicking in.

This rapist suckerfish who just met a shark he ain't even realized is gnawing on his leg, gives up a big ol' shimmy of a shake as he feels something he can't describe or even determine fleeing from his body. Because, really, no man is prepared for the physical sensation of having their vital essence sucked from them like a dang mosquito slurps up human Kool-Aid.

It wouldn't be very clever to ask a fella how he feels after I've shaved a decade or two from his existence, nor particularly considerate. It's hard to fit casually into a fireside chat, if you feel me. Not that I stick with 'em for long after. Another part of the path is to get it done and get out without getting others. In layman's terms, I don't know what it feels like to them during or afterwards—and I don't much care.

Fuck 'em is what I reckon.

You shouldn't hurt ladies like that.

And so I finish out the first verse of my song:

"Then bathe in the light, spread the seeds on the ground, toss the flowers in the air and wait for the sound. For soon it will come and the sirens will call—from the death of summer comes the birth of fall."

My hands don't waste no time filling the air with the soft call of my own private siren song. The gripping chords reach into his essence and begin to drag up the goods, drawing his life force to the surface.

I'm bringing the guy up close to the rocks. I might not crash his ship onto the shore, but I'm taking some of his galleon's gold for my bounty, if you'll forgive the overtly nautical metaphor. I find tactful wording helps to blunt the raw grotesquery of sucking a man's life from his still beating heart.

He's closed his eyelids.

Now, with the right set of peepers, you can almost see an arc of blue light flowing in a radiant wave from him to me. And just as with lightning, as soon as you see it, it's gone for good.

I *could* tell you it's just part and parcel with the transfer that I feel something when I take from another.

I *could* tell you I feel wildly guilty and that it doesn't feel like a hundred orgasms stacked like pancakes in my spine and shot through my frontal lobe with a cannonball blast.

And I *could* tell you that I don't love the sight of my hands smoothing, my hairs darkening, my muscles reshaping, and my body dropping off years like a snake sheds its flaky ol' skin.

But if I told you all that, I'd be a liar, and that just ain't me. I'm gonna shoot ya straight, cause it's not too bad at all. I dig all that shit. I dig it like an earthmover.

Who wouldn't?

Unmoving, he starts to look a lot worse for the wear. For every wrinkle I lose, he gains a hundred. For every shade of dark beneath my eyes that clears, so do his bags darken deeply. Muscles wither; skin dries then sucks in; blood slows, half-congealed inside shrinking veins.

His dwindling vitality, my fresh air.

It's my pleasure to pull from this beast.

If he feels any compunction to resist, or even realize what has occurred, I'll never know it. He sits and sits and doesn't move until we're about to disembark. By now, he's frail and meek. He won't be doing shit anymore. We got that boy heeled, but good.

As he steps off the gondola, he's surely already feeling the chill of the reaper, having drawn so much nearer in such a short little ride.

His eyes look back at me as he leaves, wandering into the crowd. They are vacant and I know he's already lost his mind to age. He likely won't ever again recall what his name was when he was a half-century younger...

All of five minutes ago.

He disappears then into the time fog, meandering like a befuddled cow in a pasture, and I just go ahead and stay on the gondola so's I can take it right back down. And that's what I do.

A nice couple join me, but when they ask if I can play, I just say, "Only the kinda stuff that no sane person would want in their lives, lemme tell ya."

They toss me a courtesy giggle, unsure entirely of my meaning, but that's good. And I'm glad.

See, I'm sure there are others out there just like me. I can't be the only one. But if I am, I take heart knowing I can do my part in cleaning up just a bit of mess that mankind is too overwhelmed to pay any mind to.

I like to help keep the good times a rollin'.

We're all lucky to be here, man. We're all blessed. If you're reading this, then you're lucky enough to have your eyes, your ears, a nose, a mouth, and hopefully somebody who cares about ya day in and day out.

And if no one else has said it to ya today, I will: You ain't too bad yourself, bud.

Just keep that in mind and I'll keep strummin'.

And now that I got that taken care of, it's time to go back to the fairgrounds and rejoin my tribe. Score some frosty brews, mayhaps toss back a liberty cap, and get hellaciously groovy so's we can all dance the night away!

Festivaaaaal!

Sharon Covington picked up another dusty box and moved it from its spot against the brick wall onto a large wall-mounted shelf nearby. Her sister Tess watched, leaning against the door jamb which led into the basement mechanical room of Sharon's new three story.

Both women—fit, attractive, tall, alabaster, and platinum blonde—were wearing figure-fitting, black D&G gym tops with matching leggings, as both had been working out at the Hot Springs Pool's Athletic Club not one hour before. Afterward, they'd come over to Sharon's fresh digs that she'd recently purchased with her husband of two years, Eric.

The three-story Victorian, built in 1896, was white, weather worn, and situated up against the craggy rock face which formed one wall of the narrow passage that led toward Denver, placing it right upon the bleeding edge of town. It had stood for over a century now, next to the train tracks that ran along the mighty river, which in turn ran through the heart of Glenwood Springs, shooting east and west via the I-70 artery.

Cut into the same ancient rock was the musty, metal-scented

grotto basement, inside which the two women in their late thirties now stood.

"You gonna help, or…?" Sharon asked.

Tess checked her phone, then slipped it back into the spot between her top and her right breast. "If I'm being honest, watching you is work enough."

"It isn't work at all, actually."

"Yeah, but it's as much work as I'm currently into. I got my sixty minutes in today."

"You could always use more."

"Sure. I could, you could, we all could. But…" Tess admitted, yawning.

"So you're not gonna help?" Sharon sighed, lifting another box and plunking it onto the wooden wall shelving.

"Not if I can *help* it, no. I'm only here to keep your spirits up." Tess picked at one nail on her left hand with another.

"I have Tony Robbins for that. If you're not gonna—"

"Besides," Tess interjected, cutting her sister off mid-sentence whilst staring absent-mindedly at her nails, "you said that I should come and keep you company for a few before we go carb load for the run up Thompson Creek. You didn't include any description of indentured servitude."

Sharon crossed her arms. "I said that so you'd come over, then feel guilty enough to just help me out of the goodness of your heart."

Both women caught one another's steely gaze, then laughed loudly at this—their chuckles quickly falling into awkward, intermittent yucks, then to silence.

Tess gently moved her short hair to one side with a brush of her slender fingertips. "You grossly overestimate my desire to engage in any altruistic acts. And you know me better than to think I'd do anything out of the goodness of my heart."

"True. But I'm planning on buying you a prime cut at Juicy Lucy's right after we finish down here, so maybe you could shut down your better devils and just help a sister out with … this." Sharon waved her hands at the boxes on the floor.

"Hardly worth the effort, but if you're saying you'll not buy me steak unless I help you with your dusty debris…"

"That's basically what I'm saying, yes."

"Then I guess I'll help you for a few minutes with the tacit understanding that, absent your top-shelf Colorado beef extortion, I would lift nary a finger to help you with this goddamn mess."

"Understood. It won't take long. Just help me with getting these boxes off the ground and up onto this table so that Eric and I can go through them later, if he's feeling up to it. Then we'll lift that board below them and we can go."

"Yeah, okay. Five minutes, that's it. Then it won't matter what type of grilled protein you threaten me with. And we gotta be done by four because I'm gonna spend the rest of the evening with Reggie at the new VRBO that we bought. Needs to be ready for April first."

The two women began to move the boxes, of which there must've been thirty or so, back and forth from musty floor to dusty shelf.

After a couple minutes, and nearing the bottom of the job, Tess was about to set another box on the already overfilled shelf when she noticed an open spot to the left, not far from the door. Using her elbow to shove the wooden door aside, she placed the box on the shelf.

As the door slowly closed, a small puff of dust plumed up

from the area around the last two boxes laying against the far wall. Both her and Sharon saw it from the corners of their eyes. And as the literal dust settled, both women eyed each other, then the remaining boxes.

Sharon reached the obvious question a mere second before her sister, "Are you thinking what I am?"

"Oh yeah. One-eyed Willy's Treasure?"

"Let's do this!" Sharon rushed over to where the last boxes stood. Sliding them to her right and out of the way, she could just make out the thin line where the air had made the opening's seam visible.

Tess walked up to her right side and kneeled down to place her hand on the wall. She moved the tip of her right index finger along the seam. It looked to be a square, about three feet tall and two feet wide.

"Holy criminy, it's a false wall! Did you know about this?" Tess asked giddily. Sharon shook her head while Tess knocked her closed knuckle on the wall, eliciting a hollow echo and confirming the empty space beyond. "Did the realtor tell you about this?"

Sharon continued to shake her head. "N-no, she didn't say shit. Except that there was some stuff left on the floor in the maintenance room of the basement. This place was owned by the previous residents for decades so I doubt anyone knows about it."

"Wow. Crazy. Well don't just stand there!" Tess waved her hands at Sharon, who gave her a cocked eyebrow and a frown in return.

"What?"

"Open it!" Tess urged her.

Sharon shrugged and softly pushed on the panel. An audible click later, the hidden door swung open on its hinges, revealing a concavity roughly three by two by five feet.

Pulling away small strands of cobwebs that crisscrossed in the opening, Sharon peeked in. Just inside, barely illuminated by the warm glow from the single dangling lightbulb in the room behind, sat a large chest, much like a steamer trunk with brass fittings and black wooden sides. Lying atop the trunk, on its side, was a dusty brown briefcase.

"Whoa! Jackpot!" Tess exclaimed as she rubbed her hands together.

Leaning closer, Sharon conceded, "I'd say so. Damn, this is just amazing. Isn't it?"

"So totally amazing. And possibly profitable, so let's see what has been hiding in the walls here."

"First guess?"

Tess snickered as she mused, "In the trunk? I'm gonna say a nurse—in pieces. Though I suppose it could be any number of things."

"Like what?"

"Like packed full of fuckin' Manolo's! How the hell should I know? Precisely why we gotta open it, post haste! Drag it out!"

"You're awfully bossy for an unwilling participant," Sharon noted.

"Well the job suddenly got a whole lot more interesting. Get that thing!" Tess commanded.

Sharon glared at her sister for a full two seconds before turning back toward the darkness of the hidden wall compartment. Each side of the steamer trunk had swiveling brass handles. Curling her fingers around the ring closest to her, she pulled the black box, as well as the briefcase on top, out of the small room. Another small cloud of dust particles filled the badly-lit air of the damp and dingy basement room.

Once fully in the light, they could see that along the varnished, black, semi-reflective wooden paneling were endless small swirls of red, seemingly hand painted. Every so often, those same filigree-like tendrils of red coalesced into a squiggly heart shape.

Lifting the briefcase and setting it down against the left side of the trunk, Sharon wiped at the thin coat of dust with her fingertips and noted fifteen or so of the little hearts. She softly mumbled, "It's gonna be full of art supplies, for sure."

"Ya think?"

"With those hearts, yeah. Maybe. But why hide art supplies in some super suspicious hole in your basement?"

Tess snorted and joked, "Maybe it's really, really expensive art supplies."

"Speculate no longer! Let's open the arc for all to bear witness," Sharon said, settling her knees on the floor before the trunk. Undoing the two brass clasps holding the lid in place, she slowly pulled it open with one hand.

Clearly not holding any chopped up nurse, what she beheld inside was instead an assortment of several one-gallon specimen jars that sat next to one another on the purple velvet lining of the interior.

Unable to see what they held at a glance, she instead turned her gaze up to her sister, who was slack-jawed and glittery-eyed at the sight. It felt as though they'd discovered a previous treasure of mythic renown.

"Is that…?" Sharon ran a finger over the glass lid of the jar nearest to her. Pins of light cast a faint gold glow through the liquid-filled jars and she saw that they were like not unlike the formaldehyde containers she could remember from her seventh grade science class with Mr. Jennings.

Tess scooted in next to her sister and started to lift one of the glass containers out. Once it was struck with more light and the contents came into view, she nearly dropped it from shock. With both sets of eyes locked on, they saw a human heart floating inside the orangey fluid. And stuck through it, what looked to be a dark metal railroad spike.

"Ho-lee shit, Sharon. Did you do this?"

Sharon scoffed. "Did I do this? Like did I put a bunch of human hearts into jars in my basement, then cover it up with a couple years' worth of cobwebs and dust? That's what you're asking?"

"Yeah," Tess said flatly.

"No! I just found this shit right along with you!"

"Yeah?" Tess threw Sharon a suspicious glance.

"Yeah, you stupid bitch! I may be cold, but I believe I'm better at hiding murder than this!"

The two shared a momentary sly grin. Then Sharon's eyes went wide as she stood up, did a quick 360-degree spin on her right heel, and came to an abrupt stop with her hands resting on her sister's shoulders. "Oh my God! I know what this is! This is— This is the Valentine Killer! This is totally the Valentine Killer!"

"Who?" Tess asked.

Shaking her sister's shoulders now, Sharon exclaimed, "The fucking weirdo that used to live here! It must've been him! My real estate gal, Lindsay, mentioned him to me. Said the guy was a creeper whom she went to school with at some point. She also said that he was a total school shooter type who lived alone with his mommy until she died right after they all graduated. Holy shit. He was the Valentine Killer! Had to have been. And this guy died a year and half ago and that's why there's been no deaths for two years! Oh my God, Tess! This is nuts! The Valentine Killer lived here! Holy fuck, we're gonna be famous!"

"Famous how? That can't be the name … the *Valentine Killer?* Really? That's pretty fucking trite and smarmy, isn't it?"

"So are you, but we all manage to tolerate it."

"Cute. And who, pray tell, is the friggin' Valentine Killer, anyway?"

"How do you not know about it?" Sharon asked, hands still clasped on Tess's shoulders.

Tess wriggled free of her siblings' firm grasp, then took one step back, rubbing her collarbone. "Cause I have a social life, such as it is. Who is he? A serial killer?"

"Indeed he is—or was. And a semi famous one to boot," Sharon happily declared while peering down at the macabre collection inside the velvet-lined box.

"But for real, the *Valentine Killer?* That's his name?"

"Well he obviously didn't choose that shit! Some dipstick yokel at a local newspaper or some internet troll probably conjured up that tragically inert title."

"And how'd you hear about it?" Tess asked, still rubbing her shoulder lightly.

"Because I actually educate myself about the world around me," Sharon shot back.

Tess sighed, tapping her foot for effect. "I'm waiting…"

"Okay, smartass. It was on one of those *Dateline*-type shows I've been mainlining lately. The one with Keith Morrison. He's got that ridiculously creepy voice. Anyway, they—meaning law enforcement—aren't certain that it's all connected. But I watched the whole two hours and it was some riveting shit, I'm telling you."

She lowered her voice ever so slightly and leaned in toward Tess. "There are like fifteen or more girls who've gone missing along the I-70 corridor over the last fifteen years. Always on Valentine's Day. And whenever the keystone cops do manage to find a body, the heart is always missing. That's his modus operandi. The killer takes the hearts of his victims on Valentine's Day. Cool, right? Or he did until he died a couple years ago. Wow. Just … wow."

"That's stupid," Tess tossed back.

"It's not stupid. You're stupid."

"No, it's stupid. And that shit can't be real or I would have heard of it."

"Oh, it's real. And your consummate ignorance of local history hardly diminishes it."

"Though if wishing made it so…"

"Yeah, well, sure. Okay. But back here in reality, these are the hearts. These are his trophies. I'm positive of it. We found his trophy case, literally and figuratively." Sharon nudged the black and gold trunk with her shoe, jostling the jars in a chorus of rattling glass.

"Fucking ghoulish, is what it is," Tess quipped, grimacing at the unsettling collection of amber fluid-filled containers.

"I suppose a good serial killer trophy collection should be that, shouldn't it?" Sharon asked playfully, nudging her sister's arm.

Cracking a grin, Tess admitted, "Fair. And this is truly off-the-deep-end crazy. No other words fit the occasion. This is just one big ol' bowl, chock full o'nuts."

"That means that there were two serial killers who operated in and around Glenwood! Not one, but two! *Dos!* How crazy is that shit?" Sharon asked, lifting up another jar and examining the contents.

"As we've said, ad nauseam, yes. And trouble often comes into twos, doesn't it?"

"Indeed it does."

"Three if you count Capone," Tess added.

Sharon scoffed and scrunched her nose in intellectual disapproval, "I don't count Capone. Capone was a mobster! It's notably different." She set down the jar next to the others and stood back up.

Tess stared into space for a moment, then added, "Meh. Still killed people. Who was the other one?"

Rolling her eyes, Sharon answered loudly, "Ted Bundy, of course! You know that shit. If they'd have kept him secure in the jail just four blocks from here, he never would've killed his last, like, seven or eight victims."

"Oh yeah, yeah, that whole thing. I remember. Through a ceiling vent, right?"

"Yeah. But that's GSPD for you. Bunch a bumbling fuckwits with the blood of Bundy's victims on their butterfingers."

Tess chuckled. "Can't help but notice they never caught this fella either."

"I rest my case."

"This guy's a big deal, then?"

"Only to those who believe he's actually a thing. Sorta like that string of murders up in Alaska that they don't know for sure are connected, but are fairly certain they are. Same thing here except for one massive difference."

"Which is what?" Tess asked.

"We can, with all this, easily confirm the Valentine Killer's existence to the world once and for all. Maybe even turn this into a museum, *a la* the Deetz in *Beetlejuice*! How cool would that be?"

"Unseemly, untoward, though possibly profitable. You'd still live here?"

"Hells no! Perish the thought. No, I'll take out a loan and finance another place nearby, then run this house of horrors from there. Make a go of the novelty haunted murder site industry."

"What about Eric's thoughts on the matter?"

Sharon snorted. "They don't matter. He's along for the ride. For now."

Tess redirected her eyes to the brownish business luggage. Nodding at it, she asked, "So … the briefcase."

Sharon picked it up and lowered the lid on the trunk. She then put the briefcase back on top and turned it to face them. "It's your standard issue case." She wiped off a small metallic manufacturer pin. "Basic Samsonite with a combo lock."

Tess scowled. "It's quite the case."

"So are you."

Tess rolled her eyes.

"I just mean that it's not gonna be easy to open, sans combination."

"Maybe not too hard." Tess stretched her arms above her head, as if warming up for a jog. Sharon began to fiddle with the lock to no avail. "What do you think is in it? Jars full of brains?" Tess asked, trying and failing to sound disinterested.

"Doubtful, as it wouldn't fit the M.O. Shit! How exciting is this?"

"What?"

"*What?* What do you mean, *what?* Just the whole thing! We found the missing trophies of the Valentine Killer! A box full of his preserved hearts and a mysterious briefcase, probably with his confession inside. We are now inextricably tied to the lore of him! We're part of the legend. We gotta call and get some representation!"

"Representation?"

"Are you only going to ask dumbass clarifying questions all night? Yes! Some representation! Someone else to handle the ins and outs of our burgeoning celebrity!"

"Not to put the cart before the horse or anything…"

"No one likes a cunt, my dear." Sharon warned playfully.

"You gonna see what's in the Samsonite first?" Tess asked about the case, which Sharon noted.

"Sure, yeah. Why not? What do you think it's gonna be?"

"A million dollars," Tess said without hesitation.

"That would be fucking wild. But it has a GD combo. How do we get into it? Should we Google that shit?" Sharon asked.

"Maybe." Tess's eyes traced round the small room and quickly came to rest on a length of metal pipe that was leaning up against the concrete corner, next to the water heater. She stalked over to it, snatched it up, then quickly returned and said, "Move!"

Sharon took several steps back as Tess cocked the pipe like a Louisville Slugger and let rip a mighty swing. The cutesy lock popped in one crack, and without missing a beat, slowly opened in front of them.

Inside, to both and somehow neither of their surprise, lay stacks of hundred dollar bills, bound in bank tape and piled up as though it was being readied to pay a ransom.

The sisters did not look at each other, only stared directly at the money. The pipe dropped from Tess's hand and hit the concrete floor with a jarring *clang*.

Taking her right hand and running it along the top of the stacks, Tess quivered all over. "It's gotta be… Jesus, if each one is ten grand then there must be a little over a million in here."

"Holy shit, Tess. How'd you know?"

"I didn't; I was guessing. I was just … I was guessing. That's fucking crazy."

"I know. Jesus, I know." Sharon leaned down and pulled one of the musty stacks of hundreds from the brown Samsonite and flicked through it with her thumb, rolling the bills in a swoosh. "Easily a million. Easily."

For another thirty seconds, neither of them said anything. They simply stood side by side and took in the awesome beauty of the bounty that lay inside the briefcase.

Tess suddenly stepped away, spun in a circle, and clapped her hands. "Well, shit. We aren't gonna be able to tell anyone about your nasty heart collection over there now, will we?"

Sharon shook her head and half-frowned. "Shit. I guess not, cause I'll take this money over the silly cottage industry any day of the week. I can't believe I found it."

Tess stopped spinning on a dime and faced Sharon. "Well, *we* found it."

Sharon also turned to face her sibling. "What do you mean, *we?*"

"I mean we found it, you greedy beotch. You didn't find it, *we* did. In fact, I'm the one who closed the door which made the dust kick up!" Tess's hands unconsciously began to ball into small fists. Sharon took notice.

"I could have and eventually would have done the same," Sharon snapped back.

"But you didn't, so don't get it twisted; we whack that booty up fifty-fifty! Wham bam, thank you ma'am!" Tess lifted one hand and snapped twice to really drive her statement home.

"Do we, now?" Sharon asked, her eyes narrowing.

"Oh, we do. You know we do, dear sister." Tess met her sister's icy gaze, then promptly raised her a piqued brow.

Sharon murmured, "And do tell me why I would just hand over half a mil to you when this is a discovery on my new property, and therefore the sole property of me, alone?" Her eyes quickly scanned the room.

Tess's tone shifted dramatically into one of serious reproach. "I need that money, o' sister of mine. You're too caring to not share the spoils. Fair is fair, so let's not get all touchy. We know what happens when you get touchy."

"Yes. Yes we do, Tess. We know exactly what I do to those who trouble me, which makes it so curious as to why you'd ever deign to test my patience. Besides, you don't need that kinda scratch, anyway, so—"

"Oh, but I do! I really, really do." Tess paced slowly back and forth as she spoke. "With that money right there, my life unfucks overnight. And that isn't hyperbole, I mean it literally takes a one-eighty, instantly. With it, I can easily pay off the seventy K that I owe Vito out in Vegas, so he doesn't keep threatening me. I can bribe the cop who's investigating me for money laundering. Try to pay him off with another hundred large, maybe two. And with the rest I can possibly find a hitman to handle Reggie's sister who won't stop saying she knows that I killed her dog. Which, you know, she can't fuckin' prove, but still, it's an unwanted stain upon our good name just the same. And you—"

Sharon waved her hand dismissively. "The one thing that all those line items have in common is that they are not my problem, Tess. Those are your problems. *Yours.* My problem, which I assure you takes precedence, is the four hundred thousand it's going to take for me to clean up the mess I made in New Orleans."

Tess smirked, narrowed her own eyes, and asked, "The thing with the chainsaw?"

"Yeah, *obviously* I mean the thing with the chainsaw, Tess! Thank you for that unsolicited specificity, really. And after the four hundred grand, I'd only have one hundred thousand left and that's hardly enough to scratch my online gambling itch with now, is it? Hmmm?"

Having stopped pacing, Tess slipped her final passive attempt at sweetness into the convo, "Still, I'm pretty sure you wouldn't leave your dear ol' sister out to dry. Or would you?"

"I just might, depending on how negotiations unfold. Why do you ask?" The corner of Sharon's mouth raised and Tess knew the game was on.

They both did.

Tess smirked. "Because if you did that, I would feel that my only recourse might be to tell your husband that you've been having an affair with Dr. Darcy down at the hospital."

Sharon grinned and took a wandering step away from the center of the room, keeping her eyes locked onto her mother's daughter. "Then I'd have to inform you that he knows. Of course he does. I'm barely hiding it at this point. And he knows he's powerless to do anything about it. He's under my thumb, and that's where he's gonna stay. Empty round in your gun. Soft flex, even for you."

"Only an opening gambit. For then I might wonder aloud if he knows that those spells he keeps having every so often—that you're in turn heavily medicating him for—are actually the result of you and your physician fucktoy removing parts from his unconscious body and selling them on the dark web?"

Sharon giggled and crossed her arms as she took one step toward Tess. "My retort then would be to point out that he doesn't miss them, clearly. And ultimately he won't. If all goes well, the life insurance will go into effect next month, I can give him that final dose of paralytic, then *boom!* The good doctor and I will be whisking off to Antigua to spend the spoils while you stay here, fleecing the single, over-fifty dot-com'ers in Snowmass and Beaver Creek."

"Not worried about the risk?" Tess queried, glaring through reptilian eye slits. She pulled free her phone once more and started to click in a frenzy.

"Little risk, little sis. My fucktoy doc—as you so tactfully refer to him—has assured me that it's neigh undetectable, and given my soon-to-be-departed husband's legally documented penchant for stepped-on cocaine, it will look like his heart just took one final cardiovascular dive off the suspension bridge of life's excesses. No muss, no fuss."

"He wouldn't like to hear that you're plotting to off him, though, would he? That's why you would do well to give me half the money. Not like you need it anyway with your grim plot afoot."

"Oh sissy sissy sis. Sweet sissy sis. As though you're any stranger to plotting the death of a spouse? You shouldn't have the money, or I just might feel the wicked compunction to tell the authorities about what you used to poison poor Matthew before you collected the insurance on *him*."

"No, no, we certainly wouldn't want that. Any more than either of us want the police to discover anything about your previous life as an expat black widow in Central America. We wouldn't want them re-opening the cases into your former husbands' disappearances, right?"

As they spoke, the women began to walk around the trunk in the middle of the floor with the open briefcase on the top. Circling one another in slow, deliberate steps.

Tess stretched her taught, trim, porcelain arms and cracked her spiny knuckles in a roll of clicks.

Sharon tilted her head from side to side, audibly popping her neck, and warned in a semi-raspy tone, "We don't want them thinking about your history with pharmaceuticals."

"Nor yours with amphetamines," Tess concurred.

"I should say not, no." Sharon's eyes, now narrow as a viper and unable to let loose of Tess's, seethed.

"I really don't want anyone finding out that my sister, our dear Sharon, used to burn small animals in the woods behind the school when she was just thirteen years—"

"Fifteen. I was fifteen when you caught me."

"Okay, fifteen! We wouldn't want that making the rounds, right?"

"No, and I couldn't bear the thought of anyone discovering the truth about your role in the death of that tennis player from Aspen."

"That would be unbearable, truly. And we don't want those dips at the police department to know what happened to mommy dearest, or what you did to hasten her demise. Would we now, Sharon?"

"No more than I want them to know about you killing Daddy, Tess."

"Great! So it sounds like we have an understanding, don't we?" Tess finished clicking on her phone, replaced it in her sports top, and had started to walk toward the briefcase lying on the cold concrete floor when her sister swiftly snatched up the metal pipe from the floor and casually lay it over her shoulder while casting a crocodile eye her way.

Tess smiled at Sharon anew, seemingly undaunted by her sibling's act of treachery.

Sharon lifted the pipe, gripped it with steely resolve, and looked at her sister with a cocked head. Calmly, deliberately, she asked, "And wouldn't the prudent thing be to simply hit you over the goddamn head with this thick metal pipe, ditch it in the river, and then make it look like you just took a tumble down the stairs?"

Tess flashed a cold grin as she pulled her phone free from her top and held it out for Sharon to see her text stream.

"It likely would be, but for the fact that I already texted Reggie and let him know that I'm coming back with half a million dollars and that if I don't arrive within the next half hour, to call the police and tell them that you buried me for the bounty, you bloodthirsty bitch."

"Did you now?" Sharon asked, cold-eyed and half-doubting.

"You know that I did." Tess held up her phone for Sharon to survey, and sure enough, she'd sent her man a message reading exactly as she had explained.

Sharon sighed, lowered the metal pipe, and tossed it aside. As it clanged, hollow and hard on the concrete floor, a wide-toothed grin of pure pride crossed her mouth in a Glasgow smile. "Well played, sis. Must say, well played."

"Thank you. I learned from the best." Tess withdrew her hand, slipped the phone into her slim leggings pocket, then walked over to the corner and grabbed a reusable grocery bag covered in sunflowers that had been filled for who knows how long with old *National Geographics*. Carefully, she removed and set aside the stack of musty, dusty periodicals. Returning to Sharon, she pulled a little less than half of the money from the briefcase, piling it into the impromptu moneybag.

Sharon said nothing, just watched as the cash was transferred into the flowery sack. Once Tess had finished, she started to walk towards the exit.

"Dinner on Thursday with the boys?" Sharon asked after her.

Tess paused mid-departure, turned heel, and replied, "Wouldn't miss it. We'll meet you at Juicy Lucy's at seven. It'll just be a raincheck for today since I'm obviously gonna go un-ring some bells with this money right quick!"

Sharon winced. "Yeah, okay. Go fuck yourself, sweetie."

"You first!" Tess turned and began to depart once more, sliding the bag straps onto her elbow and rubbing her palms together excitedly.

"The fuck do I do with these dumbass jars full of hearts?" Sharon asked after her disappearing sister, not really expecting much of an answer.

As Tess walked through the doorjamb with the bag full of money in tow, she called over her shoulder, "Pitch 'em in the river for all I fucking care! Who gives a shit if anybody ever knows, anyway. Maybe it's for the best that he not be granted his fifteen minutes of fame!"

"Right. Catch ya later," Sharon hissed without looking up from the now half-empty briefcase.

From the darkness of the stairwell Tess called down, "Not if I catch you first, beotch!"

GUMBALLS

So—the way that my teenage friends and I discovered that we had ingested the blood of other children is actually a pretty funny story, really. I know it doesn't sound that way, you know, out loud or whatever—but it was.

And man, I gotta tell ya, it was a great time in our lives. We were still young and theoretically full of promise, and none of us died. Well, none of the kids from my school did. Plenty of other kids, it's true, but none of us from Carbondale did. None of my friends ever became the coloring for the candy-coated confections.

Really, the whole thing could've been worse.

It's funny how the mind works to keep us emotionally distant from things that appear obviously traumatic to others. Like you tell somebody that you consumed the blood of children—other children—not because you wanted to or anything, but because *he* made you do it. *He* wanted us to do it. And people are usually all taken aback. They say, "Well, now that's really ghoulish," and, "Are you actually serious?"

And you deadpan say that *of course* you're serious, and why would you make up such a thing? And you further declare that it really could have been worse, truly.

Then, of course, mouth usually agape, they invariably ask how that sort of thing even happens. And you have to say that it may sound awful, but at least it wasn't you that got mixed into the red dye. The red dye in the gumballs. By The Confectioner himself: the late Mr. Thadius Joseph Tayle.

The wicked Mr. Taddy Tayle.

But, as I am wont to do so often when I speak of these dark affairs, I'm getting ahead of myself. Let me rewind the reel back, back, back to where it all began.

Back before the slaughter and the sugar and the shirts.

Back to sixth grade, when we took a class trip from our half-dilapidated middle school in Carbondale, down the I-70 west route, through the gorgeous cross-mountain expanse, about two hours to the farthest west population center just over the Utah border: Grand Junction, Colorado.

Back to a time before legal reforms and massive drug busts in the early aughts largely cleared out the methamphetamine plague that had taken root in far too many of Grand Junction's residents.

Back to the Mesa Mall.

Hot damn, we sure did love the Mesa Mall back in the '90s. You would have too, I bet.

It might seem crazy nowadays to think of a mid-sized to miniscule mall in the sticks having three successful bookstores that operated independently and didn't have to compete with each other, but that's how it was. Racks and stacks of the best on wax, cassettes and CDs at the Disc Jockey or the Sam Goody, as well as a food court with both a Chopstix and a Panda Express. Aladdin's Arcade ran on quarters, kids screams, and birthday parties. Tan tile fountains always full of pennies. The building carried the aroma of fresh pretzels, fried food, and Christmas.

But the *crème de la crème*, the *pièce de résistance*, the Sistine Chapel of all the outlets that filled up the brown tiled hallways was the one, the only…

Gumballs.

At the very center of the complex, taking up the space of two stores, it was a veritable cornucopia of magic and wonder to a wide-eyed little kid like me. A massive, anything-you-could-desire repository of sweet treats and pop culture paraphernalia, the likes of which would surely have made Willy Wonka blanche with jealousy. The kind of place Nickelodeon would do a live report from. Hanging sheets of sugarplum dots and strips of taffy a mile long, rolled onto spindles. Novelty craft sodas with names like *Brainalizer* and *Love Potion #69*. Clear boxes containing any form of confection or candy the mind could conjure up lined up in rows along every wall and aisle. Rainbows of sugar in every size and shape—Taffy and Twizzlers and Tootsie Pops, oh my! Each cube containing a small spoon and tear-away bag rolls so you could easily make and take your selections.

Higher up, above the candy container cubes, the walls were filled with T-Shirts. The sort of mock-vintage stuff that kids of the mid-'90s only ever saw lethargic rockstars on MTV wearing. Bob Marley and Nirvana and Marilyn Manson and 4 Non Blondes and 10,000 Maniacs and Tool and Blind Melon and Soundgarden and Alice In Chains and Primus and Tori Amos and Beastie Boys and Prodigy and Offspring and Salt-N-Pepa and Rolling Stones shirts—with that big red floppy tongue hanging down—lined up in spectacular rows to make us positively salivate with wannabe-hipster envy.

Music piped throughout the high ceilinged space was a bleeding-edge juxtaposition of hipster musical genres. Electronica before it was mainstream cool; ragtime and big band tunes long after they had been. Naturally, "Pure Imagination" was cycled into the playlist regularly.

And by what musically attuned ne'er-do-well, you might ask? Why, by our story's bad boy, of course.

The Confectioner.

The most sought after of sacred totems in the store was the massive, ten-foot-tall gumball dispenser that filled the center of the large room. One huge gleaming glass orb filled up with the biggest gumballs we'd ever seen, sat atop a fire-engine red metal base. Each colorful sphere it dispensed was as big as a softball, every color sporting its own unique flavor that Taddy added him-self—grape for purple, cotton candy for pink, and so on.

But the ones you never wanted to see tumble down the clear spiral tube, out of the little filigree-filled door, and into your palm were the red ones.

I personally don't know what the big deal was. I liked 'em okay, but everyone else in my class treated them like the plague. They were supposed to be cherry, but always left an odd metallic aftertaste on the tongue.

We obviously didn't know what was in them at the time, you understand. How could we have? We just appreciated the spectacle of it all.

That first time we walked through the sacred and hallowed halls of Gumballs during the sixth-grade trip, none of us kids were prepared to bear witness to the magical sights our eyes be-held. For to us, it looked like heaven on a stick.

Thadius Tayle had the same lanky physical *je ne se quoi* as a tall bundle of sticks held together by durable twine. Long as red licorice with features as delicate and orange-hued as the wafer thin peanut brittle he peddled, he was in his late thirties by the time they discovered kids going missing. Eternally wrapped in a black and white pinstripe apron with a large red afro poking out from under a tall baker's hat, I still wonder if he really enjoyed wearing that garb or if it was just part of his mask of sanity. An apropos getup, either way.

Whichever it was, it did wonders in dropping everyone's guard.

You gotta understand, this was before an entire jilted generation became savvy to such nefarious goings on such as what Tayle had in store. This was before everybody binge watched *48 Hours Mystery's*, mainlined police procedurals, and developed into self-declared subject matter experts on serial killings. Back then, we didn't know any better. We were watching *Full House* and shit.

Life in the '90s for suburban kids really was an after school special. And don't let any of us bitchy millennials tell ya any different. Just don't.

Now, we all liked Taddy. Dude was a trip—always really funny. There was one section of the shop dedicated to magic and special FX stuff. Demonstrating sleight of hand or donning a fake nose for a laugh was part of his witty repartee. He had a serious talent for makeup FX, costumes, and for catching pop culture iconography just in the heat of the trend. If he wasn't quite so fixated on murdering little kids, he could've been a great MTV VJ in my humble opinion.

He was the kind of guy—physicality notwithstanding—that I wanted to be like when I grew up. The kind of guy who could charm a whole room into thinking he's just as happy, wholesome, and lacking in homicidal impulse as they.

Whenever we came home with a fresh NOFX T-shirt or *Texas Chainsaw Massacre* fridge magnet, we knew we had become cooler through this cultural osmosis, and thus elevated our perceived social status among our peers.

One year, I scored this badass Astro-Creep: 2000 White Zombie concert shirt from the wall o' shirts and felt like a total trend-setting metal maniac for all of two days—until the musically ignorant, harsh criticism of my schoolyard constituents on Monday morning informed me of my egregious fashion faux pas. The shirt never again appeared on campus.

We were just kids.

So it went for months. We would take trips or make clothes shopping sojourns—any excuse, really—in anticipation of the moment we would come around the corner next to J&M Aquatics and spot the massive neon "Gumballs" sign.

But then, the kids started disappearing. At least, the police started to notice them disappearing. It had been going on for a while by that point. A good while.

Leave it to the pigs to be a mile behind the curve.

I'd love to say that the first several had ended up on milk cartons and nothing ever came of their disappearances, but only the second half of that statement would be true. In reality, missing children hadn't been appearing regularly on milk cartons since the late eighties—and even then, we all knew that no kid ever found their way home because they were recognized from a 2% Meadow Gold carton. That shit is for the movies, and this ain't no Hollywood film. Too bad, too, because I thought those things were kinda neat, if a tad grim.

No, what caused the whole house of cards to come crashing down were the three victims he took in the summer of that year.

The first was a kid from Cherry Creek, out in Denver. He'd gone missing during a school outing and everyone thought he'd simply gotten lost at first. But as days melted into weeks, his parents became convinced something more nefarious had happened and doubled their pressure on the Grand Junction PD to develop leads or arrest a suspect.

Taddy surely must've been interviewed by the police about it. And unflinching in his steely reptilian resolve, must've waived them off his scent. How? Only he knows, and he ain't saying anymore.

After that, a couple more went by the wayside. Two girls, about a month apart from one another in July and August. I think their names were Terry and Gina. It's hard to remember the names, and Taddy didn't think it was a good idea to anyway.

Those three were taken in a period of four months in the summer of '96, and aside from the usual motions local law enforcement went through with multiple missing persons, bigger agencies were soon involved.

See, one of the kids was from Glenwood Springs, and possessing what one could describe as a checkered history with serial killers (Ted Bundy had escaped from their jail with shocking ease in '77, and aside from taking the cops seventeen hours to realize it, tragically resulted in him killing several more people, including a twelve-year-old girl) the police of that particular town quickly handed off the case to the Colorado Bureau of Investigation. The CBI wasted no time in connecting the dots with their case and several others out of adjacent counties.

Once a profile had been developed, it was only a matter of time before they discovered the common denominator connecting all the missing children. Every last one had recently taken

     ⊣ PATRICK KITSON ⊢

a trip to the Mesa Mall in Grand Junction. Specifically, to the greatest candy store this side of the Mississippi.

You guessed it.

The night that the police put two and two together, they took a small squad to the mall after hours and actually caught Taddy preparing to transport his latest victim from the mall to his warehouse, where he brought his bloody creations to life.

Though he may have been a tough guy when handling his human ingredients, he was a big ol' ball of cotton candy when the gun muzzles were shoved in his face. Heavily armed brutes had smashed through those big glass windows and discovered him counting out the drawer, of all things.

Tucked neatly behind the counter was a cage with a young woman inside. This girl was sedated and stuck, like a scared animal, in a cube of hard wire not two feet by two feet wide. Her mouth was duct taped and she had been understandably terrified since he'd abducted her a few hours earlier. Luckily, but for the lasting trauma, she was relatively unharmed.

Her name is Susie Sanders and she eventually wrote a best-seller about it titled, *Caged Girl: One Woman's Battle With a Killer.* Even got herself a talk show and podcast nowadays. Helps others. Seems like she's doing just fine.

As for getting a handle on exactly what all had occurred, this was one thing Taddy never fully allowed them the satisfaction of. Games, riddles, cryptic admonitions—even dashing delusions of grandeur with just the right amount of facts. He did everything in his power to not only draw out the investigation, but to savor his power over those investigating him.

He did a fantastic job—really, really impressive work if we're being honest—at covering up the methods by which he created his confections. *Masterstroke* is the word that comes to mind when you consider how he set a jury-jigged system up inside his killing warehouse that detonated spectacularly when the SWAT team attempted to breach it. Such immaculate planning. With that encore performance, a four-story-engulfing fireball managed to take out four lawmen and damage two adjacent buildings.

Once the literal smoke cleared—and owing to the type of flash-burning chemical explosives he'd employed—there was not much for the police to piece together. It had been a thorough scorching, leaving little forensic evidence.

Gotta admit, for '96, he was ahead of his time.

Authorities ultimately had to rely upon the testimony of The Confectioner himself to verify certain aspects of the sordid affair. In total, he speculated to investigators that he had taken right around thirty children over a ten year period, starting in 1986—the very year that Gumballs had opened its big glass-paned, neon-striped doors to the public. There was no way to confirm this, as he later claimed that he deliberately avoided learning their names so that he might never be tempted to feel any empathy for them. For to him, they were just as any other ingredient in his multi-colored tapestry of tasty treats: inconsequential pieces forming a grander concoction.

For his admissions, he sought no respite from the death penalty and was judged and sentenced within a few months. In Mesa County, there was little interest in spending money keeping a child murderer alive. The day of his execution, he had requested that he be allowed to watch Willy Wonka one last time while eating Burger King before he was led to the gas chamber.

And he'd opted for the gas himself—the total nut job! I mean, what a kook, right? What a way to go!

So then he was gone. And with him, something that—despite

its distastefulness to the average person—is sorely needed in a community to balance the scales and help strengthen its resolve: that which draws the bonds of kinship closer.

For what's light without any dark, after all?

I say all this because, sadly, people forget things. Oh yes, they surely do. They forget what others have sacrificed and fought for, and if they choose not to learn from them—which they usually don't—they forget the hard learned lessons of the past.

So it was really no surprise that, despite the community's storied history involving confections and gumballs specifically, when several small self-serve candy dispensers randomly began popping up around the mall, barely anyone paid attention. You can see them in any such shopping center, situated nicely between those little softback benches and chairs they have set up for shoppers to take the occasional load off.

And more surprising still, no one took issue with the quiet addition of clear glass gumball dispensers that now number four, scattered throughout the Mesa Mall.

That's 2024 for ya. A lack of institutional memory borne from apathy about what others suffered for.

So it's hard to feel too bad for all those chuckling dipsticks who are today, possibly even at this very moment, consuming gumballs with just a touch of human blood in them.

You see, I carry on my master's work.

Ol' Taddy Tayle, the consummate huckster extraordinaire, he had the right idea. Sure, he never got to know that his legacy would endure beyond his mortal death, but I sleep peacefully each and every night knowing he is likely smiling at me from across the stygian abyss with malevolent pride and eternal approval at my enduring transgressions.

For I keep the blood flowing and the faceless sacrificed screaming.

Mine are generally picked up from nearby Utah. Usually hitchhikers. It ain't children, sure, but it does the trick just the same—also offering the added benefit of bringing little attention to my dark deeds.

And you know that I still filter the blood the way I suspect my master did, then add it to the red dye in the small gumballs which I now make.

Lovingly, by hand.

I continue the good work of The Confectioner, because it's what the planet needs, ya know? Those soft, subtle, often chewable reminders that no matter who you think you are with your cheeky socio-digital status updates, and no matter where you try to go in this cold, cruel world, there's always going to be at least one goofy, happy-go-lucky, wildly dangerous and nearly undetectable neighborhood monster hiding just beneath a flimsy façade of sanity—waiting with feverish anticipation to turn you into a snack for some little kid in a mall with a sweet tooth.

Bon appetit.

COCKTAILS

Despite dozens of razor-sharp, forked dorsal fins whisking through the rolling ocean waves, making their way toward the wave-cresting bow of the jet black Sunseeker 88 pocket superyacht, neither Jacqueline nor Draco Rosselli actually noticed any of them.

Slicing through the surf and bathing beneath a cloud-free Mediterranean sun somewhere in the vast nautical expanse between the northern coast of Egypt and the isle of Crete, they were much too busy fawning over one another's immaculate taste in designer beachwear to pay any immediate notice.

He, a chiseled, olive-toned adonis of sculpted musculature in his Graco gold border Versace swim shorts. She, with her long brown hair carefully braided into shining sections, whilst the rest of her curvaceous body was tucked snugly into a silver, water-resistant Dolce and Gabbana belted one-piece plunge swimsuit replete with jewel-encrusted DG-logoed buckle. Each of their faces brown from the sun, their eyes shielded with bug-eyed designer shades.

It wasn't until the aquatic beasts unknowingly intruded upon the posh duo's deck-side ego-stroking session that either felt any compunction to address their possibly impending doom.

Gently gliding through the rippling ocean tides, the luxe Sunseeker may have possessed a top speed of thirty knots, but was currently cruising smoothly on autopilot at less than a third of that. A million reflections of scattered sunlight shimmering from the surface of the waves rippled into fragments as the keel cut evenly through the surf beneath the watercraft's eighty-seven foot length.

Both of the boat's occupants lay stretched out upon the finest Aegean brown Lue Bona poly-outdoor chaise loungers they could locate and have custom installed whilst anchored along the eastern Italian coast. Each nursed drinks—a classic Old Fashioned for him, and a mango vodka tonic with a kiwi twist for her.

They couldn't help but admire the postcard picturesque view.

"'Tis quite the daring thing to endeavor a Dolce plunger amid such crisp westerly winds, my love." Sitting up slightly, Draco reached out to the table between the loungers and pulled the frosted highball glass from it. Sipping his chilled cocktail, he beamed with self-satisfaction at his one and only. "Luckily your delicious design and succulent curves make it more than worth the risk of sunburn," he further mused.

Dismissively waving her hand but smiling just the same, Jacqueline replied, "If I am to suffer through sunset after grotesquely gorgeous sunset with as wanton and sexy a gent as yourself, I must make the occasion, as it were. And lest you forget, slathered in copious layers of sunscreen as I am, that burning—while optimal—is nigh impossible."

"Nothing's impossible! Not with the aforementioned wind at our backs and a crystal clear blanket of stars to gaze upon in the evenings!"

"Too right you are! Too right you are. Chin chin!"

They both raised their glasses and clinked them together with the slightest of *tinks*.

Thus far unbeknownst to the sailing twosome, nearly half a dozen of the sub-nautic swimmers were quickly approaching the hull of their craft as they were taking pulls from their frosted highball glasses.

The first of the creatures to reach and grip onto the smooth black fiberglass of the port bow—a dark humanoid form emerging from the bubbling depths beside the anchor outlet—used its cup-lined appendages to crawl up the face of the mini yacht's hull.

Slime-slicked suckers stuck steadfast to the side of the ship sent a startling signal to Draco and Jacqueline that something was suddenly seriously suspect.

"Now what could that be, dear?" Jacqueline asked, quickly sitting up and slipping the Louis Vuitton shades from her sun-lit face. Her eyes traced the horizon and she set down the glass in her grasp, then the shades next to it.

More of the slurping and sucking sounds, and Draco too raised up to attention, then stood. He wasted no time in making a hasty line toward a small nearby box built into the deck with seat padding atop it. Calmly sliding the gold-lined black cushion aside, he opened the compartment. Inside, several firearms set in brackets alongside cartons of gold-rimmed clay pigeons.

Withdrawing two silver pump-action shotguns and an unopened box of shells, he dropped the rubber-sealed lid with his elbow, maneuvered his right foot to slide the big cushion back over his weapon cache, and marched promptly back to his lady.

Watching with an unwavering, cocked smile and raised right

eyebrow, Jacqueline asked, "Did we not already do our skeet shooting for the day, Mr. Rosselli?"

"Only a precautionary measure, Mrs. Rosselli. I don't know what that might have been, but if we see anything that—"

Interrupting the tan-skinned man, the first of the things scrambled over the railed rim of the bow's pulpit and spilled onto the pristine white deck with a wet plopping sound. Semi-dazed and slow to rise, the beast straightened up and fixed its reptilian eyes upon them, but did not move. Draco nonetheless felt it prudent to point the Mossberg's business end at this most uninvited denizen of the deep.

The creature did not move, but rather seemed to search around the boat with its black eyes, as if surveilling such a grand sight for the very first time.

More sucking sounds as another two slippery greenish husks climbed onto the yacht's narrow gunnel edge and rolled over the silver railing, falling on the fiberglass foredeck and slowly, very slowly, standing up straight. They flanked the first intruder on either side.

These three humanoids from the depths—lined along their spines with sharp, ridged dorsal protuberances—cocked their heads quizzically at the wealthy duo standing armed and ready before them. Each bore two arms, ending in seemingly four digits laced together with algae-green, leathery webbing. In lieu of blinking, the reptilian eye sockets of all three rapidly flashed translucent nictitating membranes over the eyeballs. Behavior which only lent to the oddness of their appearance in the minds of the humans.

Draco grinned ear to ear, cupped his hands around his mouth, and called to the three fish-men standing roughly fifty feet away.

"Pardon me, scaly sirs? Might any of you fine chappies have any Grey Poupon?"

Jacqueline, a consummate sucker for both the timeless charm of the classic ad campaign as well as the titular mustard, allowed a pleased look of undulating approval to cross her lips at this somewhat dusty pop advertising throwback.

"Oh that's good. An odd time for such anachronisms, but who am I to judge!" Keeping her stare fixed upon the three creatures, she continued, "I do say, they look dreadfully likely to carry disease, though. We need not risk an outbreak of scurvy upon our vessel!"

"Well, but of course, my dear! But of course! Hence the armaments in hand." Whilst he spoke and cradled the shotgun under one arm, he started to pull shells from the box and slip them into the tight pockets of his posh bathers. He only could fit four extra slugs total between both sides. The harsh cost of fashion.

He handed off the extra shells to Jacqueline. Taking the box, she set it down next to her in the lounge chair and started to load her own gun, tucking several rounds into the ringed straps of her one piece.

Watching as the things stared, unmoving, Draco continued, "Scurvy or any likewise malady would be a dreadful thing to carry back to port with us. The kind of thing that could negatively impact our burgeoning status within the ranks of our island community!"

"Precisely, my love. Precisely!" Jacqueline finished loading her shotgun and pumped the stock once, standing up and taking aim at the thing on the right. It seemed, at a glance, to be somewhat closer to her than the others. "At this early stage in the game, we cannot risk forfeiture of our sought-after place upon the board of trustees! Why, these nautical interlopers, as likely as not, haven't so much as passed any proper medical screenings!"

The three dripping-wet creatures cast one another languid yet curious glances, then returned their gaze to the loud, chatting humans before them.

Draco laughed at this. "I should say not! And who knows what other flesh-souring plagues might lay in wait within the flaky folds of their scaly skin?"

From the front of the boat, the clamor of more creatures attaching themselves to the hull sounded.

"Oh, joy. More boorish philistines approaching. No doubt possessing the same distinct lack of regard for basic maritime decorum as their kraken kindred. It's unacceptable, Draco! Un-acceptable!" Jacqueline reached down with her free hand to take another sip of her drink, then set it back down next to her designer sunglasses. "Nor do they seem in the least bit concerned for what their ill-timed attack may mean for our own expected attendance at the Gala premiere in Cyprus tomorrow evening!"

"You took the words directly from my lips, honeydew." Draco raised his voice as he spoke to the creatures, "I do say, have any of you the slightest of consideration for our Gala premiere in Cyprus on the morrow? Hmm? Any of you? Don't be coy, now. Speak up if you're able!"

The creature furthest to the left rolled its eyes briefly as it shuddered along its entire body, then opened its drool-slathering maw, expectorating a baseball sized glob of yellowish crud onto the bright white top deck.

Draco shook his head in disappointment. "Okay, well clearly they've no manners."

"Clearly," Jackie agreed, tightening her grip on the shotgun barrel and wrapping the index finger on her right hand around the Mossberg's trigger. Her left hand clicked the safety off. "They simply mustn't be allowed to interrupt our divine libations."

"They shan't, dear. Rather, despite having already done so, they shan't be allowed moving forward. Nor shall we tolerate our much delayed trip to the Mediterranean being made a mockery of—not even by heretofore unknown denizens of the deep such as these rude reptiloids appear to be! Hah! For this unprovoked intrusion, there is but one course of due response."

The first creature to have boarded their vessel without any formal invitation took a single tentative step toward them, its head cocked to one side, seemingly curious about the humans.

"Oy! That drippy bugger seems to want us dead forthwith!" Jacqueline pointed an accusatory heavily gold-ringed finger at the creature, eliciting from it a soft click and cooing sound. Jackie's eyebrows narrowed. "Do fire away, my love, for I can taste the reaper's breath upon my cheek with each scaly foot drawing nigh!"

"As do I, my treasured dew drop! As do I. Tally ho!" Draco aimed at the central figure and fired, blasting the scaly, humanoid thing away from them in a spray of semi-translucent purple slime.

Flailing backward, it tumbled into the rail with such force that its back bent backward at an unnatural angle. The audible crack of its spinal column filled the air as the momentum further carried it over the railing. It splashed into the water against the ship's bow—presumably pulled quickly underneath and likely diced into sushi by the yacht's durable twin propellers.

The two mermen on either side whimpered and backed up a step at the horrific sight of their compatriot's all-too-rapid demise.

Without waiting for a cue, Jacqueline emptied a roaring barrel full of blast into the creature on the right, likewise casting its lifeless body over the railing and into the water as though it were the Heart of the Ocean.

The sight of the second thing being launched outward from the deck of the yacht into the air before crashing into the sea caused the third thing to hasten a retreat. Tragicomically flopping its wet flipper hands and feet about, it was nearly able to roll its body over the silver railing when Jackie's loud voice behind made it pause, hesitating for a split second too long.

"My, my. Now that right there was quite fun! What are these silly things again?" she called to Draco.

"What things?" Draco asked.

"What things? Why, darling, these maritime marauders we're dumping slugs into, naturally!" Jacqueline's rings clicked along the wooden grip as her fist pumped the shotgun once more, letting fly a spent shell. She took swift aim and fired at the remaining creature. It crashed over the bow railing, swiftly sailing into the salty sea with a satisfying splash.

Running to the railing, Draco peered over the side—Jackie quickly reaching her opulently festooned, albeit largely nude hubby a moment later. Beneath them, on the hull, several more of the aquatic denizens clung as barnacles would to the side of the ship. One crawled straight up the bow keel toward the pulpit at the front.

Draco's eyes slowly raised to meet his lady's, which were likewise unamused.

"No manners," she flatly declared.

"Zero," he concurred.

Both began to shoot down at the six or so creatures. As one was hit, the remaining five, in what looked like defiance of the laws of gravity, turned 180° and began to scuttle hurriedly back toward the water in clear retreat.

None made it to safety.

As buckshot rained down like hellfire, Jacqueline pumped and pulled, pumped and pulled, cackling like a banshee all the way whilst her shotgun exploded toward the sea.

Draco, cleft chin and white teeth jutted out in preening, malevolent smugness, grinned like Gaston and fired in rapid succession without aiming at anything in particular. Simply pleased as punch at the violent volley of death breaking up the monotony of their day, he hollered a string of obscenities at the nautical creatures, who surely understood none of it.

He paused his mad attack briefly—just long enough to pull some shells from his skivvies, rack 'em up, and aim at the final scaly marine monster that was scampering along to climb back into the water. The buckshot pellets filled its chest cavity, carrying it off the hull and through the air into the sea below. It hit the water, but like the others, didn't immediately sink, so Draco fired the remaining rounds at the floating corpse. Purple slime began to color the water around the boat, leaving a gooey wake of fluorescent carnage and dead fish men bobbing about.

Emptying the final round into the remaining sea-slithering creepy crawly nearby, Draco realized he had exhausted the last of the ammunition that he had prepped when he first engaged with his aquatic quarrel.

His gun clicked. "I'm dry."

A few moments later came the audible click from Jackie's gun. "Me too." Her eyelids scrunched to diminish the fierce glare that the shimmering water was casting into her eyes. Not too far away, maybe a hundred yards, she could just make out a fair-sized grouping of the creatures, congregating and watching the unfolding shitstorm. Treading water, a good twenty of them or more were watching in abject horror as their aquatic friends fell under the unyielding authority of Mossberg Industries.

Draco caught sight of them too. "Well, well. More unchecked medical scourges!"

Jacqueline leaned onto the railing and stared out at the things in the water. "Oh, yes. Well, I do fear the loss of preferential range for maximum damage. They're simply too far away. What with so much more to do here, we must adapt our tactics, forthwith. For whom are we to give up such a bounty in live target practice?"

"Why, we'd be rightly mad! And that is not us."

"Never us."

"Agreed. So what say you on this front, my dear?"

Jacqueline shrugged and pumped the shotty again, popping an empty shell out of the chamber.

"There have to be dozens of them at the ready out there. I'd say that we have the run of the lot at this point, but then I would be failing to state the obvious, wouldn't I?

"Indeed, my dear. Too true. Ducks on the pond; fish in the proverbial barrel. How about it? Shall we introduce them to the punch-packing pirate perforator?" Draco stood tall, slung the empty shotgun onto his shoulder like a big game hunter, raised a closed fist, and closed his eyes, rocking his head up and down. Without waiting for her reply, he finished, "Oh yes, we shall! We've been wanting to see how much actual punch it packs, and no time like the present for a field test! These bastards won't mind! They won't live long enough to!"

"Smashing!" Jacqueline called out as she turned and began to hustle along the side deck on the starboard side, next to the bridge. Passing her previous spot on the lounger, she spied her drink. "Lemme just..." She reached over and snatched it up. Slipping the kiwi from the glass's rim, she finished off her drink, ate the fruit slice, and set it back down.

Continuing along the side deck and opening the smooth doorway that led to the helm cabin, she slid into the chair and began to tap at the dual twenty-four-inch touchscreen control consoles to wake them up. Placing her thumb onto the biometric scanner, the controls opened up. She pushed the icon to disengage the autopilot and hit the dial on the right to adjust the engine speed. Tracing her finger up the screen, she moved the needle icon along the virtual dial as the engines below began to churn. This sent the Sunseeker flying forward, toward the terrified beings in the water dead ahead.

Draco, steadied by an iron grip on the bow pulpit rail, turned toward the bridge, and waved at Jacqueline through the dark, tinted panel glass. She smiled and nodded.

Calling loudly to her, Draco bellowed, "I'll handle the turret if you want to steer us toward the slimy bastards."

She gave him a thumbs up, then used her left hand to tap on the port control console. With a few more motions, she pulled up the toggle for the turret and shifted it from "locked" to "armed."

Draco stepped aside as a sliding panel on the white deck, not three feet from the edge of the bow, opened, allowing a large double-grip machine-gun-like turret to emerge from the bowels of the ship. Draco took position at the steer bar controls and rested his thumbs atop the big red firing buttons. A cross-sighted metal targeting pip sat atop the barrel to give dead reckoning aim to the operator. Old school turkey shootin'.

A frozen, toothy grin crossed his lips.

Just like in the Pacific Theater, but funner, he thought.

Taking note that her tanned man was loaded down for bear

and donning one of *those looks*, Jackie sat back down so that the seat cushion would keep her in place while she gunned the engine as much as she could. She slid open the small window in the helm door, calling out to Draco.

"Hey, hunky killer man, shall we run the bastards down?" she asked.

"Too right you are, my dear! Smash any that I don't rightly sink with these searing slugs!" He bent his knees and steadied himself, taking aim.

Looking back toward the ship, the sweeping cadre of little fish-men made soft, fear-filled chortling sounds to one another through their water-logged gills. But crying out to warn one another did nothing to inhibit the momentum of the V-shaped hull rapidly approaching with deadly intent.

Draco began shouting much like one would imagine a blood-frenzied Viking to have done amid some smoke-filled, gore-stained battlefield of yore. His transfixed eyes became his targeting system. Visually locking onto the fleeing things, he did not hesitate to drop his thumbs and rain a torrent of .50 caliber fire down upon them. Spent casings flew in a thin stream from the side of the rocking barrel as it swallowed up the ammo belt from the bottom.

This engagement was short, and it was bloody. Mr. Roselli knew that with this buckin' bronco of a death-dealer, he didn't need much to do a whole lot. Five seconds of sustained gunfire, and nearly everything that had been trying to escape them was dead.

The yacht was now cruising at such a speed that, within moments, the few creatures still left alive after the bullets peppered the water were struck by the keel and hull of the watercraft crushing its sizable weight upon them. A few sickening thumps rattled along the yacht's side as the bow split the puddle of dead, dying, and fleeing mermen in two.

Splats and yelps and chortles and *thump thump thump.*

Jacqueline could see little of the carnage, but sensing that the end of Draco's gunfire spelled the same for their largely helpless victims, she slid a digit across the starboard console screen, decreasing the craft's speed as substantially and deftly as she'd earlier increased it. Draco still held onto the dual handgrips and was ready for the dramatic shift in velocity.

As the ship slowed, he released his hands and turned toward the bridge once more. Spreading his arms out, he waved them in concentric semi circles. Each appendage became rubbery with the vibrations of impending dance moves. A flesh wave began with his right fingertips, then rolled along his arm, toward his sternum, and out the arm, finishing with his left hand. He started to go into disco-robot break-dance maneuvers and Jackie made an effort to raise her clapping hands up so he could see them through the bridge's tinted panel windows.

As the mighty roar of the engines became a dull hum in the periphery, a familiar sound emanated from the port side hull.

Draco was mid-swivel hip shift, hearing the sound of "Backstreet's back, alright!" in his head, when he paused the farcical celebration and caught the sound. The one signaling the approach of more guests.

He wasted no time in dispensing with his Saturday Night Fever, moving along the side of the bridge and past the cabin window.

"There's a pistol in the cabin glove box, babe. Aim for their beady eyes when you blow their fucking skulls open! If they have skulls. Shoot those fuckers! *Bang bang,* baby. You get it." Draco winked as he strode past the window.

"Oh, I get it." And got it, she did. "Just like these fucks are about to."

Flipping open the storage compartment near her left knee, she pulled out a silver Walther PPK semi-automatic pistol. Checking the clip, she popped it back into place, snatched two extra, and tucked them into her bathing suit. She then exited the bridge helm through the starboard door. Strutting around the bridge's exterior, she saw two coming up on the bow, off to the port side. Crossing the deck and taking aim, she quickly emptied the entire clip into the two creatures, five into one beast's slimy chest, then the remaining slugs into the other.

Thumping along the opposite side of the yacht were several more humanoid forms. And just as they crested the yacht's edge, Draco reappeared with a hook on a pole. Coming back around to the foredeck, he stepped between Jacqueline and the last two. Draco raised the short gaff hook above his head, then swung his arm in an arc, flashing glinting metal before burying the hooked end several inches into the hard skull of the thing nearest him. It instantly went limp.

Crying out, the thing standing just behind it whimpered. It wrapped its arms around the other reptilian being and attempted to pull the quite dead creature away from Draco. But his grip upon the gaff hook held fast, and the business end remained embedded in the skull. That is, until he forcibly retracted it with a hard crunch and a squishy pop. He then swooped it into the side of the other creature's face, opening a hole that sprayed bright slime from the opposite side. The nictitating membranes over its eyes covered them up, signaling its demise.

Behind him, Jacqueline giggled. "I didn't aim for the head, babe."

"Yeah, well, they're still hella dead so all's well that ends well, one supposes." Draco tossed aside the gaff hook and turned to face his one and only.

Jackie smiled. "What are they? Rather, what *were* they?

"Dead and dead. But if I'm being totally forthcoming, one could surmise them to be of a heretofore unexplored—or rather, undiscovered—form of fauna not native to the larger islands in the Mediterranean Sea. Surely we'd have heard of them by now. Nary such a construct to be found in the history of animalia."

Clicking the safety and tossing the gun onto the padding of the nearest lounger, Jackie asked, "What, other than their ostensible rarity, assures you of their absence from the fossil record, my love?"

"Only a passing, and dare I say perfunctory, comprehension of cryptozoology, genetic evolution, and theoretical Darwinism. Additionally, if they weren't dead and gone before, hopefully we inched them one notch higher upon the endangered species list. Gooey fucks could have taken off my head with those claws! Yuck!" Draco walked to the nearest husk and kicked it hard in the side, eliciting a small gurgle from the dead creature's scaly mouth.

"Good God, yes, the claws! What ugly claws! Nasty things. I thought it might be a problem at first, but…" Jacqueline trailed off.

Gazing at the blood splattered foredeck, Jacqueline surveyed the bullet-ridden bodies. There were several, but moreover, there was the bright purple filling that let loose from every hole they'd made in their maritime visitors. Gallons of viscous ooze, drying and caking under the sun's uninhibited rays, were splashed every which way. Brief panic set in at the bloody mess before her, then soothing relief washed it away as she recalled that this yacht model had several freshwater bibs to hook hoses to along the bridge walkway. Perfect to rinse off the decking. Crisis well and truly averted, in her estimation.

Squinting at the nearest deceased thing, she used the tip of the harpoon in her hands to lightly stab into the haunches of the beast. She pierced deeply into the flesh, turning it over and revealing the back of its greenish-brown spine and legs. Rows of small, iridescent scales, rolling colors down their backs and along their bodies.

Eliciting the slightest of giggles, she instantly brought her palm to her lips in an attempt to stifle more that followed. In this regard, she was largely unsuccessful, laughing out loud. "Oh my my," she got out between chuckles, "do you see that nub of a tail they've got there? That's just untoward! Do you see that, darling? My goodness, they look to be shaped like little pointy paddles, or even mushrooms, don't they?"

"I should say they do! Wee mushrooms! Almost like, well, I dare say…" He stifled a laugh and his eyes met hers with a knowing look.

Jacqueline embraced him, concluding the thought along with her tan man in malevolent unison. "Cocktails! Bahahaha!"

They cried out in delighted harmony, wrapping their well-toned, well-tanned arms around one another and twirling around on the white and purple-smeared fiberglass deck. Dancing and spinning, they laughed heartily amid the bullet-riddled corpses of their aquatic victims, while the clear Mediterranean sun continued its slow march toward the distant, rippling western horizon.

DEEP

As the fishing rod rattled about something fierce and his reel spun out in a frenzy, coughing up yard by yard of clear line into the bluish-green pond's murky depths, Blake momentarily ceased staring up at the wispy clouds and baby blue skies above.

He quickly finished, set down his empty Bud Light bottle and stood. His foldable lawn chair throne stuck, sweat-affixed, to his ass as he walked over to the spot where he'd braced his rod between two large rocks. Falling off about halfway to his destination, the folding chair collapsed into the dirt.

Blake neared the rod, the line still flying from the spool.

It was the sorta thing one didn't expect to see when they were minding their sky-gazing business on a perfectly fine Thursday afternoon in August. Fine and dandy, really.

His hand deftly flipped around the forest-camoed trucker hat covering his short brown hair so the bill didn't obscure any of his vision, and took the rod into his grasp. He set the reel and it immediately bowed the rod in an arc toward the waters of the pond, roughly fifty feet away. Cranking back the spool slowly, he found it was not moving much and gave it a good tug to straighten the rod back up.

What happened next was also unexpected. Because he watched as several bubbles, inches in diameter, rose to and popped on the water's surface near where his line entered the murky depths. Before he could blink at the sight, the line in his hands went loose and the rod swept up vertically, forcing him to steady it, nearly avoiding a whip-crack to the bridge of his nose.

Around him, the birds were chirping their final songs of departure as fall was making its colorful, all-too-rapid way toward the first snowfalls. Rustling along the leaf-strewn grasses and rocks nearby was all you usually heard here at the Beaver Ponds.

This trip right here was intended to be some much deserved R&R.

Blake Bunford had needed a break, by golly, and he was determined as can be to have one. See, BB's Bait 'n' Tackle had seen better times.

Or mayhaps it hadn't, if we're uh-shootin' straight.

Despite the surrounding area being a mountain-nestled paradise filled to the valley rims with trails, treelines, and rich topography, business during the small shop's short two-year turn at the Sopris Shopping Center in Carbondale, Colorado had hardly been booming. *A smidge tumultuous* might've been a more honest read of the land to the casual observer.

Now, this might've been on account of the fact that he was competing with several other well-established shops of the same type within a few miles. Or it could've been because his first manager had been replaced by himself less than four months into opening up his doors. The man he'd thought of as a friend had been embezzling a stunning amount of money from the company coffers. Ergo, his Grade-A financial investment had rapidly de-volved into a laborious, time-consuming, Grade-A pain in the ass.

It certainly wasn't because he had no idea what he was doing. Never that.

Advertising hadn't helped much. He didn't have many regulars and those he did mostly just bought Styrofoam cups of worms, spare spools, and hooks. And sure, the business caught a fair flurry of pass-erby foot traffic resulting from Sounds Easy Video & CD as well as the Wok-Inn Chinese Restaurant being situated on either side of it. The latter made the slow-to-grow tackle store—the one Blake had dumped the bulk of his life savings into—smell eternally of egg rolls and wonton soup. But his proximity to the Chinese food joint and video store were hardly able to help make a dent in the rent.

Instead, for the last few months, Blake had been floating on the guilt-drizzled, curmudgeonly generosity of his parents. A gift which was quickly running its own course, he knew too well.

Such stark realities left him as the only shop owner in the small mini-mall on Highway 133 to be in financial dire straits, by all accounts.

Was it really bad luck? Or was he just kidding himself with this whole cottage industry into which he'd thrust himself?

He didn't know and he had no idea.

Either way, he needed a break. Generally several a week, in fact. For a working man needs his peace, by golly. And no place on God's green Earth to find your place and peace with the boun-tiful natural beauty around you than to drop a line into one of the state's hundreds of thousands of fishing holes. Snag a nice spot to kick up your heels. Time-a-plenty to put back a few brews and keep anything that made noise back in the truck.

The world had been noisy lately. Too damn noisy. But one

thing that wasn't so loud was the Colorado wilderness—so long as you knew where to look. And Blake knew where that good shit was, you betcha.

For such unwinding, he was partial to one specific hidden gem. A manmade fish-catch situated a good ways up Thompson Creek Road which led up the western hills outlying town.

Not that there was much to worry about outside of work these days. Of course, that didn't stop people from tryin'. Despite it only being August, many folks were already getting up in arms about the fast-approaching dawn of the new millennium. *Y2K* was what everyone had taken to calling it. To hear the TV chat atcha about it, you'da thunk the world was about to cut the house lights and shut right on off.

So some techy knuckleheads forgot to add a digit to a silicone diode, or some such buffoonery, and now we're expected to worry about our collective doom?

Nope. Not in the cards for our man, Blake. That was one line he wasn't gonna bite down on himself. His gut told him that it was, likely as not, some fat cat ploy—mayhaps a sly tactic by Duracell and Energizer to prop up global battery sales headed into the uncertain monetary waters of the third millennium.

Could be.

But back in the here and now, he had a real odd thing to address, alright. Because after the line dropped down into the water and the surface ripples subsided, Blake wondered if he'd snagged a log that had some trapped air in it. And maybe rolling it over had caused the bubbles.

That still left the line suddenly snapping, which he couldn't quite square. It was possible something had taken the bait at the last moment, but…

Parked about twenty feet away from where his lawn chair had been set up was his 1995 Ford F-150 truck that his father had gotten him for his 18th. He'd spent the last year retro-fitting it with any and all modifications that struck his fancy. The thing had a winch, roll bars, diamond plates, and satellite radio—all after-market additions and rarely utilized. But it was nice to have 'em just the same.

Reaching inside the bed, he yanked out another fishing rod (this one black with a thin red trim highlight) and went to his modest tackle box to reset the line. He tied on a hook, cut said line with his trusty 3" pocket knife, baited it, and sauntered back to the double boulder brace he'd fashioned earlier.

Shutting his eyes, he allowed for the pleasing whizzing sound of the reel's casting to sing its sweet siren song to him. Hearing the satisfying plunk as it connected with the pond, he wedged the rod's base in the space between the two rocks.

Realizing he was now beerless, he walked to the bed again and retrieved a fresh Bud Light. Using his Bic to pop the cap, he flicked it into the truck bed and made his way to the lawn chair. Straightening the chair out and setting it back down, he took back his cozy place along the shore.

There we go. Back in business. Now where was I?

Oh yeah, trees.

Watching the branches of the lodgepole pines that surrounded him on all sides lull and sway in the soft breeze, he tilted his head back and let his mind continue its long journey to nowhere.

Chirping birds. Clear skies.

But then…

His reel began to rapidly deploy its line again. Wasting no time, he rushed to the rod. He nearly reached over to grab the pole and give it a finger brake to slow the running, but thought better of it. Lucky thing, too, as not another three seconds of the reel hissing passed before the rod jerked free of its mooring in the ground and shot like a lawn dart past Blake, vanishing straight into the pond's depths.

Standing there slack-jawed like some damn fool, Blake could not quite reason out what had just happened. There wasn't anything that should've been able to give up that kind of struggle in this little watering hole. Not here at the damn Beaver Ponds.

But now that he thought about it, those same eponymous little critters that you'd usually see or hear at some point during a visit had been wholly absent during his time there. Much like his old high school football locker room, there weren't a single beaver in sight. It'd only been about thirty minutes on this particular sojourn, but generally he would've heard the furry buggers gnawing upon a felled bit of log. Or maybe catch sight of 'em running along the emerald grasses of the opposing bank's shoreline, on a fishin' mission of their own.

Not today, though. The place was suddenly even more absent of noise than usual. And he was the sorta fella who certainly noticed that kinda thing.

A surge of bubbling foam surfaced in the middle of the pond, sending ripples toward the pebble-strewn shores.

This newly lost rod had been part of his take-home prize for winning the Roaring Fork Anglers Association's Golden Reel Award for the third year in a row. Now vanished in the semi-murky waters of the pond, Blake was confronted with a situation he'd never faced before.

Well, now what?

He pondered this as he scratched his stubbly chin and turned the hat around on his skull.

Crossing the gap to his trusty steed of a Ford, he moved toward the back of the cab and reached into a white cooler that sat just inside the bed. The lid creaked as it flipped open, and he reached into the meat cooler. He drew forth a large chunk of bloodless flesh atop a bed of two ice blocks. It'd been in there for a day or so, just waiting for the right fire grill to slap it down on.

Deer meat. That good shit.

Setting it aside, he reached past the cooler to his truck bed toolbox and opened it up. Fumbling for a moment, his hands soon struck gold. Rather, a spool of cable wound up into a handheld feeder. Lastly, he moved further down the truck's length to the back gate and snagged a large painted hook, about as thick as a #2 pencil and several inches long.

Returning to the front of the truck, he began to unspool the cable into a lasso in his other hand. Then, dropping to his knees, he secured one end to the draw-spring on the winch while attaching the other end of the thick metal wire to the hook.

Sinking the orange-colored tip in the slab of deer meat, he loosened his grip on the thick cable and gave some slack up so that he could cast it into the water. Whatever was down there, it would not be taking any more rods from this fisherman.

No way.

Near the center of the lake, another massive glug of bubbles belched forth in a frothing semi-spray that reached a height of several feet. Like something down there was trying to breach.

Whoo-boy, this is gonna be a whopper. A real wall filler. The catch to end all catches. How a biggun' like that got into this tiny hole, who knows. But here we go!

He stood up and spun the rope above his head, then squarely flung the hooked chunk of animal meat out into the middle of the pond. A small, flat splash and it immediately started to sink.

That should do the trick. Ain't nothin' down in that hole to give my rig a run for its gears. No siree.

He rushed to the cab and jumped into the driver's seat, closing the door behind him and securing his seatbelt out of habit. Turning the keys, he revved the engine for a moment. Then he flicked the switch for the winch to draw up the slack on the line.

It went taught a moment later, squealing and freezing in place.

The entire truck jostled forward slightly, startling him. It was as if he was being pulled toward the water's edge.

Okay, that's quite a lot of tug it's got there. Probably should just—

Blake reached down for the smaller stick shift in the console flooring that engaged the four-wheel drive and flung it up. Taking up the taller shifter, he tried to move the stick into reverse, but found it wouldn't budge. Not a bit.

The truck shuddered and slid another inch toward the green-blue waters of the pond.

Blake doubled over as much as his spine would allow so he could throw the full force of his arm into putting it into gear. Yet after another fruitless shove, he knew it wasn't going anywhere.

Unlike the truck—which was dragged another inch toward the pond.

His finger once again flicked the retraction switch for the winch, however it did not squeal as it had before. Just as with the shifter, it now simply did not move. The truck was slowly being dragged another few inches forward, then jerked to a rough stop as Blake pressed his foot down hard on the brake.

He reached down and wrapped his hand around the small

black lever, engaging the emergency brake. His body whipped against the steering wheel and he felt the breath leave his chest as the truck pitched forward a good foot this time, hopping up and crushing the wheel into his sternum.

Gasping, his hand fumbled around.

Through the windshield, he caught a brief glimpse as another whoosh of water sprayed skyward from the center of the pond.

He tried to exit the truck but was stopped by the hard restraint of the seatbelt holding him steadfast—conveniently engaging at exactly the wrong moment for his needs. His right hand wasted no time in slipping the three-inch Smith & Wesson knife from his pocket, flicking the blade open with his right thumb. Carefully aiming the edge away from his body, he pulled it through the belt fabric with little resistance, and as the vehicle began to stutter-shake toward the muddy shore at a steady clip, he pulled open the door and rolled away from the truck.

Leaves, debris, and freshly wet mud clung to his clothing as he rose to his feet, brushing it away and watching the truck slowly move away from him. He picked up the small knife from the ground nearby, rubbed the blade against his jeans, clicked it shut, then pocketed it.

A half-grin of defiance crossed his lips, but a single thought banished the short-lived self-satisfaction from his face.

Oh shit!

Remembering that he'd left his shotty on the rack inside the cab, he scrambled to the still ajar door and leaned in, snatching the Mossberg pump-action shotgun from the back rack.

Thanking the good Lord that he'd known well enough to keep the lock sprung for such a need-it-now occasion, he withdrew the gun. Backing away from the departing vehicle, he watched as it was drawn along the shore and into the rippling waters. Bluish-clear liquid filled the grill, then the cab, and finally the bed as it disappeared into the depths with startling speed, just like the two trusty fishing rods had.

Probably not your average fish we got here, he thought wisely.

But before any other obvious thoughts could run through his mind, he beheld a sight like no other he'd ever beheld.

A single muscular, iridescent, violet-shaded appendage as thick as an oak tree breached the surface at the pond's center and rose up into the air like a totem. It looked to Blake to be a tentacle or some such thing. Wriggling to and fro as it ascended skyward, it shook free the water clinging to it, then straightened out.

From slimy, padded tip to where the base hit the pond's surface, it must've been a good hundred plus feet in length.

Dumbfounded, Blake aimed his barrel but didn't fire, instead watching in awe as the massive limb crashed down like a chopped tree in the forest, noticeably shaking the ground as it landed on the opposite side of the lake. Water and dust kicked up, and Blake knew what was coming before it moved. He crouched instinctively, ready to drop.

Dripping, viscous sheets of watery, translucent ooze fell to the leaf-strewn earth from the full length of the purplish tentacle. After another moment, and just as Blake had anticipated, it began whipping around the perimeter of the lake, sweeping in wide, searching arcs.

Instinctively tumbling backward at the sight, Blake rolled to his left just as a horizontal swipe cut through the air above his head. The nauseating wet clicking of suckers—untold numbers of small suction cups lining one side of the massive appendage—whizzed by his ear.

Roughly positioned on his butt about fifty feet from the water's edge, he scooted backward and rolled again, this time behind the two rocks he had been using to brace the rods, and held as still as he could. Hoping that it was using sound or movement to aid its search, he held his breath and listened. Branches cracked, water splashed, and rocks flew through the air as the huge squishy arm smacked and tore through the nearby forest.

It paused in mid-air for a moment, slathering tendrils of slime about, eliciting smaller splashes into the water below. Then, a slight rustle from a nearby tree caused the appendage to shoot across the water to some distant trunk. It ripped it, roots and all, from its earthen mooring. Branches cracked like a thousand whips striking in a choir of crunching wood as Blake watched it sail overhead and crash into another several large lodgepole pines that bracketed the dirt road winding through the woods—his only exit.

As he contemplated how to get there without becoming, well, meat for the beast, as it were, the massive arm made a swift *slurp* sound—and then, silence. Not even the air being disturbed above the pond's surface.

Must've gone back down.

Cautiously, he turned and placed his palms flat against the rock, peering over the top as the still rippling and bubbling surface of the water churned less than the length of a football field away. Too close to make a run for it. It could reach out and snatch him in an instant.

A rupture at the pond's center momentarily opened into a wide chasm as his F-150 came flying from the liquid hole, careening through the air and spinning like a top along its length. Bent and crumpled, it landed, thumping against the water's edge.

The ferocity of its impact carved a huge blast from the sand like a mortar hit on an enemy shore. It rolled several more times, striking a grove of trees, not far from where the other tree had struck before, and stopped.

Quiet descended upon the area.

Without a moment's hesitation, Blake stood and started to walk quietly yet steadily in the direction of the break in the trees that the road intersected through. Careful not to step on any smaller sticks and make too much noise, he hurried along for all of fifteen seconds—just long enough to think he might be able to pull off his little exit via stage left—before the respite was quickly dashed by the tentacle breaching the waters again.

With shocking agility, it sought and found him in an instant, picking him up and lifting him several feet into the air while slowly drawing him nearer the pond's edge. The shotgun remained snugly pressed against his side in a way that rendered it wholly ineffective for the time being.

The compressive force of the slimy arm was nearly enough to cut off his air supply. He wriggled in its hard grasp just enough to force his chest above the fold of its grip, allowing airflow to continue unabated. He tried to pull his arm free, finding it impossible with the shotgun still tightly clung in his grasp.

Making a faster decision than he would've suspected himself able, he dropped the gun. After a fifteen-foot drop, it fell onto its side on the embankment, below Blake's dangling Doc Martens. Carefully slipping the knife from his pocket, he managed to slide his right arm above the fleshy vice grip of the suckered tentacle.

To that point, the sensation of all the little cups clinging to his flesh was making his spine crawl with the sensation of a million tiny nerve bugs marching along his vertebrae.

Never again will be too soon for this feeling, he mused as his right thumb flicked open the serrated three-inch blade. He spun it into a stabbing position in his palm and thrust it into the tentacle surrounding his waist. The flesh gave way easily under the sharp edge and oozed with fresh violet blood from the foot-long gash.

Immediately the suckers clasping onto his arm, stomach, and thighs withdrew and he felt himself fall. He came down hard on his right leg and his knee nearly buckled, just barely taking the impact. The left absorbed the remaining shock of landing as he wobbled, waving his arms to regain his balance.

The tentacle shook twenty or more feet above him, twisting and untwisting, covering him with tiny droplets of purple rain.

He knelt down and grabbed the shotgun. Not hesitating, he fired a round into the middle of the writhing mass. This blast opened a much larger hole along the spiny ridge that ran the length of the serpentine appendage, gushing forth purple blood in thick spurts.

Blake had only enough time to pump the barrel and take aim before the paddle end of the thing's arm hit him in his ribcage, sending him backward into the dirt. His head tucked into his chest to avoid cranial impact with a nearby rock as he hit the ground, tumbling several times.

Conscious but dazed, he slowly pulled himself around to sitting. The shotgun lay a few feet to his right.

Struggling for equilibrium and unaware of where the thing was, he was disturbed and surprised to feel it ensnare his right ankle and wrap around his leg, as a snake might, heading toward his groin.

Jerking hard at his lower half, his body began to inch toward the water's edge, just as his now-dilapidated truck had. Feeling something in or around his knee finally sound off a disconcerting pop, then giving way to an exasperating wash of fiery hot pain shooting along his thigh, he knew that his right leg was now basically useless.

"Fuck!" he hollered in agony, the likes of which he'd never personally experienced. "Oh goddamn it, that's some real shit! Goddamn it!"

Pulling him along the grassy, muddy ground with less than half of its original strength (if that), the arm spurted a wide gush of thick, black-violet blood from the wound. Hitting the ground, a splash of it spattered onto Blake's blue jeans.

His frantically casting eyes caught sight of the Mossberg in his periphery. Clawing fingers reached out to grab the shotgun, but it was about a foot too far away. He continued sliding along the mud, jerking his body to the right. Snatching at the barrel, he missed it again—stopped by the red hot alarm bell of his right knee preventing him from another inch of pursuit. He cried out in pain, dropped hard onto his back, and still inching along, noticed he was now but a few feet from the pond's embankments.

Blake figured that he had about five seconds before he was at the Pearly Gates, staunchly arguing with his creator about the utterly ridiculous circumstances surrounding his premature demise, so it was time to giddy-up.

Now or never, little doggie.

He threw all of his weight to his right side, taking his knee-cap to another threshold of suffering he'd only ever heard about in war stories, and willed his hand to draw the gun to himself. Reaching the rubber grip, he clamped on with two fingertips and yanked it to him. It came another few inches his way, which was all he needed. Grabbing the barrel, he took the gun into both hands and aimed at the biggest, nearest chunk of it that he could.

"Let go, you slimy mother-trucker!" He racked the shell, then squeezed the trigger.

Despite being a licensed hunter and seasoned hand with most firearms, even he was surprised at the deafening crack the blast let out with his target poised at such close range. Echoing electric hums permeated his brain as his eardrums fell into temporary deafness. Only the faintest of muffled sound was now penetrating the auditory miasma in blurbs and babs.

Erupting more blood and bits of shredded purple flesh, the grasp of the tentacle-tipped arm gave up. Receding away from Blake's lower half, it shot out one last spasm, cracking like a whip and splitting from the spot where it had been blasted at close range.

While most of the arm fell to the shore with another hard thump, the thick, gushing stump withdrew back to the center of the lake, quickly vanishing below the rippling surface. Shimmering purple plumes of blood blotted out the clarity of the pond waters, rising up and leaving floating, viscous slime patches.

Blake exhaled loudly and dropped his head and arms, outstretched, back to the wet earth. His eyes watched leaves fall from the highest canopy above and land all around him. He noticed how silent it was again. Just the way he liked it.

Nice 'n' quiet.

Whatever had been down there, it seemed that it had finally figured that the juice wasn't worth the squeeze on this one and had presumably beat a hasty retreat to the dark place from whence it had come. Blake imagined it now, swiftly retreating though the same network of underwater tunnels and grottos it had utilized to arrive at the Beaver Ponds.

He couldn't be sure of anything, but for all he knew, he'd delivered it a mortal blow. For all he knew, he'd just slayed a damn Kraken. Though that last one seemed a bit fanciful.

Fanciful.

Shit—fanciful? What the hell is fanciful now, after all this shit?

After another five minutes of letting his knees numb up, and with no more bubbles breaching the pond waters, he unloaded the remaining rounds from the gun. Then, as one might utilize a crutch, he used it to prop himself to his feet once more.

Looking back up the shore in the vague direction of his crushed and mangled mess of vehicular metal(Found On Road Dead), his weary eyes locked onto the still-twitching purple appendage lying severed and caked with muddy dirt and grass. Wriggling and jerking at several spots along its length, the motions were slowing and diminishing in strength. Pinkish, black ringed cups zigzagging its inner arm still reflexively sucked at the air like a thousand gasping mouths. The muscles gave the occasional twitch, the odd spasm, but he was satisfied, having watched more than a couple things die in his day, that the bastard was done for. This fight, such as it had been, was through.

Only God Almighty knew for sure what happened to the rest of it.

Blake didn't know and he had no idea, which was just fine and dandy with him. He was still in one piece and that'd have to do.

Squinting at the rays of light shooting bolts between the thicket of the surrounding forest, he rubbed a small nick on his cheek and licked the blood from his fingertip. And then, at last, with his mental clouds parting, the silver lining fluttered to the front of Blake Bunford's mind.

One thing is for sure though, he thought with a wry smile passing over his cut and bloodied lips. *That puppy right there is damn sure to attract a whole lotta foot traffic once it's up on the wall in the shop! Shoot—might be high time to ring up the ol' boys over at Field and Stream and tell 'em we got us a cover story in the makin'!*

Whoo, Nellie!

BUBBLES

The first time that it fed on one of the pale skinned fleshy things in the large stone basin, no one knew that it had. No one even realized that young Tommy McGuinn had gotten into the water of the Hot Springs Pool.

Since no body was ever found, his mother, father, and older brother were left to assume the worst, without ever knowing of his true fate. They imagined any number of horrific scenarios; that he had been kidnapped, or murdered, or had wandered outside of the fence surrounding the resort's property line, tragically falling victim to the deadly undertow of the nearby river.

They knew nothing of the thing beneath their feet. They did not know it was responsible.

For untold generations, it had existed in what the original inhabitants had called the Yampah (or "Big Medicine") Spring. The fount from which earth-warmed mineral water rolled forth through the many outlets dotting the side of the mountainous ridge that formed the northern perimeter of Glenwood Springs, Colorado.

At first, it—*the being*—was but a simple function of form. It simply was.

Then, movement.

Much later, darker-skinned fleshy things arrived and bathed in the spring's waters. Creatures that it observed but never fed upon.

And finally, stunning changes all around as the soft patter of the darker, quieter fleshy forms was rapidly replaced with innumerable louder, pale-skinned ones that brought explosions and machines and what it would eventually recognize as railways.

Rails ceaselessly rattling the hard ground with the tremors of modern conveyance. Large transports, filling the surrounding area with more and more fleshy things. More noise.

Widespread electricity arrived by the 1880s so that darkness never again swallowed the valley by night. Electric twilight reigned.

For a century or longer, some had noticed the disappearances, but all seemed to assume them to be either the sublime will of a deity or a tragically random act of nature.

A lightning strike.

Yet it was the form. The deep force. The nameless, faceless, gaseous being—invisible and incomprehensible—that had been able to slip in and out of the maze of dense iron water pipes that had connected the subterranean Yampah Spring to the bathing pools of the resort since they had first been installed in the mid-1800s. Partitioned pipes, cutoff valves, and gasket-sealed apertures did nothing to inhibit its ability to smoothly slide along any such space.

It was neither liquid nor solid, but something able to reform and reconfigure its foundational essence to suit its need to move. For that drive was something–moving was something. Moving was most of what it did for the first few years, because it did not know at first. *Could not* know. Then, after some time that was impossible to comprehend or quantify, it began, very slowly at first, to know things.

Before then, it simply was. Now, it was and it moved and it knew.

It wasn't until the summer of 1899 that the seven-year-old son of Merrimer and Trudy McGuinn disappeared. A family trip with a plan to spend the day eating ice cream between dips in the hot mineral pools, then dinner and a show on Grand Avenue. But freckle-faced little Tommy was there one minute—waiting to take a dip in the healing waters provided by the vast, underground sulfur-tinged spring—and was simply gone the next.

Not a trace.

It was neither an act of hatred nor malice nor sexual predation by some human perpetrator. It wasn't the modus operandi of a career criminal, nor was it pre-planned. Unknown to his family for the remainder of their lives was the fact that it was simply a tragedy born of opportunity. The opportunity for the form to assimilate something larger than the insectoid life and small rodents that it had before. When it had fallen upon and enclosed itself around the scared and shivering little boy with the sandy blond hair, it was, at last, able to connect physically in a way that was stimulating.

It did not feel. *Could not feel.* But still, the very stimulation— the brush against what feeling must be—was something new, and it gave it a goal where before it had possessed none. And so it sought more of the new stimulation. More connection with the physical things that filled the pool during the daylight hours.

It would retreat to the confines of the slick grottos and branching water arteries that ran beneath the town, sometimes for a year or two. Sometimes several years. To commune with the spring.

Time was not something it felt, for it could feel nothing. It was eternal, for all it understood. It knew, it moved, and it sought.

Every few years, when it would emerge from its hibernation among the aqueducts and underground rivers, it sought to assimilate more of the fleshy things in the pools at the mountain base.

The second time it sought to commune with the flesh of a human, in the year 1903, it attempted to take two at once, but found it could not. So it sought a fleshy thing in the hotter of the two large pools.

By this time, the unseen thing in the pool knew that they—the fleshy things—also knew. And moved. And sought. But it had also slowly begun to know that they did something which it could not.

They felt.

Glenwood's eternal electric twilight, supplanting the night's darkness, had shrouded the nearby township when it had taken the big woman in the striped black and white bathing suit from the hotter pool.

She had felt fear and also tremendous pain. It could not feel this directly, but it did know through her feelings that this sensation was something new. And it sought the new. It sought to feel. By communion with the fleshy things, it could almost taste the emotions glowing under the surface of their subdermal layers.

Almost.

A nearby man had reacted fearfully to the sudden disappearance of the woman beneath the waters, and the formless thing from the Yampah Spring had moved to take the man as well. As the creature pulled the large woman apart, it formed into a vortexing column of water and tugged the man toward it. The shouting man had fled.

Without waiting to see what the outcome of the man's out-burst would be, it rapidly completed its absorption of the woman and retreated through the iron pipes and back toward the spring.

It began to know that the fleshy things called themselves "people," and they traveled from the world over to soak in the natural mineral solution that spewed forth from the spring. The very spring that emptied out into the pool, where it was treated with chemicals and provided hours of relaxation and leisure to tourists and locals alike.

The creature would have traveled, if not for a preternatural need to commune with the spring. To stay close to the spring.

The spring was the source.

So it remained, hidden from the world's view, communing with and assimilating what it could, when it could.

Once, in the year 1909, it took a local police officer who was walking by the edge of the pool after breaking up a scuffle between two of the resort's drunken visitors. It had nearly been discovered as the source of the lawman's disappearance. The fleshy things, several watching with horrified expressions as it assimilated the lawman, described the awful sight to the other police officers who came after. It knew that it had to be more careful, and retreated again to the spring for three years.

To hide.

If it was to feed again, it sought to choose a more suitable, less noticeable target. Prey that was less likely to arouse suspicion. Prey that few would miss.

Like a tourist.

For now it knew of such things. The more it fed, the more of their consciousnesses it absorbed, the greater the acquisition rate of its own burgeoning knowledge. It knew much after so many decades, and with this understanding, the closer it drew toward the elusive state of feeling.

And now it understood caution.

So from 1909 forward, it never again assimilated a local resident, nor any law enforcement officer. Though the policemen, as it eventually knew to call them, always came to see if they could find the person it had taken soon after it had taken them. But it discovered that people were quick to forget tragedy and even less likely to rectify such issues. It aroused little suspicion so long as it did not take too many at once.

By what the humans would describe as the early 1920s, the surrounding community—bolstered by the natural spring—was rapidly developing into an ever-expanding resort area of some renown which filled one side of the narrow, stone-walled valley to the other. Being a stopover on the way to some distant place called Aspen did little to deter its growth, either. The rare disappearance of a visiting vacationer did not disturb the locals, nor the police officers.

In the 1960s, a fresh wave of people with novel biochemical signatures flooded into the area, leading to a new boom of population growth. With it, more visitors. More tourists. More food. And most importantly to the thinking, moving being—more opportunities to sense their feelings. To strive to feel for itself.

Foreign-born humans and their warm, easily disintegrated bodies carried chemicals which they themselves assimilated to escape their own feelings. They used the chemicals to throw their feelings away. To discard that which the thing sought for its own. The only desire it truly fostered.

Yet with its own development and expanding consciousness came both an increasing need to consume more and more of the fleshy things, but also the first outlying pings of something like emotion. Something akin to sorrow. Born from its only near-constant perception that it was alone. That it could not feel and therefore could not enjoy the process of being alive.

And for nearly a century, it had tried in vain to make more of itself. Which is to say, it sought to have more than just its own company to keep. Something of its own form, of its own kind to communicate or commune with. Alas, its attempts to create an offspring or progeny were fruitless. It could not divide itself, nor could it create a structurally similar symbiote or identical organic clone. Where it wanted to feel, it could only approximate the sensation of feeling.

Ergo, its hunger only grew.

Not much had changed in the area around the Hot Springs Pool in the previous seventy years, beyond the introduction of the interstate that had been greenlit back in '56. More fleshy things at an increased pace. Which was helpful for the creature in the pipes.

During the following decadent decade of disco-biscuit divas and drug-filled dancefloors that was the 1970s, it ate and ate and ate some more. One young woman who passed through the area and that it had consumed was revealed by a later meal to be an assumed victim of a notorious serial killer (another odd thing it could now vaguely comprehend) who had traveled through the valley. A human predator using the long road nearby, much as the formless being in the warm mineral waters had used the Hot Springs Pool.

As a hunting ground.

The human monster in question had even escaped from the local jail and was of some infamy to the humans.

The being had the faintest flicker of curiosity.

Is the human monster like me? Is it alone? Does it feel?

Then it thusly returned back to the fabric of time, breezing past its ever-increasing need to feel, to consume.

1992 was the year that the slow-to-evolve fleshy things finally caught on to its voracious appetite for humans and their squishy, succulent emotions.

The thing that had given it away was bubbles.

While it knew much more than it had even a decade before, it was wholly unaware that for many years its expanding mass had taken on some specific physical properties that it hadn't previously possessed. Attributes it could not yet fully comprehend.

When, by the late 1980s, it crossed between the rubber-gasket-sealed apertures and through to the resort's bathing pools, seeking another tourist to consume, it was generating a barely discernible trail of minute bubbles in the stead of its movements.

And on that cold December evening, someone had seen the bubble trail wriggling under the water's surface like a sea snake searching for snacks.

Falling through frozen air down to Earth, raindrops crystalized into trickling snow above the fog blanketed waters of the larger swimming pool, while wispy columns of swirling steam vortices twirled to-and-fro, like mist-made ballerinas along its rippling, emerald-hued surface.

The being had already taken two people that night. A couple who were not in the pool itself, but rather just outside its borders, making use of the large concrete outlet for the leftover water that was regularly cycled out from the pool's million-gallon plus capacity shell: A six foot in diameter tube jutting out from the hill next to the interstate and steadily depositing into the Colorado

River. Using this outlet, locals had formed rocks into bathing pools along the river's edge.

The creature had watched from inside the pipe many times, observing humans making sounds and movements which clearly expressed that which it could not yet.

Feelings.

Once it assimilated its victims thoughts and memories, it was able to understand that the town's residents called the area "The Hippie Dips" because "hippies" took "dips" there—though it did not exactly connect with what this meant.

And that night, despite having already taken two, it sought more. Just one more.

For something new had happened.

Rushing with the current through the pipe's slick interior, the invisible creature of molecular ambiguity had intellectually glimpsed the precipice of emotional understanding with the devouring of the first "hippie's" shuddering flesh and fear-drenched mind.

Screams and fleeing did not help to prevent it from wrapping unseen yet impossibly strong pressure around the second "hippie," crushing and instantly reassimilating its carbon structure, depleting the cellular fuel and expelling skyward the faint mist of exhausted molecular refuse. The byproduct was invisible.

What it had experienced through the immediate assimilation of the second "hippie" was something … new.

It was new and it was good. It was almost like feeling.

Now, it sought to commune with a third human and perhaps finally partake of that one limit to its existence.

But then … them ol' bubbles.

The deep form had returned through the cavernous tubes

that connected the river outlet to the resort's larger network of plumbing running beneath the concrete vessels, and entered the smaller hot pool where jets of foaming water often masked its approach. However, no jets churned the waters as it entered from the easternmost bottom drain.

The deep thing from the Yampah Spring could sense only one body in the water. It did not hesitate.

Perhaps that was its initial folly and the moment it crossed a line with the human things.

It made hasty work of the small screaming child, and after so many years of seeking and feebly attempting in vain to attain, it finally tasted what fear was.

And it was, to the thing's admittedly "virginal palette" (if you will), obviously terribly delicious.

Not because it was good—but because the feeling of it was real. For once, it was as the humans were.

Lasting a mere second or two in reality, it might've been a lifetime to the creature. A vibrant arc of reddish-hued emotion ran through its formless link of molecules and thoughts.

If this is bad, then how good is good?

This emotion—this *fear*—was something it wanted more of. Despite fear being something the humans thought of as a nega-tive, the being from below could not have enjoyed its first shock of feelings more.

However, the child in the hot pool was ultimately the last thing it ever assimilated. The humans had realized, at long last, that something was rotten in the state of Glenwood Springs. Someone or some creature was killing off visitors to the area at what should have been an alarming rate. But only alarming if you knew it was happening. Which before, they had not.

A lifeguard, shouting and running alongside the pool, had watched and pointed at it as it dragged the child down and structurally dismantled the fearful young boy on a molecular level within thirty seconds.

Just before that, the lifeguard had caught sight of the bubbles heading along the surface of the water, cascading up when the creature had taken the boy and begun to commune with him. The guard of life knew something else was down there.

The unseen thing slipped down the bottom drain of the smaller hot pool just as several bodies dove into it to try and save the now disintegrated and vanished victim, to no avail.

But the thing was now known to them. And they wanted it gone for good.

The initial strategy that the human creatures feebly employed in an attempt to rid themselves of its presence was to drain the whole million-gallon pool to try and flush the entire system. But the creature from the spring had simply returned to the cavernous source of the nourishing mineral water to avoid their actions and had waited days before checking out the pipes again.

They remained empty.

After that, they had applied a large amount of vacuum pressure to the entirety of the pipe network to remove any living thing that might have been able to scurry up into the system. Perhaps they suspected it was one of the other organic creatures that had decimated the other humans in the pool.

During this process, the resulting suction was immense, yet easy enough for the being to avoid. Shifting into a long sheet of atoms as it slithered away from the draw of the vacuum source, it clung to the walls—then returned again to the spring.

The being suspected that the efforts would cease then, as

they had so many times before, but with this the humans seemed resolved to vanquish it.

It had felt something like (though ultimately impossible to qualify as) anger when it learned from listening through the web-work of pipes that the local humans had been discussing a way to purge the entirety of the system with a mixture that would likely extinguish any and all trace of whatever it came into contact with. It could understand their words by the end. It knew what they planned for it.

And when, a day later, the viscous, tar-like ooze flooded the pipes, it could feel the fast encroachment of its habitat by the thick substance. For it could perceive, in a way akin to human hearing, the rapid approach of the corrosive chemical concoction created to clear the pipes of all organics that would normally survive.

But it realized, in so far as it could, that it did not want to perish. It did not. Whatever this thought was, it was the closest to an actual emotion that it would ever feel.

It was something…

Something like fear.

The sludge expanded inside the pipes in a flash and the thing had no chance of outrunning this liquid that moved at such speed. Just as the being had entered, filled, and inwardly devoured so many things before it, now did it finally experience the other side of that cruel exchange. The sensation was something comparable to pain, but absent the ability to truly feel, it was just a sense and nothing more.

Before it disappeared from the face of this planet forever, it created one single thought to eternally echo in its consciousness while it faded from our world:

Is it better to have been and never felt, then to have never been at all?

Then it was extinguished. Vanquished. Removed from the cycle of death and rebirth for all time.

Known by none.

A memory that never existed.

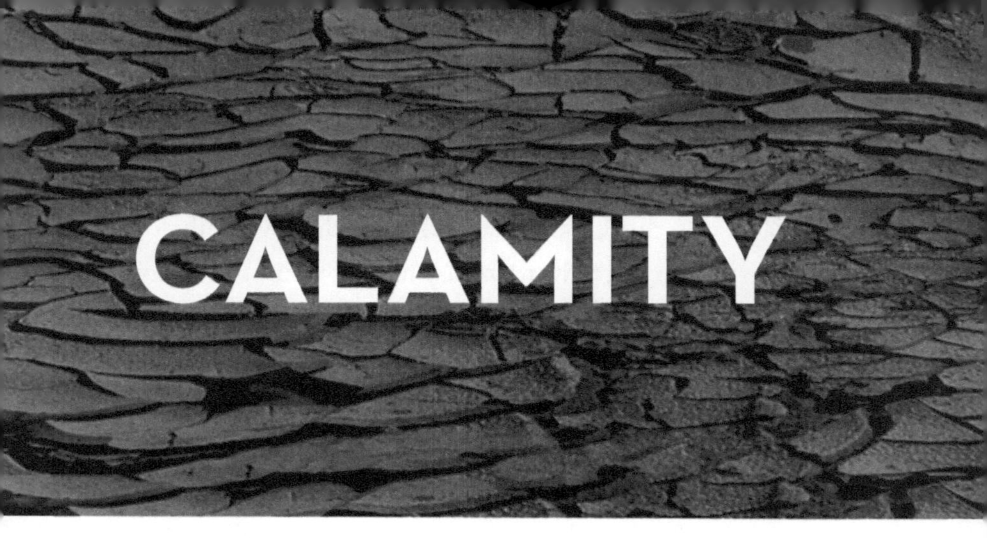

CALAMITY

"What do you mean when you say *ghost*?"

The bald gentleman in the two-button navy business suit stands inside the dimly lit office of Creed & Sons Real Estate, wondering if the man sitting behind the big mahogany desk is tugging at his proverbial chain or just being glib. "A ghost? Like a ghost, ghost?"

"Yes."

"But what do you mean, exactly?"

Long spears of orange light casting through the blinds strike the brown-haired man in his forties sitting at the desk. He is wearing a black fleece jacket and a clean shaven face singularly devoid of any humor. Nodding, he answers, "I mean it exactly like it sounds."

The standing man's reply is swift. "Ghosts aren't real."

The seated man chuckles at that one. "Yeah, well, sure. Tell me about it. Or rather, tell *her* about it." He doesn't look up from his computer screen. While they've been speaking, the sitting man has been rapidly typing on a keyboard in an effort to finish up his remaining contracts before five, when they close up. He only has about fifteen minutes to get 'em done. Luckily, he's competent enough at computational multitasking and this is no chore. No way this Uncle Fester-looking dude is gonna do anything to rid him of the burden that has kept him in second place for so many years.

Smiling, the bald man asks, "Why do you believe it's a *she*?"

"Because we—and by that I mean everyone—knows exactly who she is. She wasn't any type of lady to mince words then, nor is she the kinda ghost to keep you guessing now. It's her, alright. She was a bitch when she came to town back in '82, and she's all the worse in death. Nobody understood what was stuck in her craw. No one did, I guess…" He clears his throat, then finishes, "Until they did, of course. Now I'm stuck with that damn place."

Cody Creed has, for better or worse, spent the last seven years attempting to clear his sheet of the run-down strip mall that runs along Highway 133 through the heart of Carbondale, Colorado. It's been the bane of his existence ever since he took up as a real estate rep for his father's company nearly eight years ago.

His work largely speaks for itself: commanding a natural rapport with people, he's dominated sales every month since his arrival at the company. To boot, his record is nearly impeccable— head and shoulders above the others at the office.

And yet despite having the local market largely on lock, year after year, Cody still carries the minor yet ever-present embarrassment of never being able to clear his table of the dilapidated and disused property that sits like a festering scab on the otherwise gentrified and pristine facade of the perpetually up and coming township of Carbondale. Having a lingering uncleared property on your sheet at the end of the fiscal annum is wholly disqualifying where local recognition of real estate stature is concerned.

It is because of this that, despite his steely drive and unrelenting efforts, he has not been recognized as the top real estate salesperson in the Roaring Fork Valley.

No, that particular distinction has gone time and again to the (in his admittedly biased opinion) avarice-driven, self-aggrandized, self-satisfied, and self-declared "Queen of Valley Property Sales," Mrs. Lindsey Leopard. Seven years of the Glass House awards handed out by the Real Estates Fellows of Roaring Fork, and seven years of her taking home the gleaming, laser-etched award for top sales. Always while smiling an ear-to-ear grin with those immaculately bleached and capped white teeth. Always flexing nouveau in bleeding-edge designer outfits.

Seven long years of his father knowing that despite Cody being a veritable titan at turning properties in his own regard, he still doesn't quite match up to the woman with the long brown hair and the cheeky grin who has her face plastered up on both of the billboards on the road to Aspen.

Both. Two out of two. One hundred percent of the Valley's billboards is what she has.

The same seven years of trying in vain to offload this disaster of a destination along the two-lane road to Redstone, all while he has to drive home every night past one of those unseemly billboards with the perfectly stylized hair and the big white capped teeth.

Fucking humiliating is what it is.

Baldy smirks and barely hides his amusement. "That's quite a story." He sighs and starts to pace as he continues, "Look, I know you locals have been understandably prickly about all the recent development coming in. Changing the face of your sleepy hamlet and all that."

Cody stops typing and leans back in his chair, folding his hands in front of him. "Dunno what you mean. I've done well enough with all of it and I'm certainly no enemy of progress. What exactly are you getting at?"

"Well, you know, you say *ghost*, but what I hear is, 'Go away, foreign interloper.' Unless I'm mistaken. Am I mistaken?"

"Yeah. That isn't what I'm getting at."

"Yeah?"

"Yeah. If that were the case, I'd just say so. I'll be crystal clear here—I don't think you want to tangle with the ol' needle-jockey. That's all I'm saying. Seriously, she'll fuck you up. She fucks everybody up."

"Oh yeah? Who'd she fuck up?"

"Everybody."

The bald man cocks an eyebrow. "Humor me."

Cody can immediately recall all three confirmed onsite deaths over the last twenty years off the top of his head.

That's three for sure, though there was also this missing homeless couple who used to hunker under the bridge leading into town who mysteriously went missing one cold December evening a few years ago. Given it's close proximity to the spot on 133, he (and most local folks for that matter) suspect that they may have sought refuge from the storm in the abandoned parlor, only to vanish without the proverbial trace. One of the dude's bags was found in the dirt at the edge of the lot, but nothing has ever been confirmed. No bodies to corroborate an all-too-likely conclusion.

"A couple people. A kid from the high school was the first. That was some sorta senior dare thing, to spend a night there. Poor kid broke his neck when he jumped off the roof to his death—for no explainable reason, I might add. Never had a self-harming bone in his body before that night. And then there was this lady who tried to turn it into a beauty salon, but she died."

"How?"

Cody snorts. "If you can picture this, she threw herself repeatedly through a window in the back and was cut up pretty bad. Bled out before the medics got there. I had to hire a crew to clean up all the blood out of the dirt behind the building."

"Jesus. How'd she do that, exactly?"

"She didn't. I'm sure it was Jane. The third was some guy like yourself. A proxy, I mean. And that sad chap managed to bludgeon himself to death with multiple blows from a hammer that somebody left in a cabinet inside. Anyway—"

"The hell you say! That one seems even less believable than the window."

"Tell me about it. We have a cheeky coroner here in town. Bit of an oddball, really, but even he didn't want to put down something that invited too much scrutiny."

"And that other shit didn't?" The bald man laughs incredulously.

"Less than if he had declared in his report that a ghost did it, one imagines. Which is what actually happened. And all that was after she had died. That's nothing compared to the shit she stirred up when she was still living and taking brief fresh air breaks between chain-smoking Pall Malls."

The man standing before Cody said his name was Darryl Jessup when he first entered, and Cody's well-earned sense of such things had immediately sized him up as a proxy buyer. In this estimation, he wasn't wrong. But sadly, the guy only seems interested in the one place Cody can't put away, much as his heart wants little else. To be free of the old building on Highway 133 would be like turning eighteen all over again. The sweet freedom. Freedom he essentially gave up on sometime in the last year or so.

It isn't worth thinking about.

Darryl crosses his arms and asks, "And, pray tell, what exactly does this all equal up to? You're not gonna sell it?"

"I'd love to. I'd love nothing more, truly. But if past is indeed prelude, it seems that she wants to keep doing whatever it is her spectral ass does up in that cobwebbed mofo, and there ain't a whole lotta much that's gonna change that." It's a variation on a line he's used many times before.

Only a couple of his closest friends don't think he has a screw loose about the whole thing. It's a (mostly) unspoken town joke—the local realtor with the abandoned and haunted tattoo parlor on the edge of town. He knows what people think of his claims. And he also knows that if you ask those same jaw-waggin' townspeople to go onto the property themselves, they'll do just about anything to avoid it.

People are mighty mouthy when their hide ain't the one on the tanning table, but they tend to come correct real fast when you double dog dare them to stay in the haunted house on Halloween, yes sir. Because they know, just as he does, that Jane didn't just leave when she left. Something of her has remained stuck fast to the place like the grimy residue years of neglect has left on the peeling walls of the building's interior.

Darryl pulls a checkbook from the inside pocket of his lapel. "I can draft you a check right now."

"If wishing made it so. She won't allow it." Keys rapidly clicking under-digit, Cody hopes the emphasis he places on these last words will do the trick.

It doesn't.

The bald man's face clearly reflects his fast-growing disinterest in their conversation. He draws forth a black MontBlanc pen from his jacket pocket, clicks it, then decides to indulge the realtor in hopes of expediting the inevitable. "Okay, so who was this person?"

"A witch, maybe, if you can swallow that lure. I still don't know what I think she was all about in life. I was just a kid when the proverbial pitchforks came out and she was run outta town on a rail. Didn't take to getting killed apparently, despite everyone's best efforts. What I heard anyway. What I can attest to with all certainty is that were it not for her, I would have taken the title of Lead Sales Realtor in the Roaring Fork Valley for the last three or four years, for sure. Really, it's all her and Lindsey's damn fault that I haven't gotten my own awards. That Pops thinks…" he trails off, then leans forward again and starts to furiously type at the keyboard.

"Who's Lindsey?"

Cody's nose wrinkles. "Nobody. Doesn't matter."

The bald man adjusts his ringed glasses and, stoically stifling his laughter, says, "Okay, well, sorry you've had to deal with that. And, um, well everything really. Sounds rough."

Cody's hands keep clicking keys. "Damn thing hanging on my spreadsheet year after year is like a goddamn millstone around my neck."

The bald man smiles and claps his hands together, startling Cody enough to pause the typing for a full two seconds before resuming. "Well, today it seems like your luck might be on the upswing!"

"Yeah?" Cody asks. "How's that supposed to happen?"

"Today is the day I'm gonna take this thing off your hands."

"I somehow doubt it."

"Ye of little faith. My buyer is highly motivated."

"So's she."

"Lindsey?"

"No." Cody knows that he is required by law to give any prospective buyer the rough and skinny about the property before he can convince the man it isn't worth taking. His eyes remain fixed on the glowing Apple monitor as he speaks, hands still on the typing grind. "Her name was Calamity Jane. Like the frontierswoman. But I'm not talking about the Doris Day version from '53. No, what I'm talking about is the some-may-argue passively homicidal lunatic of Manifest Destiny, who, despite what historically glossy depictions may have us believe, was a damn crazy woman in the most literal of ways. Our girl who put ink to skin along Highway 133 was a little different maybe, but they were cut from the same cloth. Probably why she adopted that particular historical moniker. Came and opened up Calamity Jane's Tattoos on the highway there and was essentially the only real tattoo game in the valley in the '80s and '90s. It wasn't until many years after she arrived that the strange occurrences began, and not until the mid-'90s—'94 if my memory serves right—that the town put two and two together and ran her outta the place. Tried to kill her, but like I said, it didn't take—and now she haunts the building. Can't even rent it these days. Used to be able to lease it out to small upstart businesses, but they're quickly driven out. And now the whole town knows—"

"Okay, well, that's … really, really fascinating stuff," Darryl says, cutting him off. He coughs to clear his throat. "But the man I represent isn't interested in refurbishing the building."

"One hopes not! That'd be as fruitful as polishing a turd. Mayhaps even less fruitful." Cody chuckles as he uses the mouse on the desk to click between screens.

"It would be a full raze and re-dig within thirty days. We've looked up the permits and it's all sorta performative at this point. I'm really here just to close the deal." He clicks the MontBlanc pen—twice.

"You think you'll be able to break ground in a month?" Cody whistles between his teeth. "That's ambitious."

No way is she gonna allow all that bullshit to happen.

"As I said, my party is uniquely motivated. And he knows that anything in this valley can be expedited for a price. A price which, in his case, I can assure you is no object."

Cody stops typing and shoots a look at Darryl. "I don't want you guys to regret your purchase."

"You needn't concern yourself with that." Darryl's frosty eyes bear down upon Cody's.

After a mildly awkward and mercifully brief ocular parlay, Cody breaks with the other man's icy stare and stands up. Leaning over, he uses the mouse to finish closing out the programs, then pushes in his chair. His eyes meet the other man's again. "Lucky for you I happen to have just gotten the i's dotted and the t's crossed, so we can swing by and then we can talk turkey. You wanna bite off more than you can chew, fine. Just telling you it's a rough sell."

"One might almost think you don't want to get rid of it."

Cody hasn't much cared for the chrome dome stranger's general tone up to this point, but this last statement actually irks him. He suddenly wants to take an ol' college swing at dumping the lot on this smug proxy and his buyer.

Who is he to stand between this guy and the fool-hearted pursuit of imminent doom?

"If you're dead set, you have to lay eyes on her—*it*—first. Then we can make short work of the title and I'll buy you a bottle of champagne to celebrate." Cody knows he isn't going to be buying any such thing.

"Well, since you know the way, how about you drive my car?" The bald man tosses the keys through the air.

Cody does his high school baseball coach, Mr. Black, proud by deftly snatching them from mid-air with no trouble. "Can do. Like The Beatles, right?"

"What?"

"Nevermind."

They exit the building and jump into the solar-white Miata that has been sitting out front next to Cody's gunmetal gray 2020 BMW M8 for the last ten minutes, then speed away to the other side of Carbondale.

The town is only two miles end to end, so it isn't more than four minutes before the rundown structure comes into view.

His shiny-headed passenger fills the brief trip with a single, final question. "What was this broad doing that got her in so bad with everyone in town?"

Eyes fixed on the road, Cody wonders how to best summarize a whole cornucopia of intrigue and drama that spanned nearly two years and was plagued by disappearing pets, multiple teenage suicide attempts, several burglaries, one dead police officer, four burned buildings, untold stolen property, and a mess of physical altercations of every variety between various townsfolk.

It's difficult, but he gives it his best.

"To cut straight to the heart of it, during some of her tattoo sessions, she was using a sort of invisible-to-the-eye fluid—maybe ink, maybe not—to scrawl that which could best be described as hexes or even curses into people's flesh."

"Really?" The bald man's voice piques slightly.

Cody nods. "During long sessions it was never noticed and she chose her targets wisely. It led to a few good people doing a lot of crazy shit. Some folks were apparently badly hurt, and others went mad under her control. They ultimately pursued her into the southern hills, sorta near Dinkle Lake, but then lost her in the woods. It's said that they hit her a few times with small arms fire, but who knows."

Shifting in his seat, the bald man in the fine suit surprises Cody by remaining flat-faced and even toned in response. "You do know how all of this sounds to me, I would imagine, yeah?"

"Oh yeah, sure. Must be sorta amusing, though it wasn't to anyone here in town. Ask around a bit; you'll likely find that they're hard pressed to find the humor in it themselves, provided they recall the whole ordeal."

Darryl's eyes shoot a look at Cody. "You're serious? You're not bullshitting me for a cheap laugh?"

"Legally I don't think that's kosher during a real estate sale, but frankly I'm also not the type, mister. What I am is almost starting to feel some sense of relief, because if this happens, it would be great for me. Telling ya."

"It's going to happen. Rest assured."

"Okay," Cody says, gripping the wheel just a smidge tighter and putting up a few extra mph with the gas pedal. "I hope so."

Pulling into the dirt parking lot situated just off the highway, he sees the one-story building, still standing after over fifty years. Peeling white paint exposing the rain-curled wood beneath fills the length of the 150-foot-long building. If it has seen better days, they're distant and ne'er to be glimpsed again. Busted-out screen doors hanging precariously from rusted hinges, looking as a saloon in a ghost town might.

Darryl puts the car into park and they both get out.

Near the end of the small dirt lot, nestled between two rotted-out rust boxes, (one an old red and white striped Camaro and the other some sorta boxy yellow jalopy), is a big orange and brown Komatsu D-355A type bulldozer with a chipped and rust-pitted plow attached to the front. Cody moved it there himself about five years ago when one man seemed interested in buying it. It was originally behind the building, but he relocated it and has left the keys inside for years, hoping someone might steal it.

Of course, nobody has.

Closing the car door behind him, the bald buyer snorts as he scans the disjointed framework and cracked windows. "This is it? Not very scary, my friend."

"Yeah, well, this *is* it. And if you guys really wanna take it off my hands, that'd be fine." Cody looks at his watch, then checks the western horizon. He remains steadfast next to the white automobile. "So now you've seen it. Here it is. Let's go."

"Can't we just take a look inside?" Darryl asks, taking a step toward the building.

"You said you didn't want to refurbish it. Best not to go in there. It's condemned."

"No it isn't."

Cody looks around nervously. The sun is starting to fully set over the western mountain shelf. "No, it isn't. But we should go anyway. Gettin' dark."

"You really think some lady is haunting this stupid pile of wet wood?"

"Yes. Yes, I do. So let's shuffle off. I don't think I've been here for a couple years and I don't think we should've come. Let's get back to the office and I'll stay after to finish the paperwork. I can give you the keys, and if you're too hot to trot, you can come back and take a gander."

"That's ridiculous. But that's fine; I don't need the keys. This place is coming down." He leans down and picks up a small rock, which he turns over in his palm.

Cody frowns at ol' navy blue, offering up the briefest of dissuasions. "I wouldn't."

"Ghosts don't scare me, sir. And I think you might do well to chalk this one up to me sealing the deal with a dollop of adolescent amusement and real-world skepticism." Without warning, he wings the stone at the farthest right window on the building's face. Despite already having a large hole, the rock strikes the remaining window piece and makes a satisfying crash as the pane shards drop inside onto the dusty wooden decking within.

Before the echo of the shattered glass finishes reverberating through the building's innards, a sound swells up behind them—pushing past as whooshing, whipping winds carrying leaves aloft in an autumnal gust might.

But when they turn to ascertain the source of the noise, they are not greeted with seasonal floral bounty, but rather a wild-looking, sallow-faced old woman with wires of black fury punching out from her scaly, pale skull in all directions. She's impossibly seated behind the steering column and glaring at them through the windshield. Her knotted, gnarled fists curl over the top of the steering wheel. Hollow eye sockets swell as her mouth opens to an onyx pit full of swirling inky blots. Orbs of swirling fire start to kindle, glowing hot in the two black abysses of her skull.

And before either man can take a step back…

An explosion.

Both men are launched off their feet and carried through the air, tumbling onto the ground ten feet away from where they started. Each manages to miss smacking their respective heads as they fall into heaps in the dirt.

The Miata is ablaze.

Acrid, choking, billowing tendrils of black squeeze out of holes in the glass where the windows shattered outward. The small car's frame has warped from the intensity of the blast and char marks zig zag across the formerly pristine white paint job.

Cody's free hand grabs at his rib. Sharp pain causes him to wince. *Damn it, that might be a fracture right there.*

He slowly raises himself up and looks over at the car, now on fire and billowing thick smoke up into the orange sunsetting air. Fully standing, he brushes off the small pebbles and dust that covered him in the fall.

To his right, the bald man struggles to rise to his feet, stumbling once as he does. Darryl seems dazed, doubling over with his hands on knees, his suit now a light tan with clinging dust.

Cody inches toward him and holds out his own hands to the man.

Swatting the agent's hands away, the man coughs, a sound like nails jangling in a paper bag, spits, then says, "Get the fuck away from me! Don't!" He hacks again, and spits once more unto the dirt.

Cody's hands go up reflexively. "I'm really sorry about that. I told you this wasn't gonna end well."

Daryl straightens, face now contorted into something much less professional and more vengeful in nature than Cody has seen thus far. "I'm gonna wreck this bitch!" he snarls. "Look at what she did to my fucking car!" He feebly points at the burning compact. "It's not even my car; it's a rental. But still, that shit is coming outta my commission, you can bet. Fuck!" He glances down at his suit, which has several dusty blemishes and tears. "And my goddamn jacket! Shit! This thing is done for!" He throws back his shoulders and contorts his body as he wrestles the torn jacket from his arms and flips it off, tossing it aside.

"We should go before she does anymore. She doesn't run out of anger and she's pretty creative. And likely just getting warmed up." Cody glances at the flaming Miata. "No pun intended." He slaps some more dirt from his body as he watches the other man keep his steely-eyed focus upon the car fire.

"Fuck Jane!" Darryl's hand points toward a collection of broken-down vehicles at the end of the building's rocky dirt parking lot. "Does that plow work?"

"Not sure. Probably? But I really don't think you wanna go and—" Cody tries to warn the near-hysterical man, but the navy blue suit apparently ain't having all that noise.

His warning is cut short as the bald man with the haphazard plan scrambles up the stairs to the top of the yellow dozer and turns the keys. The engine instantly turns over, to Cody's mild surprise. A sputtering roar belches from the exhausts as the gears and internal machinations begin to begrudgingly churn. Black smoke puffs out of the stacks.

"She won't let you!" Cody shouts, largely unheard. "She's a cranky old broad!" He starts to slowly back up without being conscious of it.

The bald man jimmies the long stick shift at his right knee for a moment, then after a shrill crunching sound, thuds the big metal monstrosity into first gear. Black smears run over his cheeks. His eyes are a pack of wild dogs locked onto nearby prey.

"My buyer is extremely fucking motivated!" Darryl shouts over the roar of the engine as he slides his foot from the brake and slams it down on the gas pedal. Revving higher, the dozer lurches forward in two short sputters, then fully engages and careens toward the small, time-weathered strip mall.

When the Komatsu is but a mere few yards shy of the sidewall of the structure, it comes to an abrupt stop, yet remains idling. Cody continues to inch away from the scene at a steady rate, while before him, Darryl smacks his open palms on the steering wheel and jostles the shifter. He shoots a look to his right, where the frightened real estate agent is backing away, and hollers a question that Cody can't hear over the chugging of the 410 horsepower, Japanese-crafted engine.

Before the man on the ground can respond, Darryl hears a soft, impish giggling to his left. Turning his head, his eyes are only briefly able to register the unsettling and spidery way that the bony, tattoo-covered husk of Jane's purified corpse crawls over the edge of the plow blade and reaches out to pull his head into her hands.

Another small flash of heat and flame blossoms out as Darryl Jessup's body is completely engulfed in fire.

Jane vanishes.

The smoldering body shifts in the seat and crackles as it tumbles to the side. Another five seconds and it flops over the right steps, down several feet onto the ground, bringing up a plume of dust and leaving the chair of the dozer burning and spreading along the top of the machine's bulky husk.

Cody watches the plow burn brightly against the orange-gray twilight and thinks that maybe this is as definite of a sign as he is ever going to get that it is far past time to shut down this whole operation for good. Why, he could call first thing in the morning and get Joey Wheeler's concrete crew to come on down and pour three feet of vault on top of the area and maybe, if he's lucky, seal away this unfortunate thing once and for good. It is such a dead-on idea that it strikes him as kind of funny that such a plan hasn't ever occurred to him before.

In the distance, the wail of fire engines and the faint clatter of police wailers rattle through the quiet town.

Cody exhales and smiles. At least no one will think he was responsible once they see where the emergency is. Everybody knows that—

As he turns, the last thing Cody Creed ever sees is the crablike form of Jane's crooked body, scuttling in an unnatural way along the dusty parking lot dirt between him and the flaming body on the ground. As fast as a multi-appendaged insect attaches to its victim, she vaults like a leaping spider and latches onto the man with all four limbs.

They topple backward into the dirt, and as the writhing spectral woman's withered and tattooed fingers dig their nail tips deeply into the soft flesh of the screaming man's inner arms, her mouth opens wide, wide, wider—until she can wrap the blood-red lips of her slathering maw around his skull.

She closes her boa constrictor mouth around his neck and chomps down with dagger-sized teeth. Maroon fluid erupts from either side of her mouth in a thick, misting spray, punctuated by a bone-splitting crunch which disappears into the dusk, just as the daylight has evaporated from the sky.

Two weeks later, on a pleasant June day with blue skies and no wind, the Queen of Valley Property Sales pulls up to the building on Highway 133 and slams the car into park, kicking up a cloud of dust. Lindsey Leopard steps out of the silver Tesla that she rewarded herself with last year for being, well, just that good at what she does, and pulls off her shades.

In a white, custom-tailored business suit, she surveys the dilapidated husk of a structure before her. Nearby, the burnt shell of both the dozer and the Miata stand frozen like victims awaiting treatment at a hospital burn unit. A black circular scorch mark lies on the ground where the victim was found.

Though she is hardly fazed. She's turned over plenty of rough properties in her time. Even ones that were the sites of homicides. And she is known to be skeptical of the town's professed skeletons.

That is likely why she got the call to pick up the contract on the old Sopris Strip Mall on 133 after the two fires and the disappearance of Cody Creed two weeks prior. She knows that that silver-spoon hack had been unable to unload it for years and therefore hadn't been able to prove his mettle to his daddy. Now, with him going missing, everyone assumes that he joined the peace corps or maybe a cult in shame. Maybe he'll turn up in a month or two.

Despite the presence of a dead body, no one suspected foul play on his part. Not when it happened at the former site of Calamity Jane's Tattoo Parlor. And the coroner, ever vigilant in his duties, ruled it an accidental fire maiming, resulting in death. Case closed. Nothing to see here.

So the option had been allowed to lapse, and the so-called unsellable property was thusly snatched up by her firm. Now she is here to get the lay of the land and sell the unsellable.

Hah. Is there such a thing? she confidently thinks as she walks up to the building. Checking the time on her phone, she scans the place from one side to the other.

As her eyes move from right to left, her initial wall of confidence is suddenly shaken to pieces when she spies what appears to be the outline of a figure set against the dark interior of the building through one of the windows.

Wiry hair springs from the top of a small, slender shadow which peers at Lindsey from between two jagged shards of dirty glass on the far left window. Orange dots in the middle of the thing's head smolder like dying embers.

Lindsey's mama didn't raise no fool, and she certainly hasn't got this far in life on her good looks alone—though admittedly they've never exactly proven to be an impediment, either.

Or, you know, Lindsey thinks briefly, perhaps even wisely, *maybe a whole lotta none-of-this-bullshit-right-here—that's also a choice I could make right now.*

She raises her voice as much as possible whilst ostensibly speaking out loud to herself. "I'm thinking that maybe a place with such a rich history would be ill-served being relegated to the trash heap of community progress. Hardly seems fitting. Mayhaps instead of letting such a fine location fall to the all-too-cruel passage of time, maybe I go and make a call to the Carbondale Historical Society and have the site declared persona non-grata! Give this place the break from visitors it seems to desire so much."

The two reddish dots through the window glow ever so slightly brighter as a hissing whisper carries through the air in a way that Lindsey has never heard before (and frankly, after this moment, will be grateful never to hear again).

"Gooooooood," murmurs Jane's sawdust voice between the peeling wooden slats and rusted metal framework.

Lindsey nods, turns without another word, and gets back into her car. She carefully backs up and drives away from the building, leaving a dust cloud in her wake that settles slowly as the sun beams down on the old strip mall along Highway 133.

1-900

Maybe it's just me, but I don't think that people realize just how utterly fuckin' creepy the town of Carbondale, Colorado can be.

And why would they? Why would you? What with how shiny and cute and safe everything has become lately, it's somewhat understandable that you'd be comfortable letting down your guard.

Your lack of suspicion makes a certain kind of perverse sense.

A lot of folks, especially those who showed up right around the turn of the millennium, don't realize that we have a rich and vibrant history of absolutely demented shit being afoot in them hills o'er yonder.

If only they knew.

Biblical plagues that targeted children and destroyed local families in the late 1800s; serial killers and the dimwitted police who just couldn't keep them locked up in the 1970s; another cop being investigated for sexual assault who offed himself in the elementary school parking lot (*if you don't want it printed, don't let it happen*); ghosts and gangsters and cowboys haunting the local hotels from time immemorial—to say nothing of the high probability of heretofore undiscovered silicone-based life-forms lurking along the sulfur-filled gas vents situated within the subterra of Glenwood's Yampah Springs, just below the Hot Springs Pool.

Now, I *might* be exaggerating on that last line item there, but I suspect you get the idea just the same.

These days, 398 Merrill Avenue is little more than a large, retro-chic, concrete-sided industrial building, housing several small businesses, including a stone and tile outlet store. And it fits in so nicely with the ever-burgeoning gentrification of the surrounding neighborhoods, looking quite pleasantly like any number of other places.

Which one assumes is the goal.

So wonderfully, comfortably numb.

But what a good many of the town's current residents won't or simply were not here to recall is that between 1988 and 1996 or so, this dark, rain-stained building of gray stone was largely empty. Absent any and all occupants, it was but an abandoned metal foundry of yesteryear. It felt towering, imposing, threatening—like some Soviet era KGB bunker. And it left all of us guessing every time we rode up to it on our boss-ass Huffys.

And back in those days, Merrill Avenue (such as it was, at all of one hundred yards in length) wrapped around the edge of town into a hockey stick-shaped dirt turnaround (*cul-de-sac* would've been a bit too generous, perhaps), where the road dead ended in front of that downright spooky old building. Beyond a nearby fence was a rusty railroad track that ran through the heart of the town, though it had stopped serving trains decades prior.

In brighter days past, we used to spend our summers walking along the tracks, picking up rusty railroad spikes and practicing our balance on the rail beams, arms outstretched, laughing at nothing in particular.

Nowadays, that same ol' track is little more than a bygone relic, covered up by a cheeky little paved walking trail where people with seven figures in their bank accounts can locate a dog poop bag dispenser every fifty feet or so. Because we wouldn't want little Fifi to have to do her business in a bush like a complete fucking monster now, would we?

What if some J-Crew ad lookin' motherfucker wants to ride their dopey Schwinn bike on the same spot where dear Fifi just shat? Why, they might have to swerve whole *inches* to avoid this hypothetical dookie drop. They may have to adjust their lives to accommodate something other than themselves, and by golly we can't have that.

Never that.

For who could predict what unforeseen chaos such a travesty might portend for the future?

We surely all owe a debt of eternal gratitude to the poop bag dispensers of the world, and by extension the java-swilling tweebs that employ them, who truly remain the finger in the dam between us meek humans and near-certain societal collapse.

But as it happens, I—a salty-jawed cuss to be sure—digress.

Nowadays, that formerly foreboding, dusty dead end has been resurfaced with black asphalt and connected to the rest of town by way of 4th Street. Today, it's right by the chintzy visitors' center, adjacent to a real estate office and a stone's throw from several new buildings. Structures so utterly dystopian in decor and leaning hard into that bizarre new trend of outfitting buildings with the timeless, ever-posh Chernobyl look.

The creeping quasi-cuteness that consumed the whole town

in the early 2000s seemingly polished off any menace that the facility at 398 Merrill Ave had ever possessed. Though, in an ironic twist, its cold, uninviting exterior is of an ilk that is all the rage in modern-day Bonedale. Go figure.

And yet, we know that some weird shit went down there. My three friends and I found out the hard way just what happens when you go knocking on doors best left unopened.

And we know all about it for reasons that are not particularly suited for dinner conversation. But I'mma tell ya anyway.

Our childhood (and admittedly childish) desire to break-and-enter into the rain-stained brick building on Merrill Avenue—which, if we're being real here, and you know I'm all about that shit, truly looked like Freddy Krueger's fucking day spa—was ultimately born from two very specific desires.

First, after so many years of passing by this property as an outlying specter, coiled in repose along the edge of our sleepy hamlet; after so many wild stories and adolescent speculations; after all the name calling, triple-dog dares, and misanthropic meanderings by; after all the Halloween nights that ended with a multi-flashlight, glaze-eyed pow-wow in the middle of the dirt court dead end of Merrill Avenue, just the idea of finally putting eyes on what this two-story pandora's box had in wait was enough to smash apart any better sense of propriety or self-preservation we might've possessed.

Secondly—and most importantly—we wanted to see if we could use the office phone systems inside the abandoned office space to make 1-900 number calls to pornographic services.

Why did we want to do this? I don't really know. Just to do it? I mean, what the hell did we think we were gonna do, really? Stand in some dilapidated office area, phone to ear, and jerk off in front of each other while we feigned tough guy voices with fugly call center whores in different time zones?

No. Fucking gross.

But, you know, just calling them at all was *something.* And something was something where emergent hormonal drive was concerned. You'll take any toehold you can hook. Trust.

Furthermore, how did we know that they had a functioning phone system? Why, by peering into one of the few dust caked windows that wasn't covered over with cracking brown boards, of course!

We be peepin', and you know this, *man.*

Young, dumb, and full of cum, as the bard would say. The actual fuck would you expect? Sorry about being hot-blooded dudes, and all.

Our bad.

Now, a tender thing like yourself may not know this, but starting in the 1980s, pay per minute telephone services were all the rage with the kids. Really, with adults too. Used by everyone from Corey Haim to Paula Abdul to prey upon dimwitted fans by dangling the false promise of possible one-on-one contact with their favorite celebs. These silly scams somehow remained profitable until the late '90s, when waning marketability combined with their eternally lampooned and unsavory reputation within the pop culture zeitgeist led to their demise.

Unless you were, as we, a well-meaning yet naturally perved-out bunch of kids toolin' about the rough and tumble streets of Bonedale in the early '90s —looking at whatever cheap porno mags you could get your hands on (which, admittedly, was nearly as rare as seeing a real naked women in person at that point in our development), you wouldn't know this either—since despite the

Supreme Court ruling in 1992 which forbade 900 numbers from facilitating so-called "adult services," you'd still see plenty of them popping up in the rear pages of such magazines. Whoever was in charge of giving a shit about respecting the Supreme Court's edicts regarding their sex-line operations was clearly out to lunch, and giving none.

And before you get all judgy, before you even go there, just remember that there is a smidge of historical context that should be inserted here. Porn was just as sought after back then by frisky teenagers as it is today. If you think it's any less depraved now, you'd be a fool, and I got some ocean-front property just outside of Marble to sell 'ya, you sloppy fuckwit.

The real difference is that, back then, we had to earn our pornography through blood, sweat, and tears. Not by saying, "Hey Siri, please show me something lurid and graphic that I'm not at all ready for, so that I might find minimal satisfaction through sex by the time I'm twenty five."

No, our shit was hard won, by God. And that added value.

You'd try and fail to buy one through your best friend's older brother. You'd rifle through your homies' parents' sock drawer and then negotiate your damnedest to take home one of the nudie rags you'd just discovered—usually to no avail. If you were lucky, sometimes you'd inherit one from a buddy who needed it to disappear in a jiffy, lest they receive a tongue lashing from a puritanical parental figure. Or it could've been gifted as a hand-me-down from an altruistic older cousin.

To a gaggle of pubescent dipshits, they were more precious than diamonds.

So, naturally, we could only goad each other for so long before we made plans to utilize the creepy phones inside of the creepy building in front of the creepy cul-de-sac at the end of the creepy road. The place seemed terribly huge. It wasn't, but it seemed so to us at the tender age of thirteen.

As I recall, this all went down sometime in the fall of '96, on a gray, cloud-cast Saturday.

Mollifying the parental units with lip service of the *I'll be back in just a little bit* variety, we rode hard and fast to the building. None of us said so, but there was a faint back-of-the-mind concern that if we didn't get in, make our untoward calls, and get out expediently before sunset, we may have larger trouble on our hands. With none of us knowing what was about to occur, no one could've said what that larger danger might've been. It would've sounded absurd anyway.

Still does.

Arriving right around noonish, we disembarked our totally fucking rad bikes and led them behind the building to a large dirt lot. At that time it was mostly filled with a few rusty oil drums, the husk of some long-ago stripped-down pickup truck, and a small mound of split tires in a mashed pile along the sporadic chain-link fence that lined up with the edge of town.

Rolling our Huffys, we looked like the casting call for an after school special.

Darren: nerdy, chubby, striped shirt, and tan slacks with a flat brown bowl cut.

Tony: blue jeans, white tee, shoulder-length black hair.

Josh: brunette with a side part, black jeans, and a White Zombie shirt.

Me: I don't remember. Some dumb shit, probably. I dressed like piss back then. Blue JNCO jeans and a black shirt, I think.

Anyway.

"Peter," Josh kicked up his bike on its rear wheel, letting the front one spin, "you're the man with the plan. How do we get in?"

Oh, yeah—my name's Peter, by the way. Slipped my mind to say. Nice to meet you and all.

Josh was our sort of leader and de facto shot-caller. Likely because he read slightly more than we did back then, it was difficult to win arguments against him. Later in life, his verbal jousting game started slipping and he was easy to defeat in debate. For now, we were mostly *his* posse. However, when something illicit or illegal was afoot, he would, like the head of one of the five New York crime families, make sure it was someone else's bright idea. Always sure to create a buffer between himself and implicit responsibility.

The prick.

And it's not completely wrong to say that this one actually had been my big dumb idea from the get-go. We'd seen those numbers in the magazines and knew that full-fledged sexual maturation was but a few fleeting punches of the keypad from our eager fingertips away. After that, the math was easy. So once I laid my peepers on those big, yellowed, seventies-era phones— *biggity-bam!*—the idea sprung forth in a jiffy.

I rolled my orange and black bike over to the chain fence and leaned it up against the diamond holes. Looking to the building, I mused, "We just start checking doors and windows. If we have to, let's just smash one and make our way inside."

"Uh, we're really gonna break into the building? What if we get caught?" Darren asked, careful not to sound too worried, lest we tag him with the dreaded "pussy" moniker.

"I dunno, Darren. What if your mom finds out you crack off on the living room sofa when she's at her Jenny Craig classes?"

Darren Milano was the goody-two-shoes of our motley crew. A hesitant skeptic and utter killjoy by nature, he was always happy to let us know just how egregious the felonious activity we were engaging in was. Thing was, Darren also had the best sense of humor, and despite what he said, obviously *was* into whatever we were doing.

"I'm not into this." Darren said, surprising no one. "We're gonna get in trouble. And I shouldn't have fucking told you that shit!" He dropped his own BMX-style all-cross Huffy against the others, then spit into the dirt.

Tony combed back his raven hair with one hand and mumbled, "What you probably shouldn't have done is used your couch cushion as a noodle wipe, bro. But you didn't care then, so why should we now?"

Tony was our intellectually useless, smoky-eyed stoner. The one who toked three hits for every one of ours. Took too long to answer questions, but was as willing to do dumb shit as anybody. And often, funny.

Josh nodded, smiling. "A good point."

"Last time I tell you fuckers anything," Darren fumed as he marched toward the building.

Following him, our eyes darted about the dirt lot at the nothing to see.

Josh, raggedy bastard that he could be, re-engaged, purely for sport. "That's not true," he said, 'cause he just couldn't help himself.

Tony grinned. "Yeah, who else will you tell this stuff to? We aren't judging you. We love you, man."

We three ass clowns laughed at this.

Darren sighed, reaching the first marked exit. Snugly situated in the wall right next to a massive shuttered bay door that was, in turn, flanked on each side by rope chains. "No, just making me feel bad about it."

"Hey, you feeling bad isn't my fault. You could not give a shit like we do, ya know," Josh leveled at him, and to this, he had no retort. Tony and Josh looked at me with approval and it was clear by the cards that that one went to me.

Lining up before the eastern wall, we briefly studied the exterior. It was as drab as they come, trust. Two stories, gray concrete façade, some broken windows, and rain stains.

Tony was standing in front of the door, and without saying anything, he turned the knob. And it was just that easy. The door flew open, and we heard the flutter of wings—birds taking flight somewhere in the dense blackness beyond. Shooting out through shattered sky lights in the roof, they zipped off, never looking back.

The lucky bastards.

Darren dropped his head to his hands in a dramatic little turn, then grumbled, "You know what I'm thinking, right?"

"Breaking and entering? One year probation?"

Tony pulled a small metal sneak-a-toke cylinder and lit up the end, taking a puff and trying to hand it off. None of us accepted. Not that we didn't partake; we totally all did. But I know that on that dreary October midday in 1996, I personally wanted to be as lucid as possible so as to harvest the clearest recollection of the torrid things I hoped to hear from the lusty and lurid ladies of the love lines.

Why? For eventual long-term use in the ol' mental spank bank. *Duh.*

What? Oh, I'm *so sure* there isn't one thing you don't want us all to know about your formative years. Surely you can recall how weird childhood could be at times. I just don't care what other people think, is all.

Thick brown chains hung in droopy vines that crisscrossed through the air just above our heads as we walked across the wide void of dirty concrete. The dust had sucked in enough ambient moisture to form the micron granules into clumpy pebbles which crunched under our sneakers as we moved toward the office spaces at the front of the building. Exposed wiring and missing sections of badly flaking drywall greeted us.

If you've ever seen *Nightmare On Elm Street 2*, you'll get the general *mise en scène*. If not, then watch more horror movies, dude.

At first, all we saw was the three doors straight across from us. All standard, hollow core, white wood panel.

I snorted, in spite of myself.

"What?" Josh asked.

"Let's show 'em what they have behind door number three, Johnny!"

Tony cracked up. "Oh yeah! Like those shows! Funny, man."

Stepping forward, as if to lead us onward, Josh stated the obvious as he pointed toward the tri-door wall ahead. "Those lead to the offices and that's where our destiny lies, gentlemen. All of our wildest—"

Now, I'd sure love to tell you that we had a goddamn blast making our lewd little phone calls. I'm sure we would've. A right rotten bit of civil disobedience to brag to our other buddies about at school on Monday. I'd love to say it all went to plan. That we spent hours giggling whilst trying to affect as much baritone into our voices as possible, seeing as how our nuts had just barely dropped. Trying to get grown-up, big-boobed women to actually say something graphically sexual to us.

But alas, this ain't that kind story. Sorry, Pervy McPerverton.

"Uh, what were you saying, Josh?" I asked, though all of us were looking at him. Tracking the line of where his eyes were focused, we noticed something in the floor between us and the offices.

"What is that?" Josh asked as he strutted ahead of the group, taking point.

As we crunch-crossed the concrete, nearly all of us jumped out of our goddamn skin when a single bird of some type let out a raspy caw from within the darkness of a nearby corner. It quickly took flight, nearly smacking one of the dangly chains, then darted out through one of the larger holes in the paneled skylight glass.

"Guess it was a bird, looking to jump-scare our asses," I suggested, laughing nervously.

Josh shook his head as his eyes dropped from the hole in the roof to the hole in the floor. "No, I was talking about that right there."

Halfway between us and the office doors was a black circle with a narrow, reflective outline. Cruising on up, we saw a hole that was about one full foot in diameter. It wasn't enough to fall into, really, but just large enough to peer down and maybe drop a stone to the bottom of. Lining the aperture was a half-inch thick ring of a nearly iridescent golden metal.

The odd thing was that along its surface was emblazoned a relief-like outcropping of etched symbols, unrecognizable to us eighth grade dilettantes.

"What's that, ya think?" Darren asked casually as we came to stop before the black void.

"It's a hole," Josh clarified.

"Thanks. Just—thanks, dude," Darren grumbled. "Really— serious—what'cha think it's for?" Pausing to bend over a bit and squint his eyes, he added, "And why does it have all these creepy little characters filling the space between—"

"How far do you think it goes down?" Tony interjected, likely unaware anyone was talking.

"That's easy enough to figure out," I volunteered. "We just drop sumthin' down the hole and count off the seconds before it hits. It's like one second for every fifty feet, right?"

"How would you know?" Josh asked, going there.

My eyebrow cocked up, ready to meet him. *"How would I know?* Because of science class. Question is, why don't *you* know?"

Sensing the tonal shift between us, Darren cut in, "Won't the object speed up as it goes down until reaching terminal velocity, thereby altering the ratio of time elapsed relative to its descent?"

Josh did not miss the opportunity for a rapid retort, "Well, Einstein, if you wanna wax intellectual, how about we toss something in and you calculate the drop? Sound spiffy?"

"Whatever, dude," Darren grumbled (he does that shit way too much, m'I right?). "Just trying to be helpful."

Josh knew when he was pushing the tenuous bonds of subjugation by being too atavistic in his replies, therefore he shifted tactics back to passively hostile camaraderie. "I know. I'm fucking with you. We need some rocks from the yard out back." Looking over at me, he said, "You got that?"

Disinterested in being my friend's delivery service, I retorted, "Get your own rocks off."

"Clever, Pete. You should write that one down for later."

"If I wanted to have a battle of wits with you, I would've checked my brain at the door so we could start even, Josh."

"There's one we've never heard before," he said, plump cheeks slightly reddening.

"That doesn't mean it isn't brutal, cockface." I said. And I know; so, *so* lame. But yeah, I said that shit. Are you proud of everything you ever spat out?

Me neither.

Josh was, by-and-large, much more eloquent and articulate with his words. "No, it's just fucking faggoty as all fuck. And I'll fucking deck you if you keep saying shit, bitch."

He usually was.

And I'm sure he wouldn't have done shit. In fact, I knew he wouldn't have, but I didn't care. I liked to push it.

Like Salt-N-Pepa.

"Wow, didn't know you'd get so feisty so fast, bud. Maybe you should take a toke from Tony's pipe and chillax a bit."

Tony and Darren watched us with stressed anticipation. This was a thing Josh and I did. He held strained control over his court, while I regularly kept him on his toes by making like I was gonna run for the crown, though I never did back then.

Still, I was never great at falling in line with the other lemmings, so…

Before our infantile pissing contest reached a physical crescendo, Tony pivoted on heel and returned to the door from whence we'd come. He disappeared for a few moments, then returned holding several stones in his hands. He sauntered back to us and handed everyone one fist-filling rock. Absent hesitation, he dropped his own down into the narrow shaft.

It tick-tick-ticked acoustically off the walls of the hole. Noting the lack of that tell-tale clang sound you get from metal, it was surely no pipe. Just a bored-out cement hole, going straight down.

We heard another tick, then another—then a long, long, terribly long absence of any more noises coming from the depths.

All of us did not dare to breathe, lest we miss the landing. For ten full seconds we waited.

Nothing came.

At eleven seconds, Darren coughed out, then started to gasp. The rest of us followed suit.

I spoke first. "No hit. Must drop into a sinkhole or something."

Darren caught his breath and shook his head. "No way of knowing that for sure. It might've just landed on something that quashes the sound of the impact. Or it gradually rolls into a turn along the way, muffling the sound." He casually flicked his rock into the hole, and after the same several ticks along the route, silence.

Smiling, I stepped forward and curved my wrist slightly to put a little English on my own geological depth meter. It must've hit about twenty times more than the others with the spin added, but the same as the others, no actual hit onto the bottom of the dark void was heard.

We looked at Josh, who, curiosity abated, shrugged and flung his rock over his shoulder. He was taking a step in the direction of the peeling white drywall with the three doors when Darren suddenly dropped to his knees before the gold ringed void.

"Holy shit! Do you hear that? Somebody's down there!" He didn't put his ear directly to the opening, but tilted his head so it was just a few feet from it.

Josh turned around and we all half-huddled near Darren. Again we held our breathing, and again, zilch. No sound. At least not to the rest of us.

Gray clouds closed ranks in the skies above.

"I don't hear anything," I offered up.

"Me neither," Josh agreed.

"Mmmhmm." Tony nodded slowly as he snuck another toke from his tiny metal pipe.

Darren's face briefly contorted into a grimace of fear, then softly descended into more of a pacified look. The sort you might don when someone gives you a muscle relaxer to go to bed. I think Tony and Josh noticed as well.

"Darren?" I asked. He wasn't listening to us, but he was all ears.

What we didn't know yet was that the voice had simply started with Darren. Years later, upon a glut of Freudian-level self-reflection, I surmised that him being the least experienced with the opposite gender up to that point might have played a role in this. I only suspect as much because, at that time, I was the most experienced with women, relatively speaking. And I was also the last to hear the damn thing speak.

Who can say for certain, and what does it ultimately matter? *Spoiler: It doesn't.*

"It's like a woman's voice. You can't hear her? She just…" Darren's cheeks flushed red. On his hands and knees, dust globs caking his clothes, he held his hand over his mouth and whispered into the hole, "Are you serious?"

"Is *who* serious?" I asked.

"You could really do that for me?" Darren continued, speaking into the hole.

"Do what, ya fucking stoonce? We can't hear shit," shot Josh, wholly unimpressed.

Darren said nothing. He just shivered, then started to slowly move his head up and down.

"Darren? Maybe we shouldn't be talking to holes. You think about that one, haus?" Josh offered.

　　　✦　PATRICK KITSON　✦

Darren laughed, then snorted. Then, in a rapid reply he spit out, "But I want to fuck sexually deviant, big-titted Amazonian women with juicy thighs that go all the way up! The hole says I can have all that *and* a bag of chips if I listen to the lessons it wants to impart unto me!"

We couldn't help but crack up. Darren was not the type to say shit like that. In fact, I was surprised he could even say something like that with a straight face. Watching, Josh's steely resolve likewise broke and even he laughed in spite of himself. Tony even managed a little smirk.

"What kind of chips?" Josh asked.

"Don't encourage him," I scolded, then added, "Unless it's Crunch Tators." I paused. "*Is it* Crunch Tators?"

Darren didn't answer me, but remained on all fours, gazing into the dark opening.

Between giggles I said, "Man, Darren. That's not like you to be so foul-mouthed. What's gotten into you and what would your dear mother think?"

He didn't reply, but rather shot me a frosty, empty-eyed glance, then firmly reaffixed his eyes to the object of his obsession in the floor.

Looking at Tony to share in the humor, I noticed that his face had drained of all emotion. He appeared even more withdrawn than was to be expected.

"I hear it," Tony spoke quietly.

This piqued my interest a wee bit. "Oh yeah?" I asked.

"Yeah," he confirmed, frowning.

"And what's it saying?"

"Gross stuff. Weird shit. Can we go?" Tony put both hands in his pockets.

"Seriously? Like what?" I pressed a smidge more.

"Let's go," he insisted.

Josh jumped in with his standard scout-leader tone, "Like what, Tony?"

Tony hesitated, then lowered his eyes and said, "It's saying that if I feed the needs it will help me breed. Soooo we should go. For real."

"The fuck, dude?" Josh asked, and I started to laugh right along with him. However, when Tony's face stood frozen and half-flashing concern, my chuckles slowed, then fell silent. The big empty room with wafting dust particles in the air was starting to feel a little bit like a trap about to spring.

"Wait, seriously?" I asked, because his eyes did not look full of jest or glee, but rather a sickening, dawning realization that we might all be farther out of depth here than we'd want.

"Told you—weird. I wanna go." Tony slipped his sneak-a-toke to his lips, partook, then returned it to his pocket.

Josh gave me a confused smile as if to say, *"Are these guys fucking with us?"*

But then, Josh's face rapidly twisted into one of unbridled anger as his eyes met the ground and he moved closer to the opening, shouting, "What the fuck did you say, bitch?"

Taken aback but curious as hell, I asked, "You're hearing it now, too?"

To me: "Fuck yeah, I heard that!" To the hole: "Whoever you are, you better cut the shit!" He spit a glob of white, foamy phlegm into the stony orifice. "Don't say that shit! That's so gross. What the hell, man!"

Ridiculously curious now, I said, "Come on, dude! What's it saying? Don't hold out."

"Fuck that! I'm not repeating that disgusting crap! Let's just say it has to do with my mom and—" His eyes went wide, and fell back to the ground. He leaned his head over the hole and yelled, "SHUT UP! SHUT UP! SHUT UP!"

Darren's head cocked up at a somewhat unnatural, Linda Blair sorta angle, and he murmured, "If we allow it to offer its wisdom, we might only need to offer up a small bit of our flesh as a sign of our faith and—"

He stopped speaking as my hands clapped loudly together whilst I offered my humble analysis of the situation. "O-fucking-kay, that's enough! Don't you say another word! We're wildly fucking done here! All done. I don't want to hear any more of that witchy bullshit from anybody! I don't care what the voice in the hole says, we are leaving!"

I feigned a half step, like I was heading out of there, but nobody followed. They just stared at the hole. So, like an asshole, I turned back and sighed loud enough for everyone to chew on.

Darren's strange protests continued, unabated. "I don't want to leave! The hole says it can help me to enslave every last pussy in all the world. All of them! None shall escape! I shall be endowed with a fistful of tumescent glory as I rule the clitoral hordes with an iron tongue! I will drive my sexual subjugates before me like a stampeding herd of 'gasm squirting oxen!"

This finally gave us real pause. We three who were not speaking utterly fucking insane shit eyed one another like, *"What did that fool just fucking say?"*

Josh's nose crinkled as he chuckled and asked, "When did the hole say that?"

"The hole speaks true!" Darren cried out.

"Yeah?" I asked.

"Yeah!" Darren replied.

Josh laughed heartily, mockingly. "You and the hole have become that close in the last five minutes? You gonna just do whatever the hole says, now? Dude, think about this. Just stop and think for one second, man. We are talking about a fucking *hole*."

My eyes narrowed at our erstwhile moral compass, and I went for broke. "Look, we're going, Darren. And if you don't come with me *right now*, I'm going to call your mom and tell her you're over here making porn calls on these phones."

His eyes, full of equal parts rage and fear, watered as he hissed through gnashed teeth, "You. Wouldn't. Dare."

"Oh no, I *would* dare! I *do* dare! I dare all day, dickhead! Because then I don't get in trouble when some crazy shit happens to you!"

Tony grabbed Darren by the arm and started to try to lead him away. Darren jerked his arm free as he drew closer to the unholy aperture, and Tony's watery eyes gazed our way. He nodded. Josh and I got the message and surrounded Darren. We all got arms on him and started to drag his dumb ass from the mouth of the hole.

Flailing, sneakers dragging, he bellowed, "You will not take me away from this hole! I must hear what it will say! It speaks true! It's going to get me laid!"

Josh laughed as he pulled at Darren's right arm, "No, no, no. That is *not* what's gonna happen. You're—" he stopped mid-sentence and ceased pulling. His eyes went wide with rage as he looked down and yelled at the cold concrete cavity, "Stop fucking saying that about my mom, you fucking pervert! I will piss down your—whatever this is—your dumb fucking throat! I will piss straight down your fucked gullet. Don't say another word!"

At this point I was coming around to wondering if all of these dudes I counted as confidants and friends were, in fact, a platoon of auditorily hallucinating whackos.

That was, until I got my own little ugly call from the *what the fuck* down the chasm.

The voice was soothing. Soft. Like ASMR or some shit.

"Don't go, Petey my love. I have such pleasures for you all."

"Oh shit!" I exclaimed, letting go of Darren and sprawling backward like some dolt in a slapstick comedy, falling hard onto my ass. The crunchy dust globs skidded between my jeans and the concrete. Pointing one finger the way of the hole, I spat out, "That—that *thing* just said it's gonna pleasure me! Or us—*something…*"

"It told me that if I take off my clothes, it will fulfill all my desires. You don't think it would if—" a glossy eyed Tony started to say, until I cut his silly ass off.

"No! no! Keep your fucking pants on!" I shouted, standing and brushing clingy dust clumps from my probably sick-ass JNCO jeans. "We gotta go! It's nothing but a bunch of hexy, evil shit down in that there hole. We need to am-scray while we still an-cay!"

I seized Darren's arm again, and as I did, Josh and Tony both seemed to shake off their short-term daze and wrapped their own hands around our friend.

Darren immediately started to writhe and jockey about to break his arms free. But if we are being 100% here—*and you know I'm all about that shit*—he was also the weak-ass pussy of the group to boot, so the "fight" he put up wasn't much of one.

"We can't go! If we go it says we cannot return!"

Josh took up his stern, patronizing voice of authority.

Generally it meant that the disagreement had essentially reached its conclusion. "It'll say anything to keep you gazing into its inky depths, man! And who says we wanna come back? Peter is right, shockingly. This is over. Game over. We're done now. *Adios*."

As Josh spoke, it was overlaid with the voice as it took another crack at getting under my skin.

"Petey, Pete, Peter … big boy with the big toy. You know what to do with that big toy, big boy?"

The actual fuck? I shouted, "Yo! I don't who or what the fuck you are, Mister or Missus Voice Thing, but you're gross and—"

"Oh, but Petey, if you leave, I'll simply have to murder your family with dull objects under the veil of moonlight."

"What!?" I yelled, mad as hell and just about ready to not take it anymore. "Fuck you, creepy voice! Fuck you! You ain't gonna do shit!"

"Oh yeah! Oh yeahhh. Yes! Come at the hole that is me, big boy! With your big toy! Come at me! You can slide your hot little—"

Now me, I could sit here and tell you all about how unsettling it is to argue with a goddamn hole. *A hole.* Not tangible, verifiable sentience, mind you, but rather a fucking gold-ringed hole in the concrete floor of some disused, largely forgotten factory. It's *bullshit*. It's for the birds. I don't recommend it. But I'm the kinda fella that ain't got time for all that bullshit right there, so—

The voice called to me again.

"I'll suckle upon your sweet meat, my sexy treat…"

"No. Ew, no! Shut up! Shut up! I'm leaving. I'm gone from here, and that's gross and I hope somebody fills in your hole, you—you filthy little creepy-shit voice! I'm so fucking outta this place. Jesus jumpin' Christ! Fuck! Fuck!" I then threw my real weight into dragging Darren, and we moved quite expediently.

Rushing through the big open space, we easily managed to reach the door, kick it open, and remove our buddy as the voice was trailing off. What I was hearing was something like:

"…grab my fucking hair and insert those big beads into my…"

The door slammed before it could finish. Thank God.

Emerging into the yard, Josh and I pulled a still struggling Darren out. Tony picked up a discarded chunk of rebar and used it to bend through the door handle, effectively jamming it closed.

Watching in horror as if he was witnessing a loved one slip into the next life, Darren made his final desperate plea. "I won't ever get laid if we don't go back in there! It won't happen!" Darren yanked and tugged, feebly struggling against our hold on him. It was a little pathetic, really, with all the moans and groans and all. "I need to get laid, goddamn it! We have to go back! My dick will never know the touch of—"

Both Tony and I were shocked when Josh dragged Darren up by the shirt and his fist came round-housing around, striking Darren square in the face. My eyes went wide in disbelief, and Tony started to giggle like a burnout usually does—awkwardly and randomly.

However, Darren didn't drop; instead, he just yelled a lot as he held his hands to his now-red right eye. "Owww! Fuck! Why'd you do that, dude? Why the fuck—why'd you do that?"

Standing there, Josh looked sheepish and surprised. "Uh, I was actually trying to knock you out so you'd calm down. I'm sorry. I thought that would work."

"Are you crazy? I'm gonna have a black eye!"

"I said sorry! But it's better than having your dick chewed off by some demon in a hole, man! I know that whatever that was, it was bad shit. But you're acting nuts!"

Darren removed his hands from his ocular socket, revealing an already darkening spot over the lid. "What do you mean, demon? Chewing off my dick? What the fuck, bro? I wasn't doing anything!"

Tony, Josh and I, while certainly not in any remedial classes or anything, still did not get what he meant by that. So naturally, I queried him. "Refusing to leave the hole? Cause we ain't staying here!"

Darren looked at us, seeming genuinely confused. "What hole? What are you talking about?"

Our eyes suspiciously ran him up and down until Tony asked, "Did he just go all *Temple of Doom* on us?"

And this still remains the smartest observation he's ever made in my presence. Because he had the rare point.

I kicked off the necessary follow-up interview, "You just said, 'what hole?' Can't you remember? The hole you just said was gonna get you laid. It was inside that building. Then Josh popped you in your dome, and—"

Darren rubbed his head and frowned. "Do you mean the phone calls? Was this— Did I make a phone call? I can't…" his voice trailed off as he looked up into the rapidly darkening sky. Clouds were beginning to thicken up, threatening to make our respective journeys home wet ones.

Freudian slips be damned at this point.

I looked at Tony. I looked at Josh. They both looked at me. Still, none of us could figure it out.

Darren returned his eyes to us and said, "It's getting shitty. We should go to someone's house and get some food. I'm starving."

With that, he headed off in the direction of our wildly awesome bikes, still resting cozily against the diamond pattern metal linkage.

Noting the inclement weather drawing fast upon us and rapidly dimming the lights on the day, I followed without trying to belabor the oddness of the encounter. Tony and Josh exchanged glances, then shuffled after. We picked up our bikes and headed off to the closest house, which was mine, incidentally. In what was out of character for all of us chatty bitches, we essentially dropped the subject henceforth.

We never rode our bikes up Merrill Avenue again. We actually left well enough alone, which was not like us to do so.

And we didn't hear hide nor hair about anyone else stumbling upon that thing.

Years ticked off the calendar. Y2K did very little. 9/11 did a lot. After we all either moved away from town to start our boring nine-to-five march toward *the middle* or remained to do much the same, someone bought the place and filled it with new things, new people, new opportunities.

One wonders if they filled in the hole. They would've had to, right?

Right?

Likely not. They all think that place is safe. Well, it isn't. There's danger everywhere. But those are the times. Nobody sees what lurks in the shadows, 'cause they don't want to.

Today, in this guy's humble opinion, Carbondale is a picturesque postcard to the rapid influx of fresh arrivals. But slowly disappearing, all over the valley really, is the homegrown heart and soul that has long defined it. The reason why a wild man like Hunter S. Thompson felt perfectly at home here.

These days, and absent a self-administered mouthful of gunfire—*(if you don't want it printed, don't let it happen)*—the good doctor would surely be losing his shit if he bore witness to the free-spirited generational memory of yore being supplanted by a nouveau-riche, self-congratulatory torrent of fragile, uninspired, pill-popping, musically unoriginal, Instagram-famous, vacant-stare having, clickbait-hittin', hiking-selfie taking, trail ruining, hot pool clogging, mountain-view blocking, smartphone-obsessed, dystopian-metal-building-loving, pastel pretty, ingrate yuppie larva suckling at the financial teat of their more successful and competent parents.

Not that anybody should let those baby boomers off the hook, either. Sure, they're ten times better than the drooling, dead-eyed lemmings stumbling out of classrooms these days, but let's not forget that it was those self-superior baby boomers that parented us, who ultimately took all that positive, groovy, tie-dyed energy from the '60s and did essentially fuck all with it.

Lest we forget that when Dr. Thompson spoke elegantly of the failure of his generation to ride the wave to tangible change, he was speaking about himself, too.

It's a gorgeous community with a history and people like no other place. And it's also inching at a snail's pace toward becoming that which it once stood staunchly against. Maybe not those CRMS kids (they still seem as happy as pigs in slop—and what with the ride they all got, who can really blame 'em?), but us townies sure used to truly hate rampant commercialism and silver spoon suckin', social status idolatry.

The people who would tell you otherwise stand to gain, usually financially, from the perpetuation of the myth that some of the soul of the town is not, in fact, being gnawed at by fat cat interlopers and land-grabbing rich-bitch developers. The kind of cucks living at River Valley Ranch. The ones living in Aspen Glen. It's not cynical to say so; it's both facile and disingenuous to ignore it.

And sometimes that means rough takes that don't always go down easy. Like this meandering polemic right here.

So sorry, Charlie. This is why nobody ever asks for this guy's opinion.

So just you remember, just don't you forget: There has been some weird shit going on all over Carbondale. Every park has been used for drug-fueled teenage hijinks. Every school has been broken into and ransacked. Every home has had some sort of perverse sexual activity occur in it. And every district has lost a teacher due to horrific and often criminal impropriety, leading to their ouster.

I don't wanna name names to prove my point. You have Google. Of course you do. On that digital crack pipe you suck on all day? You're *that kind* of person. So go look it up yourself, bucko. Do your homework for once.

Remember that there's a deep, dank hole in your town, leading down an unknown distance to an unknown depth where some unknown thing sits all day, whispering creepy-ass shit in the pitch dark. Stuff that you'd do best to pay no mind to.

You're best served by walking the other way.

Luckily, apathy is something you clearly have a firm grasp of. Might even say you're a pro of the *doing nothing* variety.

Silly ol' you.

And I have no idea what was up with that hole, and I don't really give two shits or a fuck. We naturally didn't ever go back to hear the shifting whispering of that goddamn black chasm in the concrete floor of the former ironworks, or whatever the shit that place was. No way, José.

Truth be told, I've never even spoken of it 'til now. Hell, for all I know, the damn thing might still be there.

I'm *not* gonna go check.

RULER

In her haste to get the final paper grading of the school semester done before Christmas break, it hadn't occurred to Amanda Britz that she might be mostly alone inside of the school. That was, until she heard footsteps slowly moving down the hallway toward her.

Glancing at the wire-encased wall clock, she saw that it was actually after seven and her man John would likely be wondering where she was by now. She'd somehow barely noticed the descending sun.

From the skittering scuff sound outside, she surmised they must've been rubber soles, as they carried that high-end shriek exclusive to sneakers striking linoleum.

And that's what filled the hallways these days. Sure, it was thicker and more durable than your average residential fare, more cost effective than the previous carpeting had been, and was even rebranded as *faux laminate* in the early aughts to avoid the dated '70s home decor vibe that terms like *linoleum* tended to carry with them. But it was still cheap, crappy linoleum, no matter the nomenclature.

Another unfortunate byproduct of the ever-dwindling over-head budget at Carbondale Elementary School.

It was no surprise really, as everything in said academic institution was showing its age of late. Despite an influx of citizenry in the last decade, the money granted to the school for repairs outside of its regular operating budget was not equivalent to the correlative wear and tear. The school was hardly in disrepair, but in the year 2005 and absent a concurrent influx of funds, things like quality flooring and 24/7 security systems were not a high priority.

Later that evening—while wrapped in a thermal blanket and standing under gently falling snowflakes in the front parking lot, next to a group of firefighters frantically spraying water from a two-inch hose at the flames dancing along a section of the school's rooftop—she would recount to the inquiring first responders that it was likely the discordant noise created by that very inexpensive flooring that ultimately saved her life.

Fortuitously loud and scuffing along, the shoes called down the hallway toward her classroom, providing her five extra seconds of knowing that someone was approaching. It was enough for her to instinctively glance around inside the colorful, albeit somewhat cramped confines of her ground floor 4th-grade classroom.

She wasn't a former green beret and did not, in fact, possess some secondary spidey sense of imminent danger, by any means. However, her father had been all too eager to help his little girl be best prepared for a world full of douche-sacks just itching to make a random target of any unsuspecting lady caught with her guard down. As such, he'd coached her to never be that: *one with her guard down.*

He'd advised her to be situationally aware above all else, no matter where or with whom she found herself. *Know where the exits are. Pour your own drinks at parties. Never take a random pill.* As he'd explained, it was that extra little bit of fight or flight instinct that could spell the difference between hanging out above the ground or getting unceremoniously tossed under it.

Still, the surprise assault had yet to arrive. And as the years rolled on, she was increasingly certain that she'd never have to worry about such an attack—and certainly not on any home turf like this.

Sadly though, this night would turn out to be one of those pesky exceptions that proved the rule.

In the time between when she first heard her approaching assailant and those few precious moments before he entered, she rapidly surveyed the area around her. The many desks were not helpful—too hard to bludgeon with, frankly. Framed pictures and a pull-down map of the world were likewise useless to suit her current needs. The chalkboard had a few sticks of Hagaromo white and a useless two-foot wooden ruler lying on the tray.

Lotta good that shit is gonna do.

Her eyes quickly homed in on her pencil jar with a Broncos logo stenciled on the side. It sat on the edge of her desk, next to a framed picture of her man, John. Inside the jar: pens, pencils, sharpies, and most importantly, a pair of long-bladed shears. The type that one wouldn't necessarily associate with a classroom setting, but Amanda felt she simply could not live without when it came to crafting with her students.

Quickly snatching the shears from the jar, she brought them down to her side. Then her eyes watched the opposite side of the room, keenly aware that since the desks largely lined the other walls, it was essentially a straight shot to her from the entryway. Only the desk lay between her and whomever was—

As the door flung open and clattered against the wall behind it, she caught sight of a figure wearing puffy white unlaced high-top sneakers, dark and baggy denim jeans, and an equally loose-fitting black hoodie with silver piping. Maybe five-and-half-feet tall. Beneath the silver trimmed hood was absolute darkness. No features, no face—*nothing*. Even under the unforgiving glow of the school's long bar halogens.

"You don't look at all friendly. Where's your face?" Amanda asked, quite matter of fact. She scowled and scrunched her nose.

Her brash attempt at disarming humor, such as it was, fell fairly flat upon this dark hooded fellow. He simply shrugged, then casually waved at her with one black gloved hand that held a likewise black-handled survival knife ending in a silver six-inch blade.

"That looks pretty fucking dangerous. You got a permit for that?"

For a good five seconds, they regarded one another from across the small classroom while the faces of the many past US presidents looked down upon them from their framed pictures hung along the walls. The clock ticking—the only sound.

Grunting softly as his only warning, the vaguely menacing figure in the black hoodie suddenly shifted into a fully menacing sprint across the room, knife already in a stab-ready pose.

He took only one second, if that, to come around the desk. Barely enough time (though, lucky for her, *just enough*) for Amanda to stand up and bring her swiveling, high-backed chair around between the two. Blindly plunging down and landing the blade's sharp tip into the top cushion of the chair's padded backrest, she drew it back toward her. Throwing off his center of gravity, it brought him closer for one fleeting, albeit crucial moment.

Her use of the chair had seemingly dissuaded him of the notion that she might be otherwise armed, and as such, the next blow was hers to deliver. She buried the shears into the spot she thought would be his heart, but landed probably a bit north of it. Still, it punched a hole into the black fabric-clad shoulder.

Now, Amanda had actually never stabbed anyone. But basic knowledge of human anatomy, as well as everything she had been told and gleaned from her own use with knives, would tell her that there was something unnatural to the way the blade slid in. Too easy. It sank down straight to the cross guard without any true resistance.

She was left with precious little time to ruminate on this oddity, as the figure shoved the chair into her, which she stepped away from. He then yanked the knife right back out of the cushion between them. Flipping the knife, and strangely holding the blade as a handle, he promptly cracked the thick black pommel onto the front of her skull.

Spots of white light perforated her vision, flooding the eye field with a star shot of specks—but still a shot that fortuitously did not knock her clean out. Rather, her sight resolved somewhat quickly.

As she fell back, she raised a hand to her fresh wound. The hit had broken the skin and her hand came away with blood on it. Staggering back onto her butt, she could see the figure shove the chair away from them, smacking the wall.

She scuttled on her hands, vision still clearing. Pulling her knee back as far as she could and taking a swing at her heels with her right leg to sweep him, she caught him mid-step, knocking him back. She turned on her hands, scrambled up, and started to make for the door. But before she made good her exit, she grabbed the corner of the desk from the front and shoved it hard into the slowly rising husk behind it.

Dark Hoodie was again struck hard and crunched between the heavy wooden desk and the wall. Something had to have impacted one of the desks legs, because the whole thing buckled and bent toward him, spilling the items on the desk on top of her would-be killer. She didn't wait to see how he fared. In an instant she was out the door.

Entering the hallway, which her classroom was near the end of, she looked to her left, where there was an easy exit out. But looped between the heavy handles was a rubber-coated chain bike lock, securely fastened.

Fuck, that's gonna be a no.

She turned to the right instead. Feet flying forward, they carried her at breakneck speed down the hallway, her own sneakers now making that crunch-shriek on the linoleum. Passing by lockers and water fountains, her footfalls echoed along the corridor. A good fifty yards down, the hall veered off to the right, toward the front of the building and the admin offices.

The front office. Someone is possibly still in the front office, or maybe the janitor—

But then she remembered that that was a no go as well. She knew the janitor had left over an hour ago, since he'd made sure to peek in and let her know. Come to think of it, perhaps her being the last in the building was precisely why he'd mentioned it to her in the first place.

Damn, there's a crack in your normally steely trap of a mind. Time to get your game on, girl. Think, Amanda, think!

Still, this was her best bet. Try to get to the phones in the office at the very least.

Running past the double doors to the cafeteria, she saw that, again, the handles had been tied together, though in her rush, she didn't see by what, exactly. It didn't matter. He was cutting off her means of escape.

Hearing the overturned desk pushed aside behind her, she ran as fast as she could down the hallway and took a swift 90° turn toward the open area between her and the front doors. Off to the right was the school's administration area, from which branched the principal's and guidance counselors' offices, as well as the tiny teachers' lounge (really a glorified closet with a coffee machine atop a folding table).

As she skidded to a stop before the front entryway, she saw that yet another rubbery bike chain had been wrapped around two thick brass handles on the front doors. She closed her hands around them and pulled hard several times, knowing damn well that this effort was futile. She also figured that since the glass in both of the door layers between her and freedom were webbed with diamond patterns of metal interweaving, that breaking it was also going to be a bust, just not the type she needed at present.

Bastard's on a mission.

Glancing at the door to the office, she saw that the knob handle had been crushed and dented by some unknown blunt force upon it.

Well, not totally unknown.

Bastard's on one helluva mission.

In the corner—between the double glass-paneled doors before her, which led to the parking lot and the office area—stood a flagpole stand. It held both a full-sized American flag and, on another long wooden staff, a classic Colorado flag with the giant red *C* wrapped snugly around the burning yellow Western Slope sun. Snatching the latter, she foisted it from its spot in the metal bracing pipe, turned, and pointed the gold-painted wooden tip at Dark Hoodie just as he came around the corner. The shears—*her shears*—still stuck out of his chest.

He cocked his head, revealing nothing of a face or features. Only an onyx abyss, swallowing any and all light that dared cross into the ink blot of a black shadow void.

"Why?" she gasped, trying to catch her breath and pulling in air through her nostrils while holding the pole between them. "Why are you doing this?"

The shadowy shape said nothing, but rather tauntingly twirled the large metal shears in a slow arc that glinted the light from an adjacent classroom onto the blades, then shrugged.

Amanda scowled, scoffed, and shrugged back. "That's really ... *you*, with the whole—" She mockingly nudged her shoulders his way again. Twirling the blades, the ovoid of his face only stared now.

She suddenly felt a spot of wetness on her forehead and patted it with her left hand.

Blood.

Hopefully that *isn't too serious.*

She wiped her hand on her pants and bristled her shoulders again. "That's fine! Fine! You just go ahead and—" She shook the wooden pole gripped tightly in her sweaty palms.

Dark Hoodie stopped spinning the shears and slowly pointed the tips at her.

Amanda narrowed her eyes, utterly unamused. "What? You

got something to say, Pancho Villa? Anything? Do you have any fucking point or is this just some crime of opportunity bullshit?"

Again, Dark Hoodie, still aiming the glorified scissors in her direction, simply shrugged.

"Fuck your shrugs, dude. Fuck them all day and twice on Sunday!"

And she knew *damn well* what she was doing.

He immediately started to run at her again, as she'd anticipated. She reasoned that engaging him could be just as dangerous as before, so she didn't move. Instead, she just waited for him to come at her with the same speed, planning to hit and dodge simultaneously.

But of course, he stopped just a few feet short, and as she swung out in an arc with the flagpole, he ducked. The Colorado flag flapped in the air over his head and she felt his body crush her between his and the doorway. He pressed her against the glass, which immediately cracked into a splintering of shards that clung to the metal webwork inside the glass pane. He rocked her again and quickly stepped back, raising one fist faster than she could respond to and stuck the shears into the soft flesh of her thigh.

I said goddamn that hurts like a sonofabitch! Shit!

Teeth gnashing, she groaned, surprising even herself, and winced in unyielding pain as the reality of her injury set in.

That's gonna leave a mark. A good, er, bad one. Whatever.

Still against the glass, she flexed her arms and brought the wooden stave down onto Dark Hoodie's head. It struck before he could raise his arms up to catch it, thumping his skull. Again though, something was off. The sound was hollow, like striking the side of a pumpkin. Still, he slumped slightly.

Quickly twirling the pole so that it was braced between her hands, she brought it down twice more. Two more hollow

WHUMP sounds from his shrouded skull and Dark Hoodie fell instantly to the floor.

She stepped to the side and the gash in her leg let her know right away that walking was gonna suck for a hot minute. Eyes darting to the black mass on the ground, she noted he wasn't moving at all. Keeping her eyes trained on him, she reached down and pulled the shears from her leg. The increase in pain as she wrenched them free from her flesh caused her to shudder. The shears dropped onto the floor at her feet.

She undid the buckle of her belt and pulled it free in one swift motion from around her waist. Then she cinched it tightly around her thigh to stem the tide of free-flowing blood.

Still watching her assailant, she cautiously picked up the flag-staff and dropped it twice more onto Dark Hoodie's head. On the third strike, the pole snapped in two. A pool cue-length of sharp wood remained in her grasp. She considered jabbing it into him, then surmised that such an act might be perceived by any number of her students' parents as behavior hardly befitting of their child's primary daytime caretaker.

Backing up, she could sense that somehow, someway, in a deep recess of her mind, that this wasn't through. A suspicion confirmed almost immediately as Dark Hoodie twitched, grunted softly, then began to unfurl his tangle of limbs on the floor like a slowly uncoiling snake.

Amanda didn't wait to see how long it took for him to regain himself. She was running back down the hallway she'd come from in a flash, but for the hobble-hop she was now flexing. Scuffling along, she made sure to knock over the trash cans that stood outside of every other classroom. To throw him off her scent and obscure the noise.

She knocked over another one, then doubled back and quickly and quietly opened the door to Mr. Lui's science lab. Dark and full of lab tables with wooden stools behind them, Amanda stepped into the classroom and carefully pulled the door shut behind her. She turned the lock, knowing it was a largely fruitless enterprise as the glass spyhole was easy enough to simply break and reach into.

Noting that this room was also grounded with the same tacky laminate flooring as that which permeated the hallway she'd just stepped out of, she figured enough was enough. Sliding off one shoe, then the other, she picked them up in one hand and tip-toed over to where she knew Mr. Lui's desk sat at the north end of the darkened space. Cautiously, she placed them underneath it, then made her way to the nearest black pressure-pressed laminate science table. Once behind it, she pulled open a big sliding drawer. Her eyes were quickly adjusting to the limited light coming in through the small window in the door. She was able to make out that there were several pairs of goggles, tongs, a test tube tray, one beaker, a container of cotton swabs, and a bottle of rubbing alcohol.

Down the hallway, she heard a trash can being kicked aside and knew she only had a minute or two before he figured out which door she'd entered.

Amanda stood up and felt the sharp split of her flesh, jagged and fresh with the wound still seeping blood from her right thigh. Her thoughts went gooey and she felt as though she might pass out. Her palms pressed onto the table for a moment as, down the hall, another trash can was flung into a wall.

Closing her eyes, she breathed in deeply and exhaled quietly. Her mind allowed the dizziness to recede and her feet became steady under her once more. Pulling out the beaker, she set it onto the table, then drew forth the plastic bag of cotton balls and snatched a handful of them, stuffing them into the beaker.

Another trash can crashed into one of the doors, followed by the sound of one rubber-soled foot kicking its way into a classroom just one or two away from where she stood. Grabbing the bottle of rubbing alcohol, she popped the cap and started to squirt into the beaker. After a few seconds, she set it down.

Now her one problem: *ignition*. Looking back into the drawer, she saw there was no spark lighter or matches. Figuring Mr. Lui had to have one in his desk, she trot-limped back over to it and pulled open the top drawer. Sure enough, fortune smiled upon her once again. Lui had it ready to rock atop a pile of ungraded papers and a half-drained pint of Johnny Walker. She snatched the ignitor out.

Moving back toward the black lab table, Amanda glanced at the door to the hallway, then looked over at the northern door which led to the adjacent classroom. Every other room was connected to its neighbor by a doorway so that the classrooms were basically in pairs. Knowing she needed to get to her cell phone, which she'd stupidly left in her purse behind her desk, she snatched up the alcohol, walked to the entrance, and set the beaker down on the linoleum next to the hallway door.

The door to the classroom across the hallway banged open as her would-be killer crashed into it and began to search it. She had maybe five to ten seconds before he came busting in. As she backed away, she sprayed a line of alcohol onto the ground that led to her spot. Inching back, she reached the door which led to the adjacent classroom.

Hearing Dark Hoodie re-enter the hallway and start toward her direction, she knelt and flicked the spark ignitor. At first, nothing. Wondering if she should spray more, she decided to play the odds. Two more flicks. Another, and then *POP*, it went.

Rolling in a long blue line toward the door, Amanda only saw the flickering flame get halfway toward the beaker before she slipped into the next classroom and made for the door. This was the school's other science lab, though it was set up with half as many tables and several desks, as well as two stand-up skeletons.

Before she could even take a step toward this room's exit, the improvised bomb went off next door.

This is it. Run, honey. Run like your life depends on it. Because, well, let's be real here—things aren't looking so great for the kid right now.

The door smashed open into Lui's lab, and Amanda crossed into the hallway, careful to avoid any debris on the floor. She ran past the classroom she'd just been in, praying that Dark Hoodie was too busy investigating to see her.

Despite thinking it would only create a diversion, the fire had really taken hold. Likely aided by other chemicals nearby, the room had started to fill with smoke, obscuring the view of the hallway.

Amanda barely cared. Still hobble-hopping along, though at a steady clip, it only took her ten more seconds to reach her room and enter. Walking to the desk, she leaned over and picked up her purse. Removing the phone and dialing 911, she placed it to her ear and looked around. Still absolutely jack shit as far as good weapons went.

Just two rings and an answer.

"911, what is your emergency?"

"Hey, this is Amanda Britz at the elementary school here in Carbondale and I'm being attacked by some fucking crackpot in a black hoodie with silver piping."

"Silver piping?"

"Yeah, silver piping! Like silver trim, but just around the edge! Just…" She trailed off as Dark Hoodie came flying around the corner, shears somehow in hand. "You better get here right away cause I'm gonna throw you at him as a distraction now! Come and help me!"

And just as she'd said, she threw the mobile phone straight at him with all her might. Sadly, it missed by a mile as Dark Hoodie dodged the projectile, and it shattered against the wall behind him. Dark Hoodie stood up straight.

Shooting to the wall-mounted blackboard, she snatched the ruler from the chalk tray and tossed it at him as well. But his hand improbably flicked open the shears, then used them to split the incoming wooden stick in half. The two jagged shards fell to the floor.

Amanda rushed to the desk, dashing while her attacker held his ground. "Cops are coming, you crazy hooligan! Unless you wanna spend this holiday season fucking dead, I'd get the hell on! But leave the shears."

Dark Hoodie, as one might imagine, shrugged at her once again—this one in particular sitting not at all well with Amanda. And while she didn't say anything, she *did* give him the finger, then spat a coppery glob of blood onto the floor between them.

Crouching down into an oddly low stance, he raised his hands as though he might pounce. And then he did just that.

Jumping in an equally unnatural way—as an animal leaping onto the body of fleeing prey along some primal landscape might—Dark Hoodie landed on top of Amanda's body, carrying her skull onto the ground with a blinding white *smack*.

Semi-dazed, she feebly flailed her arms at her attacker as her senses started limply coming back from the darkness they'd been sent away to with the rough crack to her dome.

That's two too many of those for the evening.

A sharp pain on her collarbone really cleared her mind up in a flash, as the faceless form of Dark Hoodie seemingly bit down on her shoulder, causing her to grimace in pain. Even this close, she saw none of it—no face, no teeth—yet still a clear bite sensation all the same.

She would've cried out, but instead of fear or flight, she finally felt her fury flood forward in a swollen torrent of burning rage. Swatting and scratching and shredding every piece of his person she could clamp onto with her fingertips, she writhed underneath him, trying in vain to gain leverage and free herself.

Easily pinning her with his knees, she saw him raise his puffy sleeve up. She moved her head so that the tips of the shears she'd earlier stabbed his thigh meat with just missed her face and planted firmly into the floor by her right ear.

Raising a knee to his groin, he still managed to keep her securely held down. Frantically grabbing for his wrists, she kept her elbows pulled in so he couldn't lean down to bite her again—*or whatever the fuck that was.* As her eyes rolled back to the ground near her head, she caught the briefest glimpse of a piece of the broken ruler lying a foot from her.

Her fingers let go of his left hand as she tried to reach for the wooden shard. Dark Hoodie shifted his weight and used his now free left hand to clamp onto her ribs with a talon grip that made her grit her teeth. She returned her hand to defend her side, and he reached over one dark-sleeved arm to pull the shears free from the floor.

She pushed her left elbow into his throat and held him back

just long enough to free her right hand, swatting away the shears. They slid several feet away and came to rest against a chair leg. Hand still moving, her arm reached out, grabbed onto the splintered wood piece not one foot away, and without hesitation she rammed the business end into the side of Dark Hoodie's skull.

With ease that seemed unnatural, the wood went straight in and Dark Hoodie slumped heavily to one side, limp. Unlike the previous times, his muscles relaxed entirely and his full body weight remained on top of her.

Amanda croaked out a frightened gasp, then took a massive breath in and exhaled it out to steady her nerves. Inhaling deeply once more, then shoving the shrouded figure up and off of her, she loudly exhaled with the weight lifted from her chest.

For a moment, she lay there next to Dark Hoodie, worrying that he'd spring up at any moment to finish her off. But he didn't.

Ten seconds. Twenty seconds. Then thirty passed and not one movement. Not even a twitch. Nothing.

Zip, zilch, nada.

At sixty seconds, she figured that must be that.

Peering in his direction, she stared at his head void. Amanda reasoned it must be some tight face mask or something, because his features remained little more than a pitch blur.

She didn't think a whole lot about it until later, when the authorities told her that the body had disappeared from the morgue and the two deputies guarding it had been killed. She thought about how both times she had stabbed Dark Hoodie, the weapon had slid in the way a good knife slides into fruit. Not *no* resistance, but not close to enough either.

Like he wasn't made of mortal flesh.

Almost as though he was made of…

Fruit? No, that sounds ridiculous.

She shuddered and raised herself up on her palms. In what she believed to be in her mind, at least at first, she could hear what sounded like a soft, calming choir calling out from somewhere in the far distance. Like when you enter into a big church and the echoes of singing reverberate throughout the hallowed halls.

Like a siren song.

But then, she rapidly realized that rather than the bewitching call of some mythic sea enchantress, she was hearing literal sirens. Like the ones on top of emergency vehicles.

Oh thank fuck. The cavalry.

A funny thought then randomly occurred to Amanda while she waited out front for the approaching sirens to draw closer: *Budget cuts might have been partially responsible for me being alive right now. Because that floor is how I knew he was coming. Had I been caught more unaware…*

Then a simpler, rounder truth took hold. The cheap flooring might have saved her life, but those same budget cuts failed to provide ample after-hours security for staff, which would've gone a long way to preventing this whole dumb mess.

Turning and facing the building, she saw that the fire she had started in the science lab had spread to part of the roof. Not a huge blaze, but it needed putting out, for sure. Hearing the sirens of the fire engine, she figured that'd be okay.

I mean, they got this. It's their job. Fairly certain I just did mine.

It was a day she wished hadn't happened, but was ultimately sort of relieved it finally had. Her dad's fabled attacker had come, he'd seen, and he'd been thusly conquered with a broken wooden shard to the friggin' cranium.

It was a day she would recount too many times throughout her long, happy life. A day she would and could never forget.

Because, whilst gazing upon the embers rising from the science room roof into the cold air, the moonlit crests of Mount Sopris in the background, it was also the day that she finally decided, *Yeah, fuck a whole lotta this bullshit,* gave her two weeks' notice, quit teaching, and promptly started her own hairstyling business. One which has been wildly successful and financially lucrative in the many years since.

Nowadays, the only one brandishing the shears is Amanda. She can deal out one mean cut; just ask her clients.

You could even ask ol' Dark Hoodie, for that matter. If they ever found him, he'd likely agree that she ain't fuckin' around.

MORTEM

Scattered clouds list through the blue skies overhead while the clear midday sun casts down blankets of light onto the green grass lining the hills of the Roaring Fork Valley. The late march day is exquisitely bright and sunny, with the snow lines of the mountain ranges nearby already rapidly melting down and filling the rivers, giving way to blossoms and greenery along the valley walls.

Absent any consistent natural illumination, Rocky Mills is setting up his tripod-steadied halo light ring for the interview on the outdoor patio deck of the three-story ranch house when he notices Fiona Capshaw looking his way. Red-headed and porcelain-skinned, her slight and slim figure is fitted tightly within a formal-ish business-like black Vera Wang dress that flaunts as much of her womanly twists and turns as might be considered appropriate in an ostensibly casual interview context. Over her shoulders is a matching black jacket.

She sits on one of two chairs across the deck from the lighting setup that Rocky is now covering with a waterproof splash guard.

"I'm sure he'll be here any second, Rocky. Any second," she

says, breaking the silence. Her eyes are locked on the notepad in her lap, where she jotted down some questions she wanted to make sure to get in during the interview.

"I wasn't... I didn't say anything," Rocky replies without looking up.

"Yeah, but you were thinking it. In your schemy-scheming mind, such thoughts were afoot."

Rocky laughs at this. "Sure, I was thinking it—but who wouldn't be? It's just odd. A bit odd. Mayhaps even a smidge on the weird side."

"Weird?" Fiona asks as she closes the clamshell makeup mirror in her palm, affixing her gaze on his. "Elucidate."

"This. This is a little weird," he says, securing the light guard with a small bit of elastic drawstring.

"What's weird about it?"

"It's weird that he's had us waiting here for so long. It's weird he requested that only you and a single crew member come out to this, uh, compound thing. Out here in butt-fuck Egypt. I'm just saying, it's a little weird."

"First off, it's hardly butt-fuck Egypt. Aspen is like five miles that way." She points to the southeast. "And secondly, it's really not too weird for him. He's an eccentric, and/or he's cultivating an image. Likely more of the latter than the former. I mean, I suspect it's both, though it hardly matters if it's either. We're here for the scoop. The hot dish with a side dollop of human interest."

"Semi sus. Just saying."

"Noted."

Brushing the auburn locks from her face, she looks at her chic little Rolex then taps her foot twice on the wood beneath her shoes, sending the signal that she empathizes with her crewman.

After adjusting the light cover, Rocky moves across the dark, richly-stained wooden deck to where he's set up his laptop, a secondary display, his compact input mixer, level monitor, and other gadgetry required to make this remote op as smooth a ride as possible—all atop a small fold-out table. He's got all of it set up behind Fiona and the two deck chairs she's pulled out for the interview.

Taking a seat on a tall lawn chair that Rocky has used for this very purpose many times before, he begins to click through windows with his computer touchpad. This particular time-refined rig makes it so that, while the interview is rolling, the livestream of anxious viewers will be able to ask their interviewee questions in real time. Queries will fill his secondary display, which can then be relayed to Fiona and put directly to the author himself within seconds of popping up.

Rocky and Fiona took the sketchy flight from Los Angeles directly into Aspen/Pitkin airport, then caught an Uber up to the swanky and fairly elite neighborhood of Starwood Estates, located a few miles outside of Aspen proper. Passing through the guard gate checkpoint without much fanfare, it had only taken them a few minutes to reach the reclusive author's estate not far from the deep valley's high eastern ridge. A massive wrought iron gate standing two stories high, crowned with rolling spirals of hooked barbs, lay open as they passed through into a larger dirt court before the property.

Nearly as high as one can reach anywhere within the valley, at this heavenly vantage one can see Snowmass, Aspen, and nearby Basalt. Largely built into an Aspen-tree-laden hillside and appearing much as a subterranean bunker, the main part of the compound is masked from view. A half-oval bulkhead built into the flattened hill's face and fitted with two large gray blast doors is readily visible. Adjacent to the sloped mound that serves as the earthen canopy for the main facility is a small, modest ranch house and horse stable. There are security cameras everywhere and extremely high fencing that offers relative relief from any prying eyes.

"You're not wrong, though. Tad odd, yeah. But I assure you, it's a persona. I hear he's always this way with his interviews—the few he's done. It's normal enough for him. Don't worry."

"Not worried, just more eccentric than I suppose I'm used to, Fiona."

A broad grin crosses her face, exposing her perfect set of pearly whites. "But it's Danforth Daggersmith, Rocky! Danforth! When it's Danforth Daggersmith, you just roll with it, right? You roll with it. We are rolling with it. And you'll be rolling tape on it. This is one of the biggest days of both of our lives, so count your blessings!"

"I do. I *am*. They're counted. I'm counting; always counting. But that friggin' name is hella sus too. It sounds too silly, like a pen name but douchey. Painfully douchey. And I doubt it's legit."

Fiona snorts softly. "It's legit. Too legit to quit, in fact, and this is about to make us legit as well."

"You figure so?"

"I figure so. I *know* so. This is the start, right here."

"Makes you wonder how we got so lucky."

"Why question it?"

"Because it's suspiciously fortuitous."

"We got lucky. People get lucky."

"Then why does us getting lucky make me wonder if anyone else did?"

"Hmm?" she mumbles, her eyes now locked on her notepad.

The corner of Rocky's lip twists knowingly. "You didn't say before—why did Gordon hand this off to you—to us?"

"Essentially to shut me up. He figures this is a good way to get me off his back once and for all with the whole field work thing. It doesn't matter. If this goes well, I'm in a stronger bargaining position than before and—"

"Wait, did you…? You *did*. Shit, Fiona!"

"What?"

"What do you mean 'what?' You know which what I mean!"

"Still, I'm gonna pretend I don't." Fiona absent mindedly flips through her notepad.

"But you do! You did it, or should I say *him?* You just said he wanted you off his back, but it's more like he wanted you on yours!"

"Can we not discuss this?"

"Shit where you eat; that's all I'm saying, little missy. It's your business, of course—"

"Of course."

"Of course! But you don't get to say someone didn't give you the obligatory talking to, advising you to suppress your own carnal impulses."

"Jesus, Rocky! It wasn't like that. Also, that sentence was a bit hard to track."

"Ha! But you did it then?"

"Did what?"

"Did our douchey boss!"

"Of course I did! I told you if he wasn't gonna move me up of his own accord, that I would fuck him into doing so."

"I thought you were fucking around," Rocky concludes, clicking at his keyboard and chuckling.

"Now you know I wasn't."

"That's … yeah, whatever. It's your choice, Fiona."

"Yeah, thanks, Rock. I'm aware of my choice. And considering that you and I have had jack shit in the way of good stories to pursue in the three months we've been at Silverscreen, but now after one forgettable fuck with middle management, we got ourselves a one on one with Danforth Daggersmith…"

"You really gonna say his full name every time, like that?"

"Sure I am! Why wouldn't I? I took a cock bullet for our collective career advancement, so maybe you could just say thank you."

Rocky snorts, then smiles. "Yeah … no. Maybe. No, you're right; I'm sure you're right. I'm sorry. And thank you for taking the aforementioned cock bullet for me—for us, rather. For our careers. Thank you."

"You're quite welcome."

There's a pregnant silence between them as the cool air brushes against the nearby Aspen trees, causing the leaves to wiggle like a million tiny green waving hands.

"Dead fuck?" Rocky asks.

Fiona nodded. "Totally dead. Drunk and, yeah, utterly useless 'tween the sheets."

"Figures. So you're okay with it?"

"What?"

"Doing that for this? Just asking. If you are, that's all good. *Better* than good. I'm just…" he trails off.

"Yeah. Lemme ask you this, would it be gross if you indulged your more Freudian inclinations and fucked a half-attractive superior to advance your career?"

Rocky coyly smiles, but says nothing.

"Yeah, yeah. See? You'd count yourself lucky! So just you hurry and shut the fuck up, ya sexist mofo."

Smiling and nodding, Rocky says, "Can do."

At that moment, Danforth Daggersmith, purveyor of literary dread, pulls open a sliding glass door and strides out onto the patio.

His eyes lurk behind dark aviators. Above torn, acid-washed blue jeans, a black KISS Army tank top hangs loosely on his tall, wiry frame. His olive skin is complimented by a raven's mane of oily dark hair running down to the crook of his back. It's shaved on the sides and drawn up into a high, tight ponytail. His wrists are festooned with bracelets, beads, and chains of random cultural influence: cuffs of dense woven fabric, spiked leather straps, a rosary, linked gold chains, as well as turquoise beads embedded in silvers—covering all the bases.

Stepping out from a sliding doorway, he makes a direct line toward the two chairs on the deck. In one hand he has a tall glass of what appears to be whiskey on the rocks.

"Danforth," he says as he holds out his free hand to Fiona, who shakes it, noting how warm it is.

Excessively warm.

"A real pleasure, sir. Truly. Big fan. A line I'm sure you never hear. I've read several of your *Glen Glower* novels and I think two of your standalones. It's so nice to meet you. Fiona Capshaw."

"That's great, Fiona. It's really great, and I hope you take a couple of the autographed copies of novels from my library when we're all done here. You'll find it downstairs." Danforth takes a slight step back, looks over at her companion amid his high-tech set up, and asks flatly, "Who's this?"

Fiona stands and turns to Rocky. "Uh, yes, this is my running crew, such as it is. My producer-slash-cameraman for this trip, Rocky Mills. The best everything man money can buy."

Rocky holds out his hand and meets Danforth's steely gaze with his own expressionless face.

Danforth stretches a strained smile along his jaw, shaking Rocky's hand in his. "They said they were only sending one person."

"It's okay, right?" Fiona asks, surprised by his statement.

Dispensing with the non-smile, he replies, "Yes, certainly. It will have no effect whatsoever on what's going to happen. Very little would. So it's no trouble, really."

"Well that's appropriately cryptic, isn't it?" Rocky mumbles.

Danforth smiles, somehow even more reptilian than before. "Only insofar as I'm saying words which you may find disturbing."

Rocky crosses his arms and asks, "What?"

"Nothing, dear boy. Nothing at all. Dabbling in the dour," Danforth assures, drawing closer.

Rocky reaches into his pocket and pulls out a wireless lapel mic. "Clip this onto your rocking tank top and I'll handle the levels."

Danforth nods, takes the small black object, and readily clips it onto his shirt. He assumes his place across from Fiona. Lifting his glass to his lips, he takes a pull before setting it on the decking next to his chair's leg.

As Fiona sits back down, crosses her legs, then sets her hands on top of the notepad in her lap, she asks, "So are you possibly hinting at something with the new novel?"

Danforth answers, "All in due course, Mrs. Capshaw. I wanted to say, though, that I'm so sorry to have kept you waiting. I had to make sure my papers and business records were in order. Still, I apologize."

Fiona nods. "No worries. Tax season is a bitch, ain't it?"

"Tax season?" the author asks, pausing, then realizes her meaning. "Oh yes, yes. Taxes—*tax season*. When we all pay our taxes. Yeah. Uh huh."

Fiona repositions herself and straightens her back as much as she can. Then she carefully pets her hair along its length to ensure that she's camera ready. "So, Rocky over here has the group chat up and we're going to be using the questions submitted by those who donate over fifty dollars to the charity you've chosen. Which is the—"

"The Church of Scientology!" He finally gives a flash of a genuine smile as he laughs. "That's right! Anything to make the whole thing stranger and, therefore, more clickable."

Fiona shoots a look back at Rocky, who makes sure to send her a *no idea, but yeah, I heard that shit too* look in return.

"More odd quipping. Are we ready?" Fiona asks gently.

Rocky glances at the level monitor, then gives her a thumbs up. "Both of your levels look good. I think we're gold."

Turning back to her subject, Fiona affixes a thin, polite smile across her mouth. "Are *you* ready, Mr. Daggersmith?"

"To descend? Absolutely!"

Fiona's smile remains frozen. "Descend?"

"Nothing, nothing. Just a bit of ominous foreshadowing." His free hand runs down his ponytail.

Fiona adjusts the clip mic on her jacket lapel. "We're not live yet so—"

"I know. It was for you two."

Fiona rolls with it. "O-kay, that's another odd thing to say. Love you keeping it on brand, so keep it comin'. But, you're good? We can get started?"

Danforth nods, taking another sip of his drink and setting it on the ground next to him. "Ready as I'm gonna be."

She looks over her shoulder to Rocky, who gives her another thumbs up without looking away from the monitor. Tapping her earpiece, she says, "Give me a countdown."

In her ear, Rocky goes: "Got it. In five, four, three, two…"

Looking into the camera lens, which has her framed with Danforth against the western horizon, Fiona begins:

"I'm Fiona Capshaw with Silverscreen.com and Kino Landmark Theaters. We're here today with popular horror novelist and now Academy Award winning screenwriter of this year's sleeper hit, *Bonepile*—his water-cooler spookfest of last year's holiday season. Based on the first of his *Glen Glower* series of thriller novels, it was nominated in six categories, including best picture. Ultimately taking home the best sound editing and best adapted screenplay for its scribe, it was, as almost anyone with an Internet connection knows, the highest-grossing film of the last year. At his modest home in the wilds outside of Aspen, Colorado, we've got the man, the myth, the legend himself, Mr. Danforth Daggersmith, with us today to discuss…" Fiona pauses, then regards Danforth with a raised eyebrow. "Well, if we're being candid, we haven't been told why we're here, exactly. Other than to afford you the opportunity to speak directly with some of your most ardent fans who are, at this very moment, watching live via our sponsored platforms. They should be located at the bottom of the screen right now. They're also waiting with bated breath to ask you any number of questions."

"Glad to be with you. The kids at home will love this shit."

"And what shit is that?"

"You'll see," Danforth says, smiling through the frost in his eyes.

"And he's been kind enough to keep us on edge with odd comments such as that."

"Whatever I can do to drum up the anticipation," he says, casually stretching his arms over his head.

"And this is your first interview in…?"

Danforth pauses to think, then slowly replies, "Five years, two months, eight hours, and seventeen minutes. A few seconds as well, I guess."

Fiona lightly laughs reflexively. She flips her notepad in her lap. "That's a shocking degree of specificity."

Danforth confides, "I have somewhat of an eidetic memory when it comes to useless bullshit from the past."

"Well, hopefully this proves to be more fruitful than the previous one."

"Oh, I intend it to be."

This makes Rocky scrunch his nose and Fiona smile more broadly than before. "Great, that's—that's wonderful! So, you've got a lovely place up here."

Danforth snatches up his glass, taking a sip while doing an arm sweep of the panoramic valley views below. "Rocky Mountain High, Colorado."

Nodding in ascent, Fiona agrees, "Ah, yes. *Thank God I'm a country boy,* right?"

Daggersmith asks, "You a fan?"

"Yeah. Or my dad was—*is*. He used to listen to John Denver a lot. Didn't he live up here near Aspen?"

Nodding, Danforth strokes his ponytail and says, "Actually, his old place is just down the road from us. Like four doors down, essentially. His dusty old motorcycle is still in the garage."

"Hot damn. Guess that's Aspen, right? Famous neighbors in all directions?"

The author replies, "Famous, sure. Or those who see themselves as such."

Fiona eyes Mr. Daggersmith. His features now look somehow paler than when he first appeared from inside the house.

"So you've brought us out to your, well, I would say 'comfy home,' though if I'm being completely candid here, this honestly has more of a militaristic feel. Sort of a doomsday compound vibe."

Danforth sips his drink again while non-smiling and nodding. "Not by chance, either. Can't have anyone escaping."

Despite wondering what he's implying, Fiona maintains a professional sheen. "Nice. That's funny. And your humor comes out often in your writing. Do you find blending horror with comedy to be difficult?"

"Not as much as hiding the truth from the world's eyes. Too many masks to wear."

"Right. That's … again with the sardonic. I dig it. Almost as much as I love the first three *Glower* novels. Sorta the Alex Cross of the western slope."

"You've read them?"

"Sure, as I was saying before we started. I've been reading them, just like everyone else has as of late, one assumes. What with the impressive Oscar win and all. So yes, I'm getting there. But I was going to ask you about that—"

"I am the herald," Danforth blurts out.

Both Fiona and Rocky exchange glances and smirk at one another, knowing the reference, just as half of America does at this point.

"That's nice. Like in the books, right? In your novels?"

"Yes." The author picks up his drink again, but in a surprising move to Fiona, gulps down the remainder of its contents. His right eye twitches slightly as he exhales boozy exhaust. "'Scuse me."

"Is that— Do you mean that we should be expecting another visit from the evil Mr. Mortem this upcoming holiday season?"

At this, Fiona glances at Rocky, who is nodding, smiling, and giving her a thumbs up. The viewers liked that one. He speaks into her earpiece, "You got this. A confirmation will seal the deal on this and the rest is a piece of cake. You're rocking and rolling; chat is groovin'."

"Not exactly." The author's response is swift and flat.

"What do you mean?"

"I mean that my books are drawn from my truth. A truth I am about to reveal."

"And what truth is that?"

Setting down the empty glass next to his chair again, he stands and walks over to where the second-story deck railing overlooks his small backyard. Beyond that, the western side of the valley wall, where the cars running along Highway 82 look like insects at this distance.

He places his hands upon the railing and faces away from the camera as he says, "That my role is that of the herald. I am the tide which washes over the flooded denizens who would only look up on their own imminent demise with indifference and apathy. I am the tide that washes you all away." A cold, unfeeling smile crosses Danforth's lips.

Hearing him speak, Rocky feels a tingle of fear and uncertainty crawl up his vertebrae and burrow into the base of his neck.

Fiona, on the other hand, is all smiles, rubbing her hands

together in her lap. She addresses the camera directly again. "Well, okay, so—here's my spoiler alert for people watching at home, so be warned. Last chance to mute. But what our esteemed author just said, about being the herald, that's what Glen Glower's archnemesis—the serial killer known as *Mr. Mortem*—says in your first novel—"

"*The Echo Chamber of Sorrow*, yes. That was exactly what he said, because it's exactly what I said—or *say*, rather," he murmurs without looking back, hands on the railing.

"So you did. We all heard you."

"I mean that it was also what I said to my first victim. As well as most of the victims that followed, actually."

"That's"—Fiona raises a scolding finger and wags it comically—"appropriately disconcerting. I'm still digging it. What's the catch?"

"No catch. Just the truth. Hard as it may be to swallow. For that, I've prepared proof."

Fiona figures playing along is her only sensible choice, so she asks the obvious. "So, what? *You're* Mr. Mortem? That's what you're saying?"

"In a manner of speaking, yeah. Yes, I suppose I am that."

"How do you mean?"

"I mean, that in preparation for my descent to the iron core, I have been murdering people and burying them in my backyard."

Fiona claps her hands together. "Hah! Awesome! That's … that's very good. Very on brand, Mr. Daggersmith."

"I certainly hope so! And call me Dan, please."

Rocky whispers, "Oh, thank God."

"Of course, Dan. So, you've been hiding the bodies in your backyard?"

"Oh yes."

Fiona rolls with it, "And to what end, exactly?"

"Like I said, to instill fear into the multitudes before my descent to the iron core."

"Uh huh. That's, uh, some wild stuff. Really, just wild, zany stuff. And the corpses, they—what? Facilitate this in some way? 'Cause one could say that that sounds bafflingly kooky."

Dan turns his head toward Aspen, but does not turn around. "Indeed. Kooky to the hilt. Really the body count, along with other bits, are just to scare and worry people more when the news breaks. Just a way to make an impression."

"An impression?"

"An impression, sure. Gotta make a splash these days. A big one. Big splashes are what catch the public's imagination, like Armstrong and Aldrin did in '69 when they walked on the moon. Or like those Marvel movies did recently. Can't rely on old methods of reaching an audience. No way, José. Gotta shock and awe the people. And honestly, not many people care about much of anything you can throw at 'em. Their idolatry is saved for the sycophants, talking heads, and whack jobs they encounter in our debased technophile modernity. They'll likely doubt the veracity of this at first, but they'll come around. For even the murderous maniacs of the now achieve a level of notoriety most authors or artists could only dream of."

Nervously fidgeting with her notepad in her lap, Fiona says, "Uh, so that's sorta preachy. But—"

Cutting her off, he continues unabated, "And you could spend your whole life trying to make it as a musical artist, yet never getting yourself onto the cover of *Rolling Stone*. Never. However, if you're the surviving Boston Marathon bomber, you get the cover and a ten page spread!"

Shooting another look at Rocky, Fiona can see a grimace of disdain and concern has replaced his previous facial ambiguity.

Danforth continues to stand with his back facing the camera.

"Okay—" She tries and fails to regain control.

He swiftly cuts her off. "So I'm just saying, if you want to get the eyes of the world on you, it takes more than just celebrity. It takes a willingness to shed blood. To spill your own, if need be. In pursuit of that broader reach, you must be willing to do anything."

"Right. Okay." Fiona looks at Rocky for some clue as to how to proceed.

In her ear, "Dude might be more cracked than we suspected, Fiona. But the livestream numbers have quadrupled in the last three minutes. The chat is absolutely eating it up."

Since she is now quite certain from his odd behavior that her interviewee is barking up some esoteric tree that might snap beneath them all at any moment, she tries to redirect to the reason they are here.

Let this be good fodder for YouTube clip reels, she thinks.

"So, not to detract from your dialogue tree polemic or anything, but we've got a lot to cover and I figure you want to let us know when you'll be releasing your next novel. The next Mr. Mortem novel. Right?"

"Because you don't like what I was saying before? You think avoiding the issue will dismiss it?"

Fiona chuckles. "No, no. I'm just trying to give you an out before you say something that we can't edit because it's live, that's all."

Her nervous giggles do nothing to deflate the growing tension, much as she wishes it would.

He finally turns to face her and his facial features are now much more sunken—almost gaunt. Skeletal and pale as a white linen sheet.

Fiona's eyes go wide.

Rocky in her ear: "Is he for real? Ask him! Push him! The chat is saying this is a scripted promo. Make sure to press him!"

Fiona obliges. "You expect us to believe that? That you've brought us up here to announce to the world that you're like the villainous mastermind of your own novels?"

Arms behind him, holding him up against the railing, he cooly replies, "I am saying that, yes."

"Okay, well, playing along with that for just a moment, why would we be inclined to believe you?"

"That's why I prompted you to ask. They're buried here like a macabre little garden. Not because I get off on it, mind you. No, this was but a simple means to a gruesome end. The squeaky wheel gets the grease, and in this case, the corpses get the clicks. 'Least, that's the plan, anyway."

Rocky whispers into her earpiece, "The live stream is going nuts. Whatever he's winding up for, they're all locked on. We're at like fifty K right now and climbing."

Without replying, she nods, then calls over to her wandering interviewee, "So you've got bodies in the backyard?"

"Yes."

"Why should we believe that?"

"Come see." With this, Danforth quivers and shakes in a full body spasm that lasts all of one second before he moves a few steps to his right and stops in front of a small, gray box mounted on the wooden rail. Inside, a red key switch. He pops open the opaque cover and turns the key.

Just over the side of the rail, coming from the backyard, is the unmistakable sound of machine works and rattling gears.

Fiona stands and walks casually close enough to where she can see over the railing. Watching as the ground opens wide with two swinging doors, she sees what is essentially a large square metal hole in the ground, maybe thirty by twenty-five feet, with mechanical metal doors that must be qn inch thick.

"What is that?" Fiona asks, a sense of horror slowly dawning in her mind as she notices several grayish limbs peeking out of the hole.

"Why, that's the Echo Chamber of Sorrow."

Danforth stands by while Fiona inches up to the railing and is immediately gobsmacked in the nasal passage by a foul odor floating past her. She holds her nose, and behind the techie setup, Rocky suddenly catches a whiff and does the same.

"Oh my good Lord, what is that smell? It smells terrible!"

"*That* is the smell of corpses piled up in small, airtight container and left to rot for months. Years, actually."

"What … what the fuck are those?" she asks, knowing damn well that they are either ridiculously well-designed mockups of corpses doused in something that truly reeks of death, or, more likely, they're exactly what they appear to be.

"Those are dead bodies," the author confirms, unfazed by the audacity of his own revelation.

In her ear, Rocky asks, "Is he serious? Are there dead bodies?"

Surveying the twisted limbs and bloodied bits of persons jutting out from the metallic hole, she calmly says, "Yes, these look like corpses, Rocky. And they smell like it, too." She wretches and dry heaves, doubling over. "I think I'm gonna be sick."

Without warning, she barfs some of the cheap airplane salad

she had en route to the interview onto her white (with stylish black ink blotting) Manolo Blahnik heels.

Rocky says to her, "Uh oh, that meme's gonna haunt you for a while."

Wiping her mouth, Fiona hollers, "I don't fucking care, Rocky! What the fuck do I do here?" She uses her hand to clear her chin and looks at the camera as if it's going to help somehow. "Rocky, please come here." Fiona starts to move away from Danforth.

Rocky removes his headphones and sets them carefully onto the keyboard. Coming around from his setup, he walks up, suspecting he's about to be third-manned in some elaborate prank when he sees what Fiona's talking about.

"Those—" he begins, then goes silent as the color and expression fall away from his face and his eyes go wide. He rushes over to where Fiona stands, about ten feet away from Mr. Daggersmith, and grabs her by the wrist, pulling her behind him while keeping his eyes locked on Danforth. "Dude, what the fuck are those?"

"Corpses. As I said."

"You're serious?"

"I'd hoped my grim revelation would assure you of my seriousness."

Now standing between Fiona and Dan and half shielding her with his arms, Rocky feels his muscles reflexively go taught, as if anticipating an impending physical attack.

"What is this? Are you— What is this? Why did you bring us here?"

"To show you and the world something that will terrify and befuddle you!"

"Befuddle?" Rocky asks, grabbing onto anything he can

while he slowly takes backward steps away from the edge of the railing. Fiona, nearly shaking with fear, has her hands clamped onto his shoulders, employing him as her human shield.

Danforth coughs and hacks, then spits several bloody teeth onto the deck, leaving a thin line of red running down from his lips. The teeth click on the wood and fall between the two by fours. He smiles red, then responds. "Befuddle, intrigue, mystify, bedazzle, and ultimately cause you to go rightly mad with questions left wholly unanswered. You know, all that jazz."

Still backing away toward the camera, which has all three of them framed in the shot, Fiona and Rocky nearly trip over the chairs they set up for the interview.

Fiona half-whispers from behind Rocky, "Are you okay, Mr. Daggersmith? That looked like more than one tooth you just evacuated there."

"Yep, yeah. This puppy is breaking down fast. Ever seen *The Fly*? Not the old one—I mean the Cronenberg one. Seen it?"

Rocky and Fiona push the chairs out of the way without taking their eyes off of the author. And yet, both manage to nod.

Dan finishes, "Well, it's kinda like that. Sort of."

Rocky tries to go for broke and skip to the question on everyone's mind. "You gonna try to add us to that pile, Mr. Daggersmith? Is that why we're here? So you can do a murder on live TV? Cause I don't think—"

"No! Dear boy, no! Perish the thought! No, I'm not going to add you to the chamber of sorrow, as it were. Frankly, it's already over booked!" At this, he lets out a shrill, high-pitched flurry of giggles, then slaps his knees and claps a few times. On the third clap, one of his fingers goes flying from the rest of his palm, skittering along the wooden deck.

Fiona and Rocky watch in stunned silence, mouths hanging open.

The laughing man's jubilation rapidly peters out and within a few seconds he stops. He clears his throat and starts to walk along the railing, running his remaining fingertips over the top. "But *seriously*, folks. No, you guys are more like direct witnesses to the glory of the descent. You're the Greek chorus in my supernatural dramedy. And you will allow others to behold the glory as well."

While slowing down a smidge, Rocky and Fiona continue to move in the direction of the house. But as both realize they do not wish to enter, they stop just shy of the sliding glass door which Danforth came out onto the deck from earlier.

When things hadn't yet gone fuck up.

Fiona smiles through clenched teeth and whispers as quietly as she can to her cohort, "We need to get out of here."

From thirty feet away, Dan responds, "I heard that. And there's nowhere to go. Besides, I'm not gonna hurt ya, just as I said I won't. And I'll be gone in a few minutes, anyway."

"Okay. Okay, okay… " Fiona starts, but can't seem to get any traction. She stops and cowers behind Rocky, who handily picks up the fumble and runs with it.

"So, Danforth, *if that's really your name—*"

"It isn't," Danforth interjects.

Fiona jumps back in from behind Rocky. "What's your real name?"

"Unpronounceable and unimportant. Please finish what you were saying." He waves his hands, palms up, urging her to finish.

But Fiona continues, "You killed a bunch of people and buried them in your backyard and wrote books about it and now you have us here because you claim you're going to, uh—that you're—"

"Going to descend to the molten core and cease its rotation, yes. That is what I said, Fiona."

"Okay. So what are we supposed to do with that?"

He hisses back, "You can watch *this!*"

Danforth suddenly uses his fingernails to plunge into the soft skin of his forehead and pull back flesh from the crown of his scalp. He starts to tear it away from the skull, rending off viscous sinew in long, wet, red strips. Nails rip the top flap from his skullcap in one motion, then he flings it across the deck, hitting the outer ranch house wall next to Rocky's head with a sloppy *fwap.*

"Aw, come on, man!" Rocky calls out, his hands unconsciously coming up to cover the top of his own skull at the macabre sight.

"Hold my scalp for me, would you?" Dan snickers, shooting Rocky a gaze which he, in turn, takes as his cue to take several steps away from the house.

Fiona, unable to speak, stands and watches, mouth still hung open, left eye twitching.

As she does, the man (or whatever he is) who they'd traveled to Starwood to interview, plunges his bleeding hands into his own shoulders and pulls off the shroud of human flesh he had been wearing, revealing a humanoid glowing form made largely of light, but with most of its face still intact. The skin suit crumples into his glowing ovoid palms, and he tosses over his shoulder into the backyard. It flops onto the dirt next to the square pit of unnamed victims.

Finally lifting the last layer of flesh from where his face had been, he drops it to the deck. Standing before them and emanating soft lulls of white light, he points one arm toward the control center Rocky set up nearby. In a voice that remains completely human, he says, "Can you go and man the torpedoes, Rock?"

"What?" Rocky mumbles, in a daze. He looks up from the bloody face mask on the ground and is startled by the form Danforth has taken.

Now unable to make out any facial features, Rocky hears the voice say, "Go make sure the feed is still good so the people might behold the raw glory of my descent to the molten core!"

Turning on his heel and sauntering toward the monitor, he mutters, "You gonna keep saying *descent to the molten core* like that?"

"I'm certain that I am, Rocky, yes. If you please."

The softly glowing being saunters over to a box lying on the deck against the house. He leans down and pulls open the lid, yanking free a large sack. The bag is opaque, but looks to be several gallons worth of small colored specks. Like a bag full of candy.

Fiona comes out of her brief fugue state and asks, "Why do you need that large sack of candy?"

"Nerds?" The abstraction of glowing white form shakes the semi-transparent bag in his grasp.

Fiona shakes her head. "We're not nerds; that's an odd thing to say. No, I was just asking—"

"No, I mean *Nerds*. They're Nerds—Willy Wonka candy. Nerds. You know, Nerds, man!"

"Nerds?" Fiona confirms.

"Yes, damn it! Nerds!" shouts the dazzling being made of shimmering light.

Fiona cocks her head to one side, stupefied. "Why— Why are you swinging around a bag of Nerds?"

"Because if I am to burrow to the Earth's molten iron core and stop the rotation of its central mass, I will need a whole lotta glucose. I prefer real sugar, but this high fructose shit will do just fine. Fuel for the fires. I'll take it. Should be a quick trip anyway. Maybe a day or two. Then you topside D-bags are utterly fucked."

Fiona looks at Rocky quizzically. He shoots her back a weary glance, shrugs, and calls to Fiona, "People don't think this is real. They keep saying this is bad product placement."

From somewhere in the faceless glowing void, Daggersmith shouts at the camera, shaking his sack of glucose fuel, "Oh it's real, folks! Real as this here bag of candy!"

Fiona shouts, "What about him ripping his own face off?"

"Uhhh, they just keep saying it's a deep fake. Over and over. *Deep fake, deep fake, deep fake.* Along with lots of politics and shit talking. Lots of *Biden sucks, Trump sucks, this show sucks,* flat Earth stuff, 4chan crap—you know. But yeah, no one actually believes this is really happening. I wish they could smell it. Holy fuck!"

Without any warning, the light being that Daggersmith has somehow transformed into leaps impossibly at least forty feet into the air. What the now hundreds of thousands of viewers see on their many screens is Fiona in the foreground, facing the western valley shelf, with the erstwhile Danforth floating above the backyard.

While the being of light is tucking into a series of rolls, it buries the candy sack in its softly glowing belly. Morphing into a perfect sphere, maybe two feet in diameter, it stays suspended for several seconds, then shoots toward the ground.

The sphere hits the earth, creating a searing red burrow that heads straight down. Bits of dirt and glowing hot rocks fly up from the hole like a mini geyser, however none make their way over to where the two dumbfounded Silverscreen.com employees are on the deck.

Long past caring about how this all looks to the viewers at

home, Fiona turns on her heel to face Rocky, who is off camera. She raises her hands over her head and shouts. "Holy shit! That was crazy! Totally crazy. Did we get all of that in frame? Please tell me we just got all that!

"Not everything, exactly, but yeah, we got a lot of it. Nobody is buying this though."

"What? How do they explain—"

"Well, they don't. They aren't. That's the thing. They don't want to explain; they want to bitch. It's turning into *Lord of the Flies* in the chat. More deep fake claims—"

"What the hell? But they just saw that with their own eyes!"

"I guess they don't believe their lying eyes or something, I dunno. Whatever. This is fucked."

Fiona furrows her brow and crosses her arms. She stands there for about ten seconds, trying to process what just occurred and how to proceed. She finally quietly asks the only thing she can think of. "What do you suppose happens when he reaches the Earth's core and stops the rotation?"

Rocky snorts. "A good reporter would've asked that!"

"Asked what?"

"You should've asked him while he was still up here and, uh, wearing his human suit—thing. Flesh suit, I dunno. You should've asked him then."

"You could've jumped in and asked, you know!"

"I'm not the reporter! That's your job!"

"Sure, right. Okay, yeah, next time I'll ask before the interviewee takes his human suit off and does a subterranean dive to the molten center of the planet. Next time, I'll make sure to slip that one in under the wire!"

"Probably not a bad idea if you do. Next time."

"Next time, right."

"That would be bad though, right? Like, we don't want that guy to stop the rotation of the Earth's core, right? That's not good, is it?"

"Well, I'm no geologist, Rocky, but I think I recall it being integral to maintaining the Earth's electromagnetic field."

"You sure about that?"

"No."

"Some reporter you are."

"Bite me." She studies the screen before them. "I can't believe we got all that! What are people saying? They gotta be coming around now, I bet! Gonna have to eat crow on this one after that show we just gave them!"

"No, I don't think that's what's happening here. People are just—they're just adamant that this is fake. That's the hot button word in the chat right now: *fake*. People are saying that this is a stupid publicity stunt and they want their stream donations back. Some are threatening legal action. Mostly they are angry they didn't get to ask any questions. Lots of flat Earth stuff."

Fiona stalks straight up to the camera and peers into the lens. Looking straight at her own reflection, Fiona points a finger toward the viewers at home and speaks in a cold, smooth tone, "What is wrong with all of you? You all just saw that shit! We don't have the budget for any wild VFX bullshit. Me and Rocky are the only—"

Off camera, Rocky corrects her, "*Rocky and I.*"

"Thank you, yes. I should've said that, thank you. *Rocky and I.* And I'm sure I can speak for Rocky and I when I say we are outta this motherfucker!" Fiona slaps the camera from the tripod, crashing it onto the ground. The livestream view is now a tilted shot of the deck.

Rocky's hands go up instantly, unseen by the viewers. "Fuck! Why'd you do that, you wild loon?"

Now invisible to the audience as well, Fiona says, "Sorry, sorry. I just— I wanted to end it with a dramatic gesture. Sorry."

"Dramatic? All you did was knock it over! That's *my* camera, and it's expensive! You didn't kill the transmission or anything. The feed is still live."

Fiona wheezes a long sigh, and asks, "It's still live? We're live?"

"Yes, you putz. Still live in '85."

"People are still watching?"

"Yes. They're hearing this too."

By now, Fiona's head is in her hands. "Christ, well then cut the feed!"

"Okay, okay. I can do that. Gimme a second. Okay, I'm cutting it—now!"

END OF TRANSMISSION

GROUNDED

Overly-anxious teenagers swarmed upon, then promptly crashed their bodies into the entry bars of the swinging double doors leading to the multi-story, open space atrium of the Fruita Dinosaur Exploratory Reserve Dig Site and Museum—instantly injecting the indoor space with crass tones, smartphones, hormones, and apathetically inert entitlement.

Once inside, the adolescent mob spread out like a deluge of germs flooding an infected wound and seizing upon the area, attaching themselves to various spots at random. Two fast-chatting single-cells strode toward the observatory deck, snapping selfies all the way, whilst a group of amoebas made a beeline for the gift store for an early gander. A studious line of protozoa formed in front of the entry to the 4D *Dino-Craze* theater, right next to a gaggle of flagellates fawning over a display of updated anthropomorphic rubber raptors.

Feathers now festooned the reptilian flesh of many of the rubber models, as recent scientific discoveries made omission of such novel adornments impossible to deny. Accurate modern representations of the dinosaur kingdom had relegated once fierce, fanged reptiles to little more than chicken puppet rejects from the Jim Henson workshop—mayhaps just this side of too ugly for primetime.

Passing one such feathered reptile near the entrance, Cory Hodges followed casually behind the primary push of adolescent flesh, walking into the big room and gazing skyward. His short brown hair was tucked under a mesh Meow Wolf trucker hat, and he had on jeans and a white tee.

Around him, the high-paneled ceiling shot up two stories, easily accommodating a large jungle-themed exhibit. Replete with faux terraria, it filled the room from stem to stern, with the clear skylights enhancing the untamed naturalist aesthetic. The air was humid and sweet, with fake plastic trees, interactive models, and robotic dinos lining the walls of the indoor nature preserve.

Despite the overly indulgent name—long crying out for an abbreviated refurbish—the place was still recognized as the premiere location for dinosaur study in all of Colorado, and by extension, one of the largest still operating large-scale dig sites in the continental United States.

As he scanned the room, Cory nearly tripped and fell when the broad, imposing shoulder of Rusty Kleen, consummate personal-space violator and classmate-intimidator of questionable authority, crashed into his own.

Standing at a solid five feet ten with a high and tight buzz cut, stretch black tee that showed off his arms, and a pit-viper's bedside manner, he was easily the tallest, strongest, and seemingly douchiest dude in their class.

Staring Cory down as he passed but failing to immediately force a shift in the former's eyes as he had hoped, he paused long enough to mumble, "Fuck around and find out," which did the trick in a jiffy.

Cory mumbled, "Sorry," then kept his peepers down for a good five seconds until ol' Rusty passed by, quickly disappearing into the faux fauna surrounding the class in all directions.

Once the larger boy had gone, Cory trudged on, knowing full well that such passive bullying was often indiscriminate and randomized, so there was probably no real issue there.

Roughly fifty 8th graders from Carbondale Middle School (possessed of varying levels of scholastic indifference), corralled and chaperoned by their teachers, Mr. Henry Wood and Mrs. Dara Smith, had made the two-hour sojourn to the edge of the western Colorado border. Day tripping to spend a spell digging up dino bones in the desert with experts in the field. Part of the ever-fruitful pursuit of sculpting young, impressionable minds into a focused worldview.

Fruita, a centuries-old repository for the skeletons of the long-deceased reptilian beasts, was no longer the booming center of paleontological study it had been during the '70s and '80s. 1993 had been a godsend for the flagging fossil-finding business, hand delivered by Spielberg and Crichton in a nice, neat bow. But the initial five-year jump in visitors and retail sales spawned by the *Jurassic Park* franchise had settled by the end of the '90s, and since then the Museum—built in '88—had naturally relied upon the steady influx of class trips to subsidize large portions of its operating budget.

Yet, gazing out over the somewhat outdated, if not downright anachronistic dig site, Cory only wanted to be at home, working on his second novel. The one about the space freighter that he'd been tinkering with for months.

On that cloudless, sun-dappled day that the world forever changed, Cory had thought he was going to have a chance to ask Kaitlyn McGraw to the homecoming dance.

Blonde, porcelain, and distinctly sweet smelling, he had been digging on her for a hot minute. But as he'd never asked a girl to a dance before, his buddy Tim had studiously informed him that her acceptance was all but assured. Of course, Tim had attained said intel by way of asking her best friend, Linda, who'd confirmed as much. Matchmaking by proxy.

Thank God one's friends in middle school are always so eager to insert themselves casually into your burgeoning love life—oft claiming co-credit for successes, then hurriedly denying involvement in the face of any failures.

Unfortunately, Cory would never have that chance.

Passing by the large windows, he could see a group of men and women in the dig site that lay three stories below. Roughly the same dimensions as a football field, the decades of diggers had, layer by painstaking layer, methodically carved out a bathtub-shaped concavity into the earthen sandstone quarry. The walls, as well as several outcroppings of stone within the quarry, were struck with gorgeous white striations along with multicolored banding from years of water and weathering.

The attention of those assembled along the far rim were not drawn to the centralized and heavily bored sections of the pit, but rather the far wall that ran up onto a small ridge where the topside ground met the hole's rim.

Though Cory had no idea if this was the case, he supposed that perhaps they were expanding the gross size of the hole by taking down shelving stone and compacted dirt from around the perimeter.

What Cory did know was that since they'd just had lunch, it was probably just after 1:00 p.m., which in turn meant they had roughly three hours before they would depart and head back to Bonedale.

He strolled by the gift shop with its rows of stuffed triceratops, hooks of blinking LED name keychains, racks of polished dino bone necklaces, and shelves of purple geodes. Momentarily debating about buying something cute for Kaitlin—which he could, in turn, have Tim hand off to her to get a convo going—he quickly dismissed the idea. She'd likely feel obligated to thank him, and that could go either way. It might even play as a bit heavy handed. So he decided discretion might be the better part of valor in this matter.

Doing a quick lap of the room, Cory had only been wandering for a few minutes when he came back around to the windows overlooking the dig pit. Several students had taken the nearby stairwell down, and were now poking around with small tools and being instructed by a large man with high waters and a wide-brimmed straw hat.

Standing about ten feet away from Cory was his homeroom teacher, Mr. Wood. Short cropped black hair; a thick, albeit well-groomed beard; and a brown vest with matching brown tie.

Perhaps as a defense mechanism developed during adolescence to deflect any heckling takedowns of his last name, Mr. Henry Wood possessed a wicked sharp mind, a slash of dark humor, and always gave it just the way he got it from the little rubber people he got paid to chaperone.

In fact, he was planning on leaving to double his salary in a nearby district at the end of the school year, so his level of giving a shit was at an all-time low. As such, he was comfortable speaking with the kids in a way that some of his current co-faculty at Carbondale Middle School would charitably describe as "a bit outdated," and some of his students would lament as, "a bit insensitive." However, it also had the effect, rather inexplicably to the others on staff, of endearing him to the student body like no other.

"Yo!" Mr. Wood hollered over the raucous din, settling the noise a tad. "We need everybody to gather over here for a few minutes. Time to force a little education into those hard heads of yours, like it not!"

"You callin' us dumb?" somebody shouted from within the flimsy folds of faux forest foliage.

Mr. Wood nodded. "Never to your face. Gather round. Come on; *chop chop* chuckleheads. We're on the clock."

Head-hung Gen-Z misanthropes shuffled like drugged donkeys into a rough assemblage before the big windows that looked down onto the football field sized dig site below. As they did, one tall and slender figure in black slacks, a white button up shirt, a lab coat, and horn-rimmed glasses, strode up to the space between the class and the glass overlooking the dig site, facing the kids.

Cory walked by him and joined his classmates several feet away.

The man at the head of the class appeared to be in his late forties and held a clipboard against his chest as he spoke. "Hi ho, hi ho! Welcome all to the Fruita Dinosaur Exploratory Reserve Dig Site and Museum! My name, for those of you who've been dying to know, is Dr. James Dane, and I am the head of research here. Just to dispense with the nerd-o credentials, I have a double doctorate in paleo-botany as well as biology, which no doubt gives you a good sense of how sad my social life during my twenties was. Roughly thereafter, I've been the de facto dino duster at this wonderful location for, um, well I guess about fifteen years or more now."

Dara Smith smiled kindly and said, "Thank you so much for having us, doctor." Her long brown hair was wrapped up in a large back knot, and she took her blue blouse in each hand as she did a half-curtsey to the man in the lab coat. "You kids want to thank the good doctor for giving us the lowdown on the dinosaurs today?" She smiled at the group, though few—if any—joined her, and those that did, did so ironically.

One sly-looking kid with a shock of spiky blonde hair strode out from behind two other kids and raised his hand. Dr. Dane pointed, and the kid asked, "Not for nothing, but is there really any more we can learn from dinosaurs? I mean, don't we pretty much know as much as we ever will? Isn't the age of big discovery over?"

"Leo, that's not exactly—" Mrs. Smith began, but Dr. Dane waved his hand, dismissing the scolding mid-sentence.

"It's fine, really. To answer, I think you'd be quite surprised, young man. And while conceptually I don't entirely disagree with the sentiment that the age of profound scientific discovery is essentially all but exhausted, it's somewhat hilarious how much we're still learning about these specific creatures to this day. Crazy stuff. Bonkers stuff. Stuff you might even be amused by. In fact, within the last few years alone, we've essentially been made to rework a whole mess of our presuppositions about the animals we study. We had to acknowledge that us paleontologists, well, we got a whole lotta shit wrong initially."

Part of a generation that always enjoyed a good voyeuristic mea culpa, the kid—Leo was his name-o—took the hook, "Like what?"

"Oh, well, let's see. Um, yeah, so for starters, we discovered Brontosauri as a species back in the late 1800s, but then within a few decades realized that they were the same genus as the Apatosaurus, right?"

"Yeah?" the blonde kid replied.

"Wrong! Turns out that we flubbed that one big time, pun intended. A few years ago, 2015 specifically, we ascertained that they were in fact two different dinos, just like we initially thought, and we had to re-re-write the old books."

Mrs. Smith nodded and warmly spoke up, "Well now, that's very interesting, doctor. I had no idea! What an interesting anecdote."

"If you say so," some dippy zoomer grumbled from the back.

Dr. Dane missed no beat. "Well how about the fact that dinosaurs are cold blooded? Does anybody know that one?"

A hand raised, and Dr. Dane pointed at the young woman. A small brunette girl with a red beret lowered her arm and said, "Everybody knows that."

Dr. Dane smiled, having gotten the exact reply he needed to cue up the following query to the group, "How about it, everyone. Did you all know that dinosaurs are cold blooded?"

Several snide quips and a whole mess of kids saying, "Yeah," and "Of course." A ball of paper flew up from the back, hitting someone at the front on the back of the head.

Dr. Dane clapped his hands together, and with his fingers laced, pointed his indexes at the class of kids. "Then that would make each and every one of you utterly incorrect! Because as of 2022, we know that they are, or *were*, in fact, warm blooded. Likely all of them."

Despite not one of the dazed scholastic slugs saying so, the sheer fact that none of them had any fresh sarcasm or passive hostility to lend voice to told the good doctor that he had managed to offer up something they couldn't readily shit upon.

Not wanting to lose them, he quickly concluded, "We may further infer from this that not one of you has been keeping up with paying your annual subscription fees to *Dino Digest Monthly*. Hmmm?"

At this, he got several chuckles from the kids, as well as approving smiles from both Wood and Smith.

"Is *Dino Digest* even a real thing?" some crass kid near the center of the flock asked.

Mr. Wood scowled and replied loudly without looking at the source of the comment, "Is that a question you really need the answer to, bucko?"

No one replied.

Wood smiled.

Dr. Dane pointed at several of the feathered, long-taloned raptors that lay in repose along the walls. "And as a great many of you undoubtedly have noticed throughout the years, we've needed to update our ideas of what they looked like."

"They look dumber now," one pugnacious rapscallion in the back chortled.

Dr. Dane nodded and sighed, running one hand through his short, salt-'n'-pepper hair. "Yeah, no—totally. I'm no fan of that particular development. I mean, it's certainly necessary to maintain a biologically accurate fossil record, but their implied ferocity sorta dropped off a cliff with that update."

Several students laughed at this as well.

"They look like those freaky things from *The Dark Crystal*," one chuckster quipped.

"Yes. Yes, they do…" Dane trailed off, gazing at the rubber figures, slightly shaking his head. A good second or two passed, then his head swiveled back to the group. "Anyway, the point is that even when you think that you've seen everything there is to see in this life, there's usually a surprise just around the corner." He smiled and rubbed his hands together. "That was a little parable at the end, there."

Someone audibly yawned.

A few seconds of silence passed, so Cory took the plunge. "So *Jurassic Park* had it right then?"

"What's that?" Dr. Dane held one hand flat over his eyes to cut down on the light shining into them as he peered over the heads of the rest of the class to where Cory stood.

Stepping forward, Cory cocked up his head in a feeble attempt to be more visible to the man in the lab coat. "That dinosaurs probably evolved over time into birds?"

"Yeah, that seems to be the most likely scenario and we know now that they had feathers like this. But it's worth crediting Robert T. Bakker—the paleo guy they mention by name in that film—as a big reason for a lot of this. Aside from being hugely influential and partly responsible for the dino renaissance of the eighties and nineties, he was also one of the first serious voices within the field to further the theory about dinos being both feathered and warm blooded. Despite being an early outlier with some of these conclusions, over time, the more we discover, the more correct Bakker's theories seem to become. In our rarified trade, he is *da man*."

Mr. Wood walked in front of the group, past Dr. Dane, tracking the movement of one student. That student was Rusty Kleen, who had broken off from the larger cluster and was standing in front of one of the nearby Utah Raptors lying in wait behind a fake bush made of plastic leaves.

Rusty snickered, turning to face the man in the white coat. "So these were huge chickens, yeah? Really tall, fat roosters?"

"Not roosters, exactly, but yeah—really big chickens. Sure. That's essentially accurate."

Rusty smiled, having secured the setup he needed to deliver the punchline. "So these are some pretty fucking huge cocks, aren't they?"

The class burst out in laughter.

Mr. Wood snorted, but ultimately reprimanded Rusty just the same. "All that setup and that's as good as the punchline gets, Rusty? *Tsk tsk*. You can go take a seat over there now and can it. Really classy stuff. Just put your butt down and keep it to a low hum if you relish the absence of scholastic suspension in your life, Mr. Kleen."

Rusty winced and clenched his fists as he started to walk over to the nearby table. The moniker was clearly something that he didn't appreciate being called. He stared daggers through Mr. Wood, who in turn paid him zero mind.

Several of his classmates, temporarily emboldened by the safety granted them by sheer numbers, giggled as he sauntered over to the bench on one side and plunked down hard.

He took a seat, and grumbled, loud enough for everyone to hear, "Fuck around and find out."

With that, his classmates immediately went silent. Mrs. Smith put her hand to her mouth and Mr. Wood laughed. Wood then shot Dane a look and did a loop with his finger.

The doctor clapped once more and said, "Guess I'll wrap this up. All I'm driving at is that scientific curiosity is usually rewarded. It can take a while though, as was the case with Mr. Bakker. But time rewards those that keep at it. As you all cruise through the exhibits, remember that you could always be the one to discover something that no one else has."

At that very moment, per some cosmic cue, a single metal door, painted to match the jungle fauna theme and built directly into the wall adjacent to the large window panes, swung open. A man in a white coat—short, blonde, goateed—rushed in, panting, and waved at Dr. James Dane.

"Sir, we've found something!"

❦

While Cory was taking extra time to appreciate the level of detail in some of the displays that were set up in the Gallimimus Grotto, the teachers, all the scientists, and most of the students had emptied into the dig site outside. It was not lost on him that several of these displays were works in progress. The odd missing rubber limb; a few uninstalled name placards. Even some of the films playing through various wall-installed screens seemed incomplete.

As the gibbering swarm of prepubescent douchebaggery flocked to and fro outside, Cory sat before one educational console watching a short reel on herbivores. Eight VHS-quality minutes of education later, he stood up. While making his way toward the bathrooms by the gift shop, he glanced out of the big glass windows, noting that the bulk of the people outside had again coalesced into a tighter group.

This gave him pause.

Almost everyone outside had encircled one area situated high up the far wall of the stony pit where he'd seen the other museum employees earlier. It was hard to tell, but Mr. Wood appeared to be helping several other men who were, in tandem, slowly carrying some sort of dark, flat object away from the wall and toward the museum. Whatever they had was causing a stir, as several students, including his buddy Tim, seemed quite giddy and excitable, snapping photos with their smartphones.

After briefly running in and using the bathroom, he came out to see that the mob had disappeared into the stairwell and elevator leading up to the facility. Like him, a few other students were lackadaisically floating about the atrium, intellectually nibbling on tidbits of paleontological data.

Dr. Dane was across the room, using the phone behind the reception desk to make a call.

When the doors to the elevator opened, allowing the three men carrying the tablet to enter, everyone gathered around, buzzing about and chattering like hungry flies. The doors to the stairwell flew wide as bodies oozed out like toothpaste squeezed from the tube.

Dr. Dane hung up his call and waved to the three men carrying the large object. "Let's put it on the mapping table over here. It can take the weight. Come on."

The doctor led the others away from the big glass windows and toward the area that was utilized for actual scientific studies, rather than those of the money-raising or scholastically-enriching variety.

A separate room lay just beside the gift shop, not far from the front entrance. It was partitioned by tall walls of plexiglass and filled with microscopes, pressurized air blowers, vacuum hoses, dangling drills on rubber ropes, black countertops, wall-hung clipboards, and dinosaur bone fragments jutting out from unearthed mounds of time-sealed sandstone. Just outside of that room stood a very large table with a labeled mockup of the dig site under a two-inch layer of transparent epoxy.

Shuffling carefully past the gift shop and over to a large wooden table, Henry Wood and the scientists from the facility carefully held the tableau between them. The line of chirping adolescence clicked along behind them like tin cans tied beneath a *Just Married* placard.

Approaching the thick edge of the flat plank mahogany table, the three men rotated it so that they could lower the dense stone onto the wood without dropping it. However, when they cautiously removed their fingertips from beneath the slab, it dropped the remaining centimeters onto the table with an audible *thunk*.

"Holy moly!" one of the two men whom Henry had helped lug the thing in exclaimed.

All three backed away slowly, allowing Dr. Dane to come in closer and lower his head to the surface. He pulled a small magnifying glass from his pocket and scrutinized the face of it.

Mr. Wood waved at Mrs. Smith, who was just coming into the room from the stairwell. The kids speculated about what it could be, randomly tossing out words like, "aliens" and "curse." But none of the adults reacted to them, instead treating it as the exciting archaeological discovery that it could very well be.

"I, uh—" Dr. Dane began, then caught himself, scrolling toward the bottom of the tablet. "We're just going to keep it up here on this table until we can clear some space in the Dino Discovery Den—our little hovel where we clean fossils for assembly of larger specimens or, if not possible, documented, cataloged, then stored…" He trailed off momentarily, still wrestling with the magnitude of the discovery. "Then we go from there. This is unreal! Did you already dust it off?"

One of the two men—a dirt-caked fella with dark jeans, a handbag 'stache and a blue button up—who'd helped their teacher carry up the bounty along with the goateed man from earlier, answered, "Of course not! It's odd, but it sorta came out like this. Very well polished. Mayhaps a distinct absence of a porous surface so nothing sticks? I dunno. Oddly though, it looks obsidian. Which, if true, would be ridiculous. Either way, we're heading back out because we think there's going to be some other stuff beneath it."

"Really?" some jabbering rubber person asked.

Dr. Dane nodded and said, "I'll stay up here with it and won't let it out of my sight. I'm gonna call Fitzsimmons. What do you think is beneath it?"

"We got one tap into the ground giving us ground radar and at a glance it looks like a box, possibly made of wood," the other man said, then began to walk toward the elevators again.

"A wooden box? That's … well, I guess that kinda puts the kibosh on that, doesn't it?" Dr. Dane spoke softly, winching as if in pain.

"Yeah. That's what I was telling the kids on the way up. Too bad," the man spoke without looking back as he crossed into the elevator.

Dr. Dane remained in place, scrunching his eyebrows and once again leaning over the tablet with the looking glass to study the characters on its surface. Tiny, engraved symbols, nearly undetectable to the naked eye, ran along the black, reflective surface.

Mumbling to himself, Dr. Dane mused, "So odd…"

One quick-witted teenager declared, "It's a fake!"

Another agreed, "Probably part of a scavenger hunt or something. Let's go find a real dinosaur!"

Students began to lose interest, slowly filing back out the stairwell doors to rejoin the rest of the group outside. Both Mr. Wood and Mrs. Smith, likely co-sensing some hijinks about to occur, quickly followed suit.

As the exodus continued, only two students remained.

"What's odd?" one inquiring mind ventured.

Dr. Dane noticed that it was Cory, again asking the right kind of question, and smiled. "Well, if we're breaking it down by the numbers, and supposing that what my colleague just portended ends up being the case, it can't have been there very long if it's in a wooden box. Certainly not more than a couple hundred years max, but likely a whole lot less than that."

"So you don't think this is a capstone of some type?" Cory asked.

Several of his classmates shot him looks as they sauntered away. Dr. Dane, however, leaned forward and gave him a thumbs up.

"Normally I would think so, if I weren't so dubious of its antiquity."

"So you suspect it's a hoax?" Cory asked.

"Yeah," the doctor mused, chuckling. "Yeah, I do. But an odd one, as I said. It's just, if there's a box … I dunno. I dunno. Might be a primitive time capsule, or it could just be a dumb prank. At the moment, I'm leaning toward the latter. One thing it isn't, is anything prehistoric. *C'est la vie.*"

Striding directly up to the edge of the black stone, Cory's eyes moved to James's for approval, which he subtly received from the older man. Cory gently ran his fingertips over the surface while the doctor watched. Noting that the inscription was broken up into smaller groups of characters, the young man tilted his head and it occurred to him what he was looking at.

Dr. Dane watched as Cory's eyes gleamed with fascination. He relished that look on kids' faces. For it was, just as with so many things of the past, increasingly rare to see nowadays.

"This—I think this might be a Caesar cipher," Cory suggested. He ran his finger along the surface for another moment, then concluded, "Yeah, I'm almost certain that's what this is. I can try to break it that way, anyway. See what happens."

James Dane was inclined to agree and smiled. "That's what I was thinking as well."

From a heretofore silent position just a few feet away, Rusty Kleen, who'd been waiting for the others to head off and watching with some passive level of interest finally spoke. "What's a Caesar cipher?"

Dr. Dane decided to jump in and answer. "It's a substitution code. Basically *A* equals *F* and so on. In this case, young Mr...." He motioned toward Cory.

"Cory Hodges," the young man answered.

"Young Mr. Hodges here is suggesting that it's a simple form of cryptography. Something a second grader with the right knowledge can solve. And looking at it now, I am inclined to agree."

Rusty drew a step closer, intrigued.

"May I try to decipher some of this writing here?" Cory asked, trying not to sound too excited.

Dr. Dane brought his clipboard up to his chest and asked, "Do you think you can break it?"

Without hesitation, Cory nodded vigorously. "Oh yeah. I mean, yeah, I think so. If it's just a Caesar cipher, it should be easy as pie. That's assuming it's in English, too."

Smiling, James asked, "Ever thought about a career in the scientific field, son?"

Cory astutely answered, "Yeah, a bit. And that's probably what I'm going to try and focus on in college. Might be tech, but who knows? But yeah, science for sure." His right index fingertip traced each indentation carefully, each carved to near-laser precision.

Dr. Dane looked around. Seeing only Rusty eyeballing them both from a few feet away, he leaned in and spoke to Cory in a more hushed tone, "It shouldn't be a big deal if you're mindful not to scratch the surface with anything. But as you can see, it's a big, tough chunk of stone. Looks durable. And we'll probably polish it in the coming weeks once we run it by a few others. Speaking of, while you keep from doing anything damaging to this thing, I'm gonna run over and make a quick phone call. Start cracking the code if it pleases you and I'll be back in a few minutes. But I'll be within eye shot, just there." James pointed at the reception desk not too far from where they were. "You good, Cory?"

Cory nodded, understanding and appreciating the gesture. "Yeah, we're good. I'm good. It's all good. I'll see if this thing is just an old recipe for stewed cabbage or something."

"Jesus, I bet it's gonna be something silly and banal like that, all right." Dr. Dane tousled his hair as he walked over to the reception desk and crossed behind it to use the phone.

Cory pulled out his cell phone and tapped his thumbprint on the screen to unlock it. Opening up a notepad, he tapped another icon which allowed him to take a photo, then write on top of the picture he'd just taken. After snapping a shot of the onyx stone and the symbols etched into it, he started to rapidly replace letters and take guesses at what the smaller two character words might be.

"So is it a tombstone or some shit?" Rusty had casually come within viewing distance of the onyx tablet. His eyes gazed at the symbols cut into the slab's face, his arms crossed so as to make him look like a bouncer.

Cory reflexively tensed up as Rusty drew close, but steadied himself enough not to let it show. *Probably nothing to worry about there,* he thought.

"Not exactly. Maybe a capstone of sorts, but I don't think that's what it's going to end up being either." His fingers kept clicking on the smartphone keyboard, then crossing out letters, then switching them around. As character after character was failing to fit, he suddenly realized that the message was not in English. It was, surprisingly enough, in Spanish. And serendipitously, he'd been taking Spanish for two months now. He might not have been fluent yet, but he was conversant enough to start subbing out a few characters for their letter counterparts.

It took him about two minutes to start creating the substitution alphabet along the bottom edge of the picture, so he could rapidly solve the surprisingly brief text puzzle.

Leaning over his shoulder and peering at the slab, Rusty asked, "What's it say?"

"Um, not quite sure yet. But I think it's in Spanish. It's just a basic substitution cipher like the doc said, and now that I'm looking at it, it's coming up with 'el' and 'la' and 'y', so yeah, this is gonna be Spanish. Somebody wrote this after translating it to Spanish, and then encoded it."

"Why?" Rusty asked.

"I'm guessing just a whole pile of boredom. I mean, why does anybody do anything? And honestly, why bury some encoded black tombstone next to a dino quarry? It's weird. And—"

Dr. Dane cradled the phone between his shoulder and ear

while he cupped one hand over the receiver's mouthpiece and looked over at the two young men. "What is it?"

"It looks like it's in Spanish," Cory answered loudly. "Do you have anyone who speaks Spanish fairly well in this place?" Cory thought about it for a split second then said, "I guess one of our classmates could—"

Rusty chuckled, snorted, and scoffed in rapid succession. "Dude, that's what Google is for."

Fair enough, Cory thought to himself.

"Okay, sure, so do you have a cell phone we can use to find out what I've got subbed out on this one?" he asked.

Rusty smiled and pulled his Motorola smartphone from the pocket of his jeans, then tossed it to Cory, who caught it easily.

Without looking, Cory asked, "Is there a passcode or anything?"

"Of course not," Rusty replied.

"Not worried someone is gonna go through it if they find it?"

"I figure that'll be the least of their worries if they touch my shit without my say so. They can fuck around and find out. Trust me, that shit don't play. So no code. Just fists that wail on a punching bag full of steel BBs for an hour a day."

Cory nodded and grinned. "Hard to argue with fists. But it's okay if I use it for a second, right?"

"It's cool since you asked." While saying this, Rusty reached down into his right sock. After making sure Dr. Dane was still preoccupied with his call, he pulled forth a marijuana vape pen, promptly taking a hit off of it. He stood back up and walked over to where there was a bit of dense foliage and blew thin wisps of smoke into them, apparently giving only the faintest of craps about the possibility that his subterfuge might be discovered.

Then, returning to the table, he watched as Cory finished replacing the symbols with letters.

Cory tapped for another few seconds, then stopped and held it up. Minus one or two anomalies, he seemed to have it figured out. And what he saw made his nose scrunch. He quickly started to pull up a translator on Google.

"Okay. Cool, cool."

While he tried not to show it, this side of Rusty was quite disarming and interesting to him. It's funny when someone who has classically been rude or aggressive toward you suddenly changes their stance; you're so relieved that you don't immediately question the tenuous bonds upon which your current armistice relies.

Think Stalin in WWII.

Still, Cory would take what he could get, when he could get it.

"Here." Cory handed his phone with the mostly broken cipher to Rusty. "Hold this up so I can just type in what it says there. I don't have every letter but I think that if I use Spanish auto-correct it should work. Unless it's oddly phrased, employs regional colloquialisms, whatever…"

Rusty simply stared at Cory with a blank look on his face.

Cory shook his head. "Just hold it up so I can translate it. I'mma put it in now. I know what some of this says though, and it's … honestly, have you seen the movie *The Goonies*?"

"Of course, man," Rusty rolled his eyes.

Entering the last bit of Spanish, Cory hit the *translate* button and watched bold, all-caps letters fill the smartphone screen.

"Okay, well, I think we got *sangre* and *bestia* here, so it sounds about as foreboding as One Eyed Willy's Treasure Map, though I doubt that it's…" Cory's voice trailed off as his eyes read the message he'd translated with the phones.

It was right about then that the two heard the tell-tale sound of the receiver hitting the cradle as the doctor hung up and returned to them.

"That was a colleague of mine from Denver—Dr. Fitzsimmons. Says he's gonna make a special trip out in the morning to give this thing a gander before someone talks about carting it off to one of the bigger institutions."

"They can just take it from you like that?" Rusty asked, seemingly genuinely interested in the puzzle at hand.

"Well, it's a scientific community, Rusty, so they aren't exactly 'taking it from me.' We try to share what we discover in pursuit of acquiring knowledge as we are able. So much that we seek is hard won, so we will always gladly take the small leaps if able. And the more bodies you have working a problem, the easier it is to solve."

Rusty grinned and clapped Cory on the shoulder, hard. "Well worry not, because your boy already done closed the case on this one, *righ-cheuh*. It's some ol' bullshit in Spanish."

"Really?" Dr. Dane asked Cory, raising an eyebrow. The young man nodded, and the doctor's eyes quickly darted over to the far window as he spied his colleagues surrounded by students. They were digging around the area where the tablet had been discovered earlier.

Dr. Dane began, "Looks like they're pulling something else out of the ground over there. I wonder if it's just a box, like—"

"Uh," Cory interrupted the doctor, "so this, uh, says some fairly crazy shit. I–it must be a joke, like you thought it might be…"

Genuinely excited, James Dane asked, "You got it? What's it say?"

"It says quite a lot, actually. But…"

"Well, like what?" Rusty pressed.

"It's like a warning. It's … yeah, it's a warning. Those jokers outside should not open anything they find in the ground below—"

"Looks like they already have! Or are. Whatever. But they got something!" Rusty pointed toward the glass and the three standing by the onyx tablet watched helplessly while the people digging along the far wall pulled a black box free from the soft dirt lining the pit. It appeared, even at this distance, to be time-worn, but likely not wood, as it was in good condition. The assembled outside group carefully lowered it onto the earthen floor of the pit while forty or more kids held up their smartphones as if seeing it through the screen might reveal some hidden truth, otherwise undetectable.

"Uh, so that's probably not good," Cory warned, his eyes no longer on the phone but on the box being opened outside, revealing…

"What's not good, Cory? Don't be obtuse; just show us what it says," Rusty complained.

Cory did not hesitate to flip the phone around and hand it to Rusty who, in turn, held it up for both he and Dr. Dane to read. Two sets of wide eyes began to read the translated text:

DO NOT REMOVE THE SEAL FROM THE BEAST. THE BEAST BELOW SHALL MAKE MORE OF ITSELF AGAIN AND AGAIN UNLESS IT REMAINS IN THE GROUND. IT MUST BE KEPT BURIED. DO NOT LET THE BONES INTO THE LIGHT. KEEP THE CURSED BONES OF THE BEAST HIDDEN FROM THE LIGHT OF DAY OR THE BEAST WILL RISE AND DESTROY. IF YOU VALUE ANYTHING, DO NOT REMOVE THE SEAL. ONLY THE BLOOD OF THE DRAGON TREE OR PITCH DARKNESS

CAN HINDER ITS SPREAD. DO NOT REMOVE THE SEAL. DO NOT AWAKEN THE BEAST.

Lowering the screen, Rusty and James both looked at Cory, who had an inquisitive look across his face.

"It's weird, right? Does that mean the beast is in that box out there? Are they… Are those assholes about to let loose the beast?" As he said the words, he started to laugh at how silly it sounded when spoken aloud.

Rusty smiled as well.

Outside, unseen by the three, the box now lay open and everyone around gazed upon a set of black bones, laid out within the interior.

Dr. Dane sighed. "Yeah, that's kinda fun and a bit spooky. And a damn shame it isn't something better. At the very least it's gonna be a nice little exercise to figure out who put it there and to see what's actually in the box. But if it were a legitimate warning, then why would whomever go to all the goddamn trouble to encode it as though it's hand-chiseled nuclear secrets or something that—"

Before James Dane, holder of two doctorates, could finish the sentence, howls of agony blended with screams of terror rattled the glass from the outside.

The two boys and the doctor turned from the table with the tablet and hastily made their way across the room to where the paneled glass looked down on the dig site.

People were scurrying about in all directions but not getting very far as a swirling blur of black talons spun like a centrifuge, ripping past people and tearing chunks of flesh asunder as it did. Arterial sprays from untold scores of necks flew up in a misty fountain of red. Bodies were flung about like ragdolls, randomly crashing into rocks on the hard dirt earth.

The two young men's wide eyes turned slowly toward the adult in the room.

Dr. Dane's jaw trembled and he turned as white as the lab coat that hung from his shoulders. Both eyes rolled back in his skull as his body dropped to the floor in a crumple of limbs.

"Damn. I didn't think people actually fainted like that," Rusty observed, gazing down at Dr. Dane, who lay unconscious on the floor with a trickle of blood oozing from a fresh head wound. He used the steel-toed tip of his Doc Martens shoe to nudge the lab coat-covered arm of the fallen paleontologist. It flopped slightly as the man remained on the reflective, white flooring, unmoving. "He's out as fuck."

Rusty and Cory stood side by side, watching the madness unfolding below them on the dig site through slanted window-panes. Several of the scientists had swooped directly into the fray to try and be of some help, but lacking any formal training in exfiltration of victims from violence-filled scenarios, seemingly only offered themselves up as fresh lambs to the slaughter.

The speed with which the creature sprung from body to body, ripping pieces of people apart and chomping at soft throats in red splashes of gore, was almost too fast for either of the young men's eyes to track. The handful of white lab coats were soon redder than the stone that lined the dig pit's far stony ridge and crumbled onto the ground atop the corpses of the dead men and women who now filled them.

The movement was so rapid that an opaque brown cloud, like a small vortex, began to engulf the area. Swirling dust, severed limbs, ears, and even the odd gore-stained bit of organ flew outward from the spinning chaos.

Cory watched as, amid the expanding dust cloud shrouding

the massacre, his classmates were being dispatched in startlingly short order. His eyes closed for a moment to give his mind respite from the horror before him, but he opened them again a few seconds later when Rusty drew his attention to the pit slaughter once more.

"Check out Wood and Smith, dude." Rusty pressed his index finger against the glass.

Mr. Wood had grabbed Mrs. Smith and was making a beeline for the door below that led up to the visitors' center. Whatever was killing everyone within the pit had seemingly allowed them to escape, relatively unscathed, via stage left.

Or it simply hadn't noticed. More likely that than the former.

It wasn't ten seconds before the two burst through the same painted door built into the wall that they'd seen the goateed chappie emerge from earlier.

Rushing past Rusty and Cory without slowing, Henry Wood shouted, "I'm callin' in an early retirement! Fuck all this noise; we're outta this death zone! You should leave too, boys, but I'd be lying if I said I gave a fuck anymore! Later, assholes!"

Running in stride with Mr. Wood was the frightened and meek Mrs. Smith. She said nothing, just barely managing a feeble half wave as she zipped past the young men. The pair of educators rocketed through the front doors and out into the parking lot without looking back.

Rusty laughed. "That's pretty funny."

Cory gulped, finally feeling how dry his throat had suddenly become. "Is it though?"

Cory watched as what appeared to be a pitch black skeleton started to materialize between gusts of dust. Still widening wings flapping with unnatural speed, it tore through his classmates with reckless abandon. He'd seen something like this in some zombie hunter video game once. Not this exactly, but close enough.

Bloody, brutal, and above all, brief, the whole massacre lasted less than two wildly traumatizing minutes while Cory and Rusty peered through the tilted and tinted glass onto the dig site below in abject horror.

One of the last victims taken from this mortal coil was his homecoming-date-never-to-be, Kaitlyn. He watched her make a valiant effort to reach the door two floors down from his high vantage, but she was stopped and slashed down the middle, bloodily bisected by the monster's surprisingly human hand-shaped claw.

Rusty chuckled and tapped the glass with his fingertip. "Isn't that your girlfriend?"

Cory gazed down at the two halves of his erstwhile crush and quietly mumbled, "Eh, not really. But I was gonna ask her out."

Rusty saw the other boy's empty face, lowered his finger, and nodded, frowning. "Guess that's a bust."

"Yeah," Cory agreed. "Gotta figure something else out for homecoming."

Scrunching his thick brows, Rusty asked, "Think there'll still be a homecoming?"

A thick chunk of bloody scalp was suddenly tossed free from the confines of the ruckus and flew up and toward the visitors' center window. Splatting against the glass in front of Rusty with a *plunk*, both boys watched it slide slowly down, leaving a thin smear of red as it descended.

Cory finally replied, "Guess we would be a few classmates shy at this point, huh?"

Rusty nodded, then returned his eyes to the chaos outside. "People shouldn't dig in the dirt."

"Yeah."

"Fuck around and find out," Rusty concluded.

"I'm hearing that," Cory readily concurred.

Rusty held out his fist without looking over at Cory. Keeping his own gaze fixed forward, Cory met the taller boy's knuckles with his own.

BOOM.

Outside, the literal dust began to settle as the onyx muscled beast rose up as an unholy demon, arms fully outstretched, expanding the folds of its ragged wingspan. Wet, maroon-tinged musculature and taught licorice sinew coiled around its slippery biomass as a writhing pile of interlaced black serpents. Each beat of two massive, leather-thick wings started to carry it further aloft.

Still rising, several squirming lengths of slick, black flesh—wriggling along the sternum, the thighs, the tendon-framed neck of the beast—began falling to the ground. Maybe a hundred dark serpent shapes dropped fifty or more feet upon the dusty earth and started to burrow one side of their slug-like bodies into the soft ground.

Once those fat, ugly sea cucumbers started to dig down, the creature—the gargoyle, as everyone would soon come to call them—swooped down in an arc, then used the downdraft on its wings to pull itself back up. With one more big push, it flew off into the distant horizon, flapping its wings every so often. In a matter of seconds, it was hard to see against the bright yellow ball of the setting sun. Soon, a dot—and then completely gone.

Watching the thick, black wormy things digging down into the cracked and bloodied dig site dirt below, Cory noted, "I doubt those things are gonna be something we wanna stick around for. We should get while the getting's good."

His eyes locked onto the nearest viscous onyx slug burrowing its girth into the split ground, Rusty couldn't agree more. "Yep. That's, uh, yeah… Let's get the fuck out of this bitch."

Cory nodded and they both ran toward the exit, shooting out into the parking lot.

⚊⚊⚊⚍⚊⚊⚊

On that day, the dark denizens of the midnight skies, known to most by their formerly fictionalized moniker *gargoyles*, commenced what was likely the beginning of the end for all mankind.

As it stands today, the burgeoning swarms of savage, ravenous, and blood-lusting gargoyles that plague our civilization—often in numbers great enough to blot out the midday sun—have circumnavigated the globe with no end in sight. They are capable of moving through the air faster than most aircraft, and nothing we've done as humans has hindered their spread.

They indiscriminately kill man, animal, woman, child—any living creature they fall upon. Buzzing down, snatching someone, then disappearing into the cloud cover always faster than anyone can react to. Humans, as a species, now live in unyielding fear of becoming food.

We've built bunkers and fruitlessly fired our useless weapons, but still they are winning. The terror is a bottomless void. Estimates are that they number in the millions, though no one knows for sure and global communications have become difficult, if not downright Neolithic. It is all but impossible to track them as they've disabled or destroyed essentially all airplanes, satellites, helicopters, jets, and even larger drones. Effectively anything that we can put up into the air, they readily smack right back down.

One video that was wildly popular before the internet

disappeared entirely showed a muscular charcoal-colored gargoyle one-shot punching an F-16 out of the sky whilst completely un-affected by both the jet's twin cannons, as well as one well-aimed sidewinder missile.

None of our ballistics penetrate their flesh. Neither do explosives. The sky now belongs to them.

What we do know for certain, via the radio communications that we have been reduced to, is that the population of the entire world as of 2024 was a few million shy of eight billion. Now, in 2025, after just one year of them spreading like locusts across the night skies, we are down to less than six billion, with no sign of slowing.

We are being wiped from the surface of the planet.

And you *could* say we're all pretty well fucked, *couldn't you*?

But then, for that to matter at all, we as humans would require a whole lot more concern about our own impending doom, now, wouldn't we?

Lucky for us, we are burdened by no such practical fear.

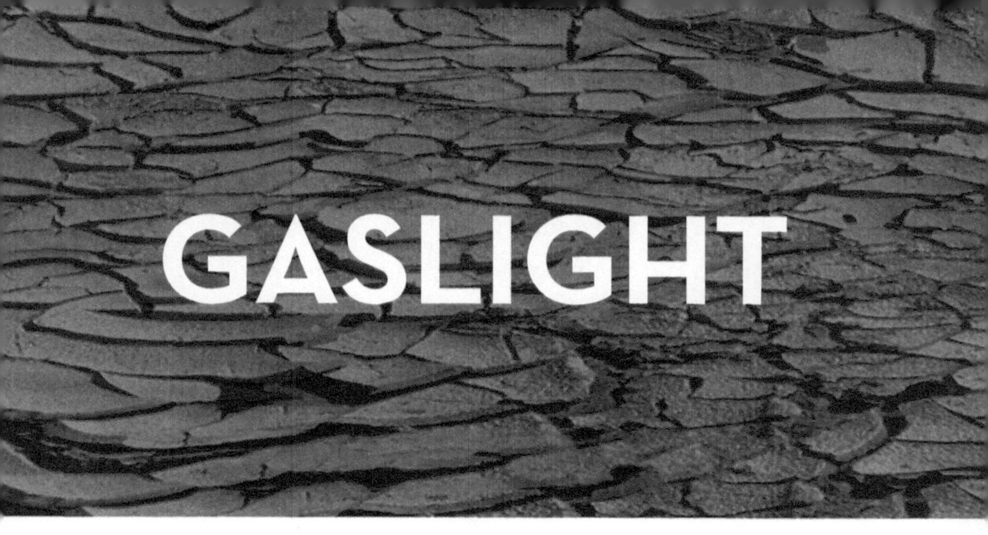

GASLIGHT

Jillian Karen Amway was always noticing how much people gaslit her. Now, she was told time and time again by her fellow residents of Redstone, Colorado that accusing other folks of gaslighting was tantamount to calling them a pervert or a wife beater or somethin'. But that damn sure didn't stop her from believing that near every other person she was forced to endure during the course of her day-to-day struggle to avoid people altogether was happy to gaslight the ever-loving shit out of her.

She could tell. They weren't fooling anyone.

The neighbor, Mr. Briggs, gaslit her regularly when she politely suggested he should strive to maintain lawn grass height that did not exceed the HOA's rigorous guidelines on the matter. *Not to be longer than three inches, unless it's fall or winter.* It was right there on page 147 of the HOA handbook.

He could've looked it up.

She was too-often gaslit by the tall, freckled lady at the post office. Every time Ms. Amway had to drop a package of sundry goods into the mail for shipment to her sister in Georgia, she'd politely suggest that they might update their systems so she could track the package in real time. But they never did. Never. She had to wait, often *days*, to find out whether the package had arrived or not. Which she disliked, a whole lot.

Her priest, the one who had been with the church and doing sermons for her and the local people every Sunday morning for over thirty years, was oft-prone to the odd *lighting of gas*. No matter how many times she politely suggested that in lieu of tap water, he might use Aquafina—or some other purified water to fill the holy water fount near the front entrance—he did *nothing* to spare her from the chemical flavor of the town stuff. It made her mouth taste as though she was sucking on a nickel. It was just dreadful, truly. But it didn't seem to bother others the way it did her.

Most people will allow themselves to be walked all over. But then again, in Jillian's view, an increasingly large segment of the population was downright amoebic in their higher-level reasoning. If they'd just listen to her, it'd be so much easier.

Instead, you know what they did?

Whether it be the "funny" mailman on her route, the "clever" zoomer who checked out her groceries at the supermarket, or even the "sweet" old lady who groomed her dog, Muffy, the story remained the same: Gaslight, gaslight, gaslight. All day, every day, she was doggie paddling, chin-deep through a murky quagmire of horseshit and endless gaslighting.

And nobody cared. They never apologized. They never made amends. They acted like it was all good.

Well you wanna know what?? It wasn't all good!! Not one damn bit!! Not that you asked or anything!!

The torrent, the flood—nay, the goddamn *Cat 5 hurricane*—of gaslighting she was made to endure on a weekly basis had left her without any other choice. After thinking for weeks about how to resolve her dilemma, the only course of deliverance became abundantly clear.

She would just have to convince the townsfolk to gather at the local meeting hall so that she could burn it to the ground with them all trapped inside.

Yep, she figured, that should do the trick. This time she would light a little gas of her own.

And so our mean little lady over here decided to set herself about the task at hand. It's amazing what you can do when you focus all your energy on a singular goal, and it wasn't three weeks before the main parts of her plan lay at the ready for execution.

Her high school acquaintance, Toby, had helped her acquire a few barrels of diesel, wholly unaware of her dark intent. She'd bought the other necessary pieces, parts, and odd bomb components from a handful of different places. Mostly small outfitters and always with cash. The fertilizer she got from Walmart.

It took her several test bombs in the woods (to say nothing of too many hours spent on YouTube, as well as Reddit), to get one workable idea that would ensure maximum damage.

Just one shot to get them all.

She chose a cold and frosty Saturday in mid-October to convince the rest of the wee hamlet's denizens to gather within the meeting hall's warm confines, under the auspices of a community-wide potluck. And to really sell it all, she'd had the women's auxiliary and the nearby chapter of the loyal order of Moose help her coordinate who would bring what. Cindy L. would bring the green bean casserole; Denise R. was going to bake several trays of sweet butter rolls; Maribel G. naturally agreed to handle the chicken cutlets in honey demi-glaze; and it was the task of Lisa A. to make sure all the plasticware, solo cups, and paper plates were stocked, locked, and ready to rock.

Jillian Karen Amway was really only there to bring the parts of her unholy concoction to the maintenance room, bar the exit so no one could run, then cleanse the narrow halls of the meeting lodge with the purifying fire of justice. And gasoline.

Justice and gasoline.

Suffice it to say, lil' Jill ain't so well.

Not that this was the sort of thing she'd ever done. Truth be told, she had managed in her forty-eight years on Earth to barely hurt any flies, let alone any other people. So she was a tad nervous in the lead up and, according to the citizens of Redstone, had been acting odd all week. Several people had commented on it. Each one of them gaslighting the hootenanny out of her, she felt.

This was precisely why they all had to go. She was Kevin McCalister and she was ready to be *Home Alone.* It was an apropos metaphor, considering how much everyone gaslit the hell out of that poor boy.

But first, she needed to place the bombs and stack the gas. She had, in fact, gotten the idea from a movie called *Heathers.* The one with Christian Slater—her yummy yummy, hunky hunky stud-muffin über-crush from the '80s. How 'ere did he make her heart throb!

And just like in that movie, she had made sure to secure the smaller eastern and western fire exits with door jambs, so that only the main, northern entrance would be available. But of course, she was going to barricade the doors closed once she was certain that they were all safely inside. Absent them spilling from the windows in a flurry of smoke and flesh being shredded by window glass, she figured she'd get them all in one fell swoop.

Then her days of being gaslit would be well and truly through.

She figured she could just make up something on the fly to tell the cops. They'd buy whatever she told them because, as her dumbass figured it, they'd just be happy to say they were doing their job. Cops were unrepentantly stupid, in her modest opinion.

And it would've gone off without a hitch, had it not been for some unrealistic shit that we'll come back to soon enough. Put a pin in that one.

Backing up her truck the night before, she used a drop ramp off the back tailgate to roll six drums of gas into the hall's maintenance closet. In short order, she placed several package-sized boxes around the big meeting chamber, tucked neatly behind the exhaust grills of the several floor register vents. Each box was filled with an explosive charge, usually sold for light demo work that she had acquired at the local co-op.

She had, through experimentation, realized that she lacked the explosives qualifications to ensure that she would decimate the whole building, unless she relied on sheer amount of blast through packed explosives. Because you better believe that she was way too nervous (or full of common sense, as Jill likely saw it) about blowing herself up to monkey around with any wires or timers or base-charges or any such gobbledygook that might require any modicum of technical ability.

After dispersing the packages and making sure the barrels were ready, she zip-tied and bolted the door to the Maintenance Room of Impending Doom so that any lookie-loos wouldn't be able to spoil the festivities ahead of zero hour.

The day of, she had a hearty breakfast of steak 'n' eggs with an apricot and a glass of OJ, ran a few miles, then started to call everyone in town to ensure they were going to attend. It seemed by noon as though everyone was quite excited and ready to relax and delight in one another's company for a fine evening of community camaraderie.

After getting everyone settled and coordinating the food layout, she ushered everyone to begin their feast while she "grabbed something out of her truck." Once outside, she grabbed a long pole she'd thought of using as a fence cross brace, but had repurposed for this evening. It only took thirty seconds for her to smoothly run it through the handle of the doors to the front of the assembly hall.

A bit nervous, she took a few rips of her small vape pen to steady her hand, then practically skipped like a girl playing hopscotch back to the rear of the building.

Returning to the maintenance room, she began tipping over the huge barrels, and gasoline instantly flooded the floor. From her right pocket, she drew forth a box of matches.

But the glugging of the gas spilling from the narrow mouths of the overturned barrels was somehow quickly drowned out by a loud march coming across the parking lot. Like someone or something was stomping toward her, shaking the ground with each footfall.

But surely no one could have such big—

Her eyes flew to the double doors as they sprung open on their hinges, nearly ripping the clasps free from their moorings. An imposing fortress of metal, humanoid in form, filled up the space between the door jambs, so that little light was filtering into the mechanical room. Its muscles were bound steel, fastened at the joints with exposed cogs and swiveling gears. From its largely expressionless face, two holes burning blue served as the thing's eyes.

Through the walls, she could hear yelling and disconcerted

screaming. The folks on the other side of it must've already discovered the front door was jimmied shut. This needed to happen, and fast.

"And what the hell are you supposed to be, now? she demanded of the supervillain-looking husk standing before her.

Massive metal limbs crossed before a plated chest as it replied in a hiss of static shot through an electric vacuum tube: "I'm the Machina. I'm here to stop you before you do something that you'll regret, Jill."

He aimed one fist of knotted ore at the barrels of gas leaking amber liquid onto the halogen-reflecting linoleum flooring. The Machine of the Gods re-crossed its large titanium arms in front of its heavy chest full of bolts and small, metallic plates.

Jill raised a trembling finger on her right hand and pointed at the steely thing before her. "Y-you can't be real. You're … made of metal? Is your body metal?"

The metal man took a large step forward into the room, making imprints in the floor where his shiny feet landed. He waved away the question with a shiny hand the size of a car tire. "Shut your fat trap, Jill. That's hardly what's important at this moment."

She clutched at a small silver crucifix around her neck and stepped backward a hair to show her insult. "Don't you speak to me like that! You— You thick metallic twat! I don't even know what you are! Why the hell do you care what I'm doing?"

Letting loose the cross, she casually started to open the box of matches in her hand, but the colossally muscular, silver-shaded man wrapped in metallic plating slapped the box from her hand. It tumbled to the ground, spilling the matches onto the linoleum floor in a deluge of tiny *tinks*.

"Because the person reading this doesn't want to see you

torch a whole building full of people, that's why. You shouldn't play with matches anyway, Jillian. Don't you remember Smokey the Bear?"

She nodded her head up and down, the movement tossing her short hair wildly. "Oh, of course I remember Smokey! Everybody remembers Smokey the Bear! I had a Smokey the Bear fanny pack when I was just a kid, Tin Man. And this dumb bitch, Holly, she stole it from me. That stupid little bitch. Wait, uh, you— Did you just say that… What do you mean 'the person reading this?'"

The Machine of the Gods pointed through the page at *you*, and said to Jill, "That weirdo. Beyond the fabric of the printed word, past the boundary of this flimsy paper leaf, there lies that person right there, watching and reading all that happens. And I can speak for them when I say that they don't necessarily want to see all that shit right now, Jill. We should keep it light. If they wanted murder, torture, chaos, genocide, fire, and death, they could watch the fucking nightly news."

Right?

"You're not real. You're just— You're *not* real. This is all bullshit!"

"Of course, I am! I am the Machina! And I can stop anything before it becomes too much of a problem. Even a curmudgeonly little imbecile such as you, Jill."

Jill rubbed her chin, then continued her unbroken streak of consummate Karen-isms by saying, "I just don't think that's a good answer. I just don't. And that's bullshit. This is *bullshit*. Really, this whole story—which was sort of threadbare to begin with, let's not kid ourselves—is basically ruined now that you just barged in and started to gaslight me by breaking the fourth wall, which I fucking *hate*. Everyone does! It's writing for hacks. Only hacks break the fourth wall, for real. I mean, who even bothers anymore? It's tiring and it's played out. It's a hard wrap on that and you should cut it. I don't know if being meta or gaslighting is more annoying. The person reading this needs to demand more from their entertainment—and the dipshit writing it needs to get a fucking clue."

The Machine of the Gods glared at her. He slowly rolled back his arm, then swiped across the air in front of her, slapping her right cheek and drawing a thin line of blood.

She cried out, "You asshole! You can't fucking slap me!"

"But I just did, so that can't be entirely accurate."

"You're not allowed to slap women in, well, *any context*. But especially in a story! You can't just drop violence against a woman all willy-nilly like that! The reader isn't gonna stick around for that ugly stuff!"

"Spake the bitchy pot unto the omnipotent kettle. You'd be surprised what they'll allow in pursuit of entertainment. They don't have much in the way of a moral compass. Otherwise they'd have left this short story collection where they found it—likely in the bargain bin of a Sam's Club with the other literary dreck. Did anyone care when Tarantino had two men brutally murder two women at the end of *Once Upon a Time In Hollywood*? Nah, that was 'high art,' because if you can justify the violence by making certain characters unlikeable enough, they'll turn the other cheek. Plus, you know, don't get it fuckin' twisted, Jill: I AM THE MACHINA. And the Machina slaps whom he sees fit. We could always just say that I am subverting expectations, and that'd probably be all the reason I need to do anything. That's what people want these days. Isn't it *so cool?* It's what the shit-sucking culturally-devoid flies want. It's what they crave.

Shall I demonstrate again?" He slowly forced his shiny silver arm back, as if to strike again.

"No! Please. Just … point taken! Clearly you're right about them, so just stop!"

At this submission, the cold-eyed Machina grinned, then lowered its arm.

As it did, she slowly knelt over and started to pick up the matches and box off the ground. Standing and straightening herself out, she quipped, "You know, you're contradicting yourself, you big dumb lugnut. You said the reader doesn't want to see what I'm about to do to this group of gaslighters, but you just hit me, you nickel prick! So just how do you square that shit?" She spit on the floor and it was speckled with red.

"I don't have to, Jill. I am the Machina. I do whatever I want, whether it makes any sense or not. Which, in point of fact, it rarely does."

"Whatever."

"Whatever with your whatever."

"That's mature," she sneered.

"Whatever."

"Okay, so if you're really some physical manifestation of an overused plot contrivance that hack bitches who can't finish stories use to get themselves out of a goddamn jam, then you can't stop me from killing all the people in this church, because you're more concept than corporeal form. Am I right? Because I mean it when I say that those pickle ticklers in there, filling their gapin' gobs with Granny's peach cobbler, have all gaslit me for the last time. Today it's me who lights the gas, ya hear me?"

"You've been waiting to say that for a while now, haven't you?" The Machina grinned widely.

"Damn right!" Her eyebrow cocked and she tilted her head like a curious creature peering out from its hole. "And I can tell that you're gaslightin' me right now, you creepy-pasta snarfin' aluminum golem!"

"I believe the word you're looking for is 'gaslight*ed*.' Plus it would be the author who would be guilty of such, if such were the case, which it arguably is. Though I'm sure he'll be the last to admit it. All this arrives us at the same conclusion, which is that you'll be stopping this now."

"Uh, you're not the boss of me! I will do what I want, I will say what I want, and if I want to murder these unctuous bitches, that's precisely what is gonna go down!"

"No, Jill," the Machina warned. "That is totally the opposite of what's going to happen. If nothing else, as I've said, the author won't allow it. A step too far, I'd say. *He'd say. We'd say*, really."

Reaching for several of the matchsticks, she fumbled, attempting to turn the strike side up. "Fuck you and fuck whoever wrote this crap! If he dropped you in, then he is trying to gaslight me, just like everybody else is always gaslightin' me! You really think you or he can even stop me at this point in the game, big man?"

"Of course! For I am the Machina! And while I cannot always speak directly for the author, I can fix anything in two shakes of a donkey's ass. Believe that shit, yo!"

Holding the box in her right hand and moving to strike the match in her left against it, she hissed, "How's that gonna happen? You bloviating, bug-eyed—"

Faster than Jill's pupils could process, his huge titanium-hued arm shot out and touched her pointy little nose with his steely fingertip. Her eyes went as big as saucers and rolled back into her skull as she exploded in a dense blur of bone, blood, muscle, fat, stupid, and ugly.

"Like that, *beotch*," the Machina croaked in a hiss of static.

THE END

Transmissions From The Campfire is Colorado's #1 original horror podcast. Spooky and irreverent, humorous and home brewed, each episode is a horror/sci-fi tinged trip into the dark underbelly of the Colorado landscape. Written by Patrick Quinn Kitson, produced, mixed and narrated by Daniel Kelley, episodes feature many stories set in and around The Roaring Fork Valley, as well as the odd interview with the genre's top tier storytellers/celebs of middling import–it's quite literally the best way you can spend your time on the internet.

> *"Unsettling, spooky campfire-like tales of a region you don't want to visit. Kitson's strong writing hits you like a chill in a graveyard."*
>
> – DALE T. PHILLIPS,
> author of the Zack Taylor mystery series.

ABOUT THE AUTHOR

Purveyor of dread, bon vivant, and scribe of middling import, Patrick Kitson has been a lifelong student of the macabre, the satirical, and the intellectually dubious. Born and raised in The Roaring Fork Valley, he's coined the term, "Valley Horror" in reference to his particular brand of homebrewed speculative fiction which largely takes place in and around the snowy climes of Colorado.

www.ingramcontent.com/pod-product-compliance
Lightning Source LLC
Chambersburg PA
CBHW032246310726
48973CB00008B/2308